The Merica Portal

Archie Cameron

Archie Cameron's website: www.archiecameronnovels.com

Copyright © 2012 Archie Cameron
All rights reserved.
ISBN:
ISBN-13: **978-1499509656**
ISBN-10:1499509650

DEDICATION

This novel is dedicated to my Children
Angus, Iain, Annabel and Francesca

The Origins of the Story…

The veiled hint that an expedition to North America had taken place at the end of the 14th century intrigued me for many years. Like many good adventure stories it began with a hoard of 16th century manuscripts discovered in an empty room used for storage. The manuscripts contained a bundle of letters among which was a map and details of a journey made across a great ocean to the west and the discovery of new lands.

The story of the map first came to light in Venice. It was found in letters written between 1390 and 1404 by Nicolo and Antonio Zen, Venetian Navigators and mapmakers who, it is thought spent many years in the service of a Scottish Prince believed to be Prince Henry St Clair, Jarl (Earl) of Orkney. During their exile they wrote to their relations a noble Venetian family about their experiences. After the death of his brother Nicolo in 1396 or thereabouts, Antonio was thought to
have replaced him as Prince Henry's chief navigator and mapmaker. It was Antonio that drew the map and continued the correspondence

right up to his return to Venice when his service ended with the death of the Jarl in 1404.

In 1398 he related in his letters that he had accompanied the Prince on a journey across a vast Ocean and discovered lands in the west mapping some of the areas they explored. Some of these letters have since been interpreted as describing a journey to parts of the North American continent. The letters became collectively known as the Zen Narrative and the map is thought to be the earliest map of part of the coastline of Nova Scotia and the surrounding lands. Letters continued between Antonio and his relations until he returned to his native City. Knowledge of the expedition might have been lost to the world among bundles of old letters stored away in a palace in Venice but for a quirk of fate.

It was another Nicolo Zeno, one of the succeeding generations of the Zeno family, who as any small boy finding himself bored and with nothing to do one day, wandered into an old part of the family's Venetian palace and stumbled upon bundles of old letters and papers. Being young he found the bundles of papers a useful distraction and used them to play games and as a result many were destroyed.

Only when Nicolo Zeno reached maturity did he realise the value of these letters. He realised that they provided a unique record of his ancestor's service with a great Prince who lived in the northern lands and who had been part of this expedition across the western ocean. Having studied the documents that remained after his youthful transgressions he felt that they should be preserved as part of Venetian history. Eventually in 1536, details of the remaining letters were included in a book compiled by Marco Babaro called "Patrician Ancestors" and they rest today in the Correr Museum, Venice.

Some experts who have analysed the narrative suggest it describes an expedition led by a Scottish Prince, possibly Henry St Clair to explore lands in the far western ocean and perhaps raise settlements there. Although it did not surpass the epic voyages of the Viking Eric the Red to the North American continent it should be noted that the journey took place some twenty two years before the Admirals of the Chinese Ming Dynasty Fleets set out to discover the known world and forty-three years before Columbus made landfall on an island in the Caribbean Sea. Others have poured scorn on the narrative and map as an elaborate hoax to give Venice part of the credit for discovering America before Columbus. They cite many other maps as sources, which together make up the original areas of land shown on the map.

I am inclined to believe the story of that incredible journey for many clues on both sides of the Atlantic exist which can be associated with this period of history. My story has for one good reason, to link the expedition with the building of Rosslyn Chapel, which still stands today on what is part of the St Clair estate in Rosslyn, near Edinburgh, Scotland.

It was during the middle of the 15th Century that Prince Henry's grandson, William decided to construct a Chapel which would replace a nearby collegiate church, which was falling into ruin. He personally oversaw the design, construction and ornamentation. The Chapel which has survived to this day is full of unusual tracery, which provides a fitting monument to both Norse and Scottish tradition, to the spiritual and the healing properties found in nature as well as a tribute to the craftsmen who worked on its construction.

Begun in 1446, the present structure took over forty years to build. Set among the ornamental tracery is a unique window in the south aisle, the upper tracery has since been interpreted as heads of maize, a Native American plant and the decoration on one of the roof supports in the south aisle looks uncannily like the leaves of a certain Aloe plant also found in America. The chapel has many surprising architectural features many of which have a strong connection with the Order of the Poor Soldiers of Christ and the Temple of Solomon or as they are universally known, the Knights Templar. The unusual architecture and much of the decoration have direct links with Templar tradition.

There has always been an underlying connection between the Templars and the St Clair family. After the eradication of the Knights Templar in 1306 it is thought that through the succeeding generations of St Clairs they continued the traditions and the rituals were later converted to form the Masonic Orders in Scotland. Many readers will already know by the many books articles and films about this mystifying Order but might not be aware of how their history combines with the history of the St Clair family.

Some Templar knights were destined to escape the Inquisition and re-establish their Order albeit secretly in various parts of Scotland. It is at this point that my story becomes fictitious, although still built on a foundation of truth.

Archie CAMERON
La Gilardie, France. 2010.

**Chapter One
A Fitting Memorial.**

Throughout the long summer days of the year of our Lord 1447 a small hill overlooking the valley of the river Esk and the Castle of Roslin reverberated with the sound of hammers dressing stone, screeching saws, clanging anvils and scurrying serfs discharging their duties. The air was filled with cries and shouts of orders being given and obeyed.

Great wooden sledges hauled by pairs of huge war horses carried stone cut from the quarry face nearby to be stacked by groups of toiling Masons bent on splitting the stone into manageable blocks and stacking them to be eventually used as building blocks. Other Masons sat in circles toiling over selected stone blocks cutting out patterns of delicate ornamental tracery. There were carpenters sawing and shaping timber, blacksmiths forming the metal work and barrowmen hurrying to and fro to keep the craftsmen supplied with materials.

Close by on the thickly wooded slopes huge oak trees were being scrutinised, selected and marked with chalk with a large "X" for felling. Foresters swinging great axes felled and stripped the designated trees and made them ready to be hauled away. Charcoal burners leaving nothing to waste recovered the smaller branches trimmed from trunks felled by foresters and used them to build their turf covered fires in the open spaces nearby to produce the charcoal for the blacksmiths.

More war horses shackled with heavy chains hauled giant tree trunks out of the woodland to an area close to the sawpits. As each trunk arrived it was placed on one of several huge stacks from where trunks selected for cutting would be quickly surrounded by sweating serfs and manhandled onto trestles above the sawpits. Pairs of sawyers one above and one below the trestles working in unison wielded their long saws slicing the great trunks into planks and beams; others deftly using small billhooks were turning wider straight branches trimmed from the trees into poles to be used for assembling scaffolding.

Sweating serfs rushed to and from the river in the valley filling and carrying water skins for the assembled workforce. Out of all this confusion a new St Clair chapel was slowly rising on Roslin hill.

The site of the previous church had been cleared over two years ago and now these Masons and labourers from far and wide drawn by the high wages promised for their labour had travelled to Roslin. Since their arrival temporary lodgings of wattle and daub capped with woven straw had slowly spread out from fields at the edge of the site. Under the shadow of the surrounding Pentland Hills these humble dwellings now stretched away from the hilltop as far as the eye could see and had the makings of a village soon to take its name from the nearby Castle Roslin.

Under the leafy canopy of an ancient elm an old man was hard at work carving a limestone block his shoulder length silver hair covered with a wide brimmed straw hat to protect his head from the sun. The deeply lined weather beaten features were dominated by a white beard and piercing ice blue eyes revealed a keen intelligence.

His once tall and well-built frame which had now succumbed to a slight stoop was clad in the long green habit made of coarse cloth signifying the livery of a Templar craftsman. Slightly overwhelming the now feeble frame the habit was tied in the middle with a belt of plaited leather to which was attached a small leather pouch. The ornate leather pointed shoes were the only indication that he came from a noble lineage.

Although Sir Guillaume de La Croix, Templar Knight and Master Mason had seen over seventy summers come and go he could still match many of the younger masons at the craft. His strong sinewy arm swung mallet to chisel in narrow arc, chipping away at the charcoal pattern sketched out on this lump of limestone which had been set on a circular wooden platform rough sawn from the girth of a large oak. Although he had been toiling at a piece of stone since dawn his energy was not as yet exhausted. This time he had chosen well, for the limestone revealed no blemish to spoil the decoration. The copy stone was nearing completion as he skilfully carved the intricate pattern drawn on the surface of the limestone. The contours of what appeared to be strange plant were beginning to emerge.

Piercing rays of sunlight penetrated the leaves overhead and rebounded from the surface of the white stone, savagely stabbing his eyes and weakening his concentration even so he willed himself to continued chiselling the fine lines on the surface drawing on his skill and understanding of its contours. Toiling in the warm sun made rivulets of salty sweat run down his forehead irritating his eyes and forcing him to lay down his tools. He removed the wide brimmed straw hat, cuffed the dust from the sleeve of his habit and wiped his brow.

It was now almost midday the sun had reached its zenith the old man's stomach began to rumble loudly signalling the need for refreshment. He stretched up and lifted a water skin from the convenient niche in the trunk of a great elm close by and squeezing the top of the skin against his body to remove the trapped air, took a long cooling drink. His thirst sated he tied the end and returned it to the niche. Muttering to himself he replaced his hat and shuffled slowly over to the nearby shelter and went inside.

The floor of the hut was covered in fresh straw, to one side was a wooden litter on top of which was a straw filled pallet covered with a large fur pelt. Nearby stood a small rough hewn bench on which was set a trencher board. He approached a large earthenware pot standing in a dark corner and removed the lid taking out a piece of coarse bread and a lump of dried fish. Carefully replacing the lid he arranged the victuals on the trencher board picked it up and headed back into the sunshine.

He sought out a nearby tree trunk recently felled and trimmed by the carpenters, laid the trencher board before him on a piece of level surface left by removing a large branch and sat down. Taking a small knife from his pouch he cut the dried fish into pieces and began his meal. He had nought but a piece of bread washed down with water since dawn and was ravenous so the food was quickly devoured. He replaced the knife and for a while lay back to rest on the broad trunk. The bright sun penetrating his closed lids became unbearable so he dragged his hat over his face and was soon dozing.

A chattering magpie brought him back to consciousness. He raised his tired body and stretched, taking up the trencher board he spread the remains of the food over the ground for the birds in particular the friendly blackbird that would appear close by from time to time. He shuffled back into the shelter and replaced the trencher board on the wooden bench.

Anxious to complete the carving he returned to the block. The dried fish had made him thirsty and once again he jostled the water skin down from the cleft in the tree raised it to his lips and took another swig and replaced the water skin. Deep in thought he fumbled inside the leather pouch at his waistband pulling out a small piece of folded buckskin untying the leather thong which secured it and turned to where the almost completed stone lay and before taking up his tools spread the buckskin open on the makeshift bench.

His eyes, now quite feeble could just make out
the two drawings on the smooth side of the skin.
Reaching again inside the pouch he extracted a
pair of magnifying lens and held them to his eyes
bending forward to examine in detail the first of
two drawings. It represented a strange seed head
covered in long neat rows of yellow seeds, part
wrapped in large coarse green leaves. Each leaf
appeared to end in a tuft of stringy fibre. Beside
the representation of the seed head was another
strange plant. This was a plant with long green
serrated leaves edged in yellow. He had made the
drawings nearly fifty years before; even so the
colours remained vibrant.

Guillaume took up a pair of wooden callipers and
checked the proportions of the seed head,
comparing them carefully with the representation
on the stone and then outlined some adjustment
to the carving with a piece of charcoal. Not
wholly satisfied with the result of his labour, he
laid aside the callipers and picking up the
mallet and chisel began to improve the detail of
the strange plant along the lines he had made in
charcoal.

Despite the heat Guillaume worked hard to finish the final copy stone. As he smoothed the surface on the rough-cut design, he reflected on the next task given to him by the noble lord. He had been commissioned to carve the tracery for the blocks of the last two pillars at the eastern end of the chapel. He knew from his study of the overall plan for the Chapel that these would be of special significance to the building. Sir William would soon be visiting the site and was anxious to see what designs his old friend had proposed for the columns.

Content at last with his changes, the old Master Mason carefully rolled up the buckskin and tied the ends securely, then folding the magnifying lens he returned both to the safety of his pouch. The two copy stones now completed could be passed to his fellow craft masons and apprentices who would begin carve identical blocks using his patterns as models.

Eventually the completed blocks would form an arch over the window in the southwest wall of the chapel. Few people alive knew what the strange tracery represented and by the time it had been assembled into the building works, Guillaume de la Croix, Knight Templar and master mason would be long dead. This would be *his* monument to a great adventure, *his* 'Merica Portal'.

As long ago as 1441, Prince William St Clair of Roslin, Earl of the Orkneys and a follower of the Templar traditions had resolved to build a Chapel to replace the nearby collegiate church of St Matthew which was falling into ruin. There were many simple Chapels in the surrounding area that had been dedicated as collegiate Churches but Sir William however, had a grander strategy for his Chapel. His intention was to create in stone a garden of paradise a building dedicated to his Christian beliefs, his Nordic connection and Templar traditions.

To this end he had drawn up special plans and had ordered them to be transferred to pine from the Baltic allowing the carpenters to carve them as a pattern for the stonemasons. The structural design he based on the Templar Cross and traditions and illustrations of the Holy City of Jerusalem and Temple. His designs for the internal tracery were copied from the illustrated herbals that he had in the castle library.

In order to explain his ideas the Earl had called a council of the senior Knights. After much discussion they approved that an agreed amount from the secreted Templar Treasury would be donated to assist the costly construction of this great Chapel. Earl William felt it would establish a permanent memorial to God, the wonders of nature, Templar and Norse tradition and a glorious shrine for the St Clair family. The site chosen already had a ruined chapel there but all that remained was a few walls and part of the crypt which the Earl would incorporate in the overall plan.

Aware of his skill in the art of masonry the Earl commanded his oldest Knight Sir Guilluame de La Croix to gather Masons from far and wide demanding the finest quality of workmanship for which he agreed to pay the craftsmen well above the average wage. Word soon spread and on hearing of the great sums offered for their skills Master Masons had travelled from all over the country and France, Belgium and the Low

Countries bringing with them their own fellow craftsmen.

Guilluame organised the work force of chosen Masons into teams each representing a Master mason, his fellow craftsmen and apprentices. Each Master and team would be allocated a particular section of the main building for which they alone would be responsible and so far the work had gone smoothly.

Guillaume who had been personally tasked to carve certain of the decorated stones in accordance with the wishes of the Earl had formed his own team of skilled fellow craftsmen under his command. From the Earl's designs the composition of floral tracery on the arches, pillars, windows and an ornate roof representing the starry firmament and the Templar flower would be the responsibility of his team.

The copy stones had proved a simple task and had been quickly completed. Now the blocks for the roof section were completed and had been passed to his fellow craftsmen to copy. For the moment this task had been set aside for it would take several years to complete the surrounding walls before the roof section was needed. He had decided that the prime task was to produce the ornate blocks that were required for the door, window and aisle arches of the Chapel.

As a memorial to Earl William's grandfather Prince Henry St Clair, Guillaume had asked the Earl for the special honour to create his own floral tracery in the south aisle forming the arch over the southwest window and on the one of the support beams along the south aisle. The Earl had granted this request so while the rest of his team concentrated on the blocks for the roof, Guilluame had begun work on this ornate tracery.

As each stone was completed it was clearly labelled with his mason's mark of a cross with a triangle at its base and section number. These had been stored by his apprentices ready for the next team of masons to assemble at the main building area. The foundation stones had been completed over a year ago work had now begun on the reconstruction of the old crypt and outer walls of the chapel. As the newly constructed foundations rose above the hill people travelled from far and wide to take stock of the progress.

It was mid-afternoon and having finished this task Guillaume felt a great tiredness overwhelming him. He had realized some time ago that he had had more than his three score years and ten that the Holy Testaments had prescribed for man but he had to complete his work on the Chapel so that it would survive him and the generations to come. He made one final comparison with the drawing and with a satisfied grunt called over to his senior fellow craft mason who was working close by.

"Aiden! Aiden! Take heed. Come at once."

A tall fair-haired middle aged man left the nearby circle of craftsmen cutting stone and approached the platform.

"The tracery blocks are now completed bid the apprentices carry them to the cutting circle and by my command set the fellow craft to make copies."

He moved to the wooden platform and pointed to the block depicting the large leaf covered seedpod.

"This will be the model for the stones making up the southwest window arch. Bid your masons to cut the left and right-hand risers in this form and I will cut the capping stone when the final measurements have been taken."

He moved to where the second stone lay at the base of the great elm. He took a last look at the three large serrated leaves. He was happy. His old drawing would at last secure permanence on the surface of the stone.

"Use this one as the model for the facing blocks on the south aisle lintels. I will take my rest now but be sure to call me should Jarl William arrive."

"By your command master it shall be done."

The senior mason strolled back to his group who were occupied dressing the faces of the inner wall stones. He began shouting orders to the apprentices in the group. In a short while the two copy stones had been removed to the circle. Satisfied that his work for the day had been competed Guillaume returned to the shelter, settled his tired body on the pallet of hay inside and closed his eyes.

For a brief moment his mind was back in the lands below the Merica star. He imagined he could hear the voice of his wife Morning Star calling him in her familiar Algonkin tongue.

"Come to me my dear Nkisikum (Husband), I wait here on the high rock for sight of your ca' noo".

Was it his tired mind playing tricks? He lapsed into a half conscious state his mind taking him on a journey back in time, summoning up the tales that he had been told of the de La Croix family lineage and recollections of childhood at Roslin. It was like a strange revelation as if suddenly an inner voice called upon him to put down in writing a record of his recollections.

Over the next few days his team finished the blocks for the southwest window and having laid them out Guillaume had calculated the measurement and was able to complete the capping stone. While plans were finalised for the inner tracery to the chapel his recent revelation dominated his thoughts so much so that he made up his mind he would obtain several parchment scrolls from the Scriptorium and inscribe thereon a permanent record of his family history and the paths he had taken on his journey through life. When it was finished he had decided that it would be hidden somewhere within the Chapel walls as his own memorial.

He spent every spare moment over the next three months writing down recollections in his bold handwriting on page after page of parchment until the completed story amounted to over one hundred scrolls. Since all the persons who accompanied him on that great adventure were long dead to his knowledge this would be the only record made of it and should by some quirk of fate the scrolls were discovered by some future generation then the great adventure could be retold.

On the day he completed the final scroll he wrote a preface...

'This a story dedicated to my Lord and friend Prince Henry St Clair of Roslin, Earl of Orkney and to my own family of de La Croix. My account will reveal how I Guilluame de La Croix was privileged to take part in a great exploration for new lands made by Prince Henry, who set out with a fleet of ten ships from his Princedom accompanied by a band of five of his faithful Knights and their followers in the Year of Our Lord, 1398. Among those who undertook this perilous journey to cross the Western Sea and with God's grace discovered a land which he named West Scotland were Priors, Chaplains and others skilled in the art of Apothecary, Metalwork, Carpentry and Masonry, humble Squires together with his Fleet Captain, Captains of ships and Seamen who played their part in establishing a settlement in this new world'.

Having finished the preface the old man felt a compulsion to read over his account so that nothing should be left out and only then decide where the scrolls should be concealed. So taking up the first scroll he began to read...

Chapter Two
The La Croix Legacy.

...My name is Guillaume de La Croix Master Mason and Knight Templar. I have compiled this history of my family from tales told by my father that had been passed down by his father from his father and as I have likewise done. I will leave the story of my life and the great adventure across the Western Sea to whosoever by some quirk of fate may in some distant future discover its place of concealment.

Thus begins my story…

From the time I was very young my father had told me how our family came to live at Roslin and the reason. It went back in time to something terrible that happened a good many years before in France. However in the spring of 1306 before this great tragedy took place it was a peaceful happy time.

My forebears were born in France and it is here that my story begins. It tells of the terrible price the family had to pay for being Knights of a most noble, gentle and pious Order of Poor Knights of Jerusalem or Knights Templar as they were commonly known. At this time the King of France found himself to be in great debt to the Templar Treasury and to get his hands on this source of income was bent on eliminating the Order. Acting on a Papal Bull obtained through false evidence many of the Knights were arrested and were forced to renounce their vows to the

Order through cruel and aggressive interrogation of the Inquisition.

My father told me how my great grandfather was fortunate enough to escape to freedom in Scotland and in this new land to bring forth new generations who would go on to serve their great Lords and benefactors, the family St Clair, fight in great battles, explore new worlds and eventually help to build a masterpiece in stone.

Just before he died my father told me a story about my great, great grandfather which had been passed down to him by his father. Alain de La Croix was one of a handful of Templar Knights who had survived the final siege of Acre where the Grand Master had been killed. He had been part of an escort which battled their way out of the fortress to take the Deputy Grand Master to the safety of a ship bound for Sidon and later to Rhodes.

Since leaving the Holy Land and returning to their native country a few trusted Templar Knights had been appointed Stewards of Manor Houses and lands owned by the Order. Although they had maintained their vow of celibacy whilst in the Holy land on their return to their native lands many Knights had taken a wife. The senior officials of the Order and Priors however had remained celibate.

Many years had passed since Acre and the loss of Holy Lands and Alain de La Croix had returned to France where he was appointed Steward of the Templar Manor of Malleyrand and Preceptor of Vouthon in Poitou Charente France. As Steward he was responsible for a workforce of about eighty souls who maintained manor house and farm and kept the land in good order, providing food for the Preceptory and for the Templar Churches to distribute to the poor in the vicinity.

And so I will begin with the story passed on to me of how my great grandfather hunted the great boar and the extraordinary events that led to his escape from the clutches of the Inquisition. My great grandfather Sir Gilles de La Croix was described by my forebears as a tall, blonde haired Knight and had passed on this story of a particular day that had changed his life.

My father called it the story of the great boar. I remember even now that my father in a tone tinged with sadness described a country he had only heard about, my great grandfather's home at Mallyrand and told the story just as he had heard it from his father.

How on that day the gentle wooded countryside of Poitou Charente was cloaked with a fresh mantle of green as April drew to a close. The forest echoed to the sound of birds chirruping their courtship songs and wild flowers spread across the soft ground in a riot of colour.

As it was his birthday Gilles' father had given him permission to set aside his tasks and join his friends. Now able to escape the confines of the Manor he had chosen to go hunting in the forest. As they moved into a more dense part of the forest the hunting party came across a family of wild boar and a chase ensued. Gilles singled out the large male a great black beast with huge tusks which at first had stood its ground but when the rest of the herd scattered it made a desperate run for cover. Gilles spurred his horse Fleche who lifted his head and set off in hot pursuit. The boar headed into a tangle of briars and became trapped in the dense mass of sharp thorns.

Gilles had dismounted and followed the boar into the knot slashing the long tendrils of thorns with his lance as he went forward. Suddenly the boar freed itself and turned, uttered a high pitched squeal and charged towards the knight who deftly stepped aside and with great force drove the lance into the back of the boar's neck stopping it in its tracks. As the boar struggled to regain its feet Gilles flung his body down onto the lance pole and forced the steel head further into the neck until the boar gave up the fight.

He had commanded his squire Gilbert to come forward and assist him to remove the boar from the briars. Gilbert secured one end of a rope to his saddle and brought the other over to where the boar lay. He deftly tied the rope around the forelegs of the boar mounted his horse and dragged the carcass out of the thicket. Gilles mounted his horse and the two men rode out of the forest onto a green sward where they both dismounted and began to busy themselves preparing the boar for the journey back to

Mallyrand. They lifted the carcass onto Gilbert's horse and tied the legs firmly together under the belly and leading the horse the squire set off for the Manor.

Gilles remounted and was about to join his friends when a cry had made him rein back. Approaching at a gallop over the hill he recognised his father's squire who drew alongside the knight, bowed his head and reported that he must attend his father at once. Fearing something had happened to his family he had spurred Fleche into a fast gallop towards Mallyrand followed by the rest of the party.

Gilles had followed the course of the valley and turned Fleche up the old cattle path that led to the Manor. Mallyrand was one of many small communities in the south west of France consisting of a Templar Manor Farm and Church and a few wattle and daub dwellings that housed the vassals and bondsmen that worked the farmland. Pausing at the church he gave a short respectful nod and spurred the horse on through the manor gates to where he could see his father Alain de La Croix waiting at the door of the

Manor bright eyed and eager to speak. He quickly dismounted and while Fleche was led away and cared for by a vassal Alain de La Croix greeted his son and in an emotional voice he broke the news. My great grandfather Gilles had been selected to be a Guardian, a member of the Grand Master's bodyguard.

The Grand Master of the Templar Order, Friar Jacques de Molay had been summoned from his headquarters in Cyprus for meetings with Pope Clement V concerning the future of the Order. He had found on his arrival in France that the meetings had been delayed due to the illness of the Pope. Because of the delay the Grand Master had made the Paris Temple the temporary headquarters of the Order and several knights had been selected as his Guardians and the appointment was a great honour for the Lacroix family. My great grandfather had been ordered to report there by the first day of May and he had just eight days to reach Paris. This gave him little time for good-byes, nevertheless his father felt they had something to celebrate and celebrate they did.

The wild boar was hung for a day while the blood was drained into a bowl to be used to make a tasty black sausage. After being gutted, the entrails taken away to where they could be separated for various uses, the body hair singed off, the head severed to be cooked separately and presented on a salver and the carcass prepared for roasting.

In the early evening the day before the celebration would begin a large pit was dug two spit rods were driven into the ground at either end, then the pit was filled with kindling and logs and set alight. In the early hours of the morning when the logs had been reduced to super heated embers the boar had been skewered on a long bar with a turning handle at one end, lifted onto the rods and was roasted. Two of the vassals from the Manor were set to turning the huge carcass so that it would cook evenly and all through the day of the celebration the scent of the roasting wild boar spread though out every corner of the Manor. By early evening a cask of wine distilled from grapes from the Manor vineyards had been tapped and the roasted boar was declared ready to eat.

The friends and family who had arrived to celebrate Gilles' appointment in style could hardly wait for the slices of pork to be served. They set to feasting, singing and dancing to the shawm, tambour and pipes and the laughter and merriment continued well into the night. I would imagine that it was a very tired Gilles de La Croix that said goodbye to his friends in the small hours and crept away to his cot to catch a few hours sleep before his long journey began.

Next morning Gilles had gone early to the church to make his peace with God then bade a sad farewell to his family and the comfortable life of the Manor and so escorted by his squire he left Mallyrand unaware that it would be the last time he would ever see his home and family.

They had been warned about the outbreaks of Plague that had spread throughout the land so on their way north they had avoided drinking water from the local wells and stuck to using flowing streams to fill their flasks sometimes mixing it with wine too sate their thirst. They stopped at many great cities including Poitiers, Tours, and the great cathedral town of Chartres but none were like Paris. Compared with the tranquillity and beauty of the Charente, Paris was a noisy, stinking, bustling place full of grasping merchants, beggars, "cut throats" and bawdyhouses. However, my great grandfather felt it was his duty to raise himself above all this and observe the customs and dignity of a Templar Knight.

Several times they were forced to stop and ask directions only to be greeted by a bawdy remark or silent stares. There were some however who were helpful and answered their enquiries with respectful grace guiding them towards their goal, the Paris Temple.

Before long they could see in the distance a tall imposing castle with round towers one of which was flying a black and white chequered flag and soon they were approaching a fortified gatehouse guarded by two Templar Men at Arms.

On their arrival at the gate they gave their names to the men on duty and were led through the narrow entrance of the gatehouse protected by huge doors at one end which were swung open to receive them. As they passed through they could see above them the sharp spear like tails of a portcullis ready to be lowered. Entering a wide outer courtyard and came upon two more great oak doors studded with metal similar to those on the gatehouse with another portcullis ready to protect the doors. The inner courtyard was overlooked on all sides by the walls of the castle. Here they were told to wait.

I can only picture the scene when the Commander of the Guardians, whose name I was told was Sir Henri de Valdonne was informed of their arrival. Before long a giant of a man with greying black hair, a beard and moustache with a black patch covering his left eye entered the courtyard and the two weary travellers dismounted and bowed. Valdonne congratulated Gilles on his appointment and told him that he had a lot to live up to. He too was a survivor the battle of Acre where he lost his eye and together with Gilles father had assisted in the escape of the Deputy Grand Master to Sidon. The Commander asked after Alain and pleased to learn that Gilles father was in good health he passed on the blessings of the Holy Mother to his family. He bade the squire take the horses to the stables where he would find accommodation with the other squires. The young knight was shown to his quarters where the Commander set out the rules under which Gilles would devote himself to his duties as a Guardian.

The quarters were in a large room above the stables and housed about forty men and their equipment. The straw filled pallets on which they slept were set along the stone walls, below in the stables was a well which provided water for the horses and also for their ablutions. The Squires slept below in the stables with the horses under their care. Gilles brought his meagre possessions into the quarters and settled them close to the straw filled pallet pointed out by the Commander. This was to be his home for quite some time and he had to get used to it.

Being from the country I would imagine that my Great Grandfather would have taken a long time to settle down to sleep in quarters with other men who snored and some who had restless dreams and would talk in their sleep. But gradually over the next few weeks, together with the other Guardians, he would have advanced easily into the strict routine of spiritual obligations and training in the various forms of fighting using the sword, staff, bow, cudgel and axe. As a small boy his father had taught him the skills of using the sword, lance and bow. He had always loved the bow as a first weapon and had tended to spend more time with this weapon at practice. The Commander noticed this and encouraged Gilles to concentrate on mastering the other weapons.

The training was hard and Gilles was a willing pupil soon achieving skill with all weapons, his body began to react to the training and he felt fitter than he had ever been. The worry of trying to sleep quickly passed for he was so tired after each days training he was asleep as soon as he laid his head to the pallet.

Aside from their spiritual and military training the main duties were to guard the Temple and provide an escort to the Grand Master whenever he left the Compound. Gilles enjoyed his position, every day there was something new to see for Paris was a large City but as time went on he began to long for the lush countryside of Poitou and most of all he missed his family.

During the month of August 1306 the Grand Master received a summons from the Pope now recovered and ensconced at Poitiers. The summons commanded him to attend the Pope to have discussions about the future of the Order. My father said that the appointment of Pope Clement had been engineered by King Philip IV of France and because of this the King had a threatening influence over him. Gilles was honoured to find that he was among the twenty Guardians chosen for the escort.

The next day they assembled in the courtyard ready to escort the wooden coach containing the Grand Master and soon they were making their way out of Paris. With overnight stops at the Templar quarters in the cities of Chartres and Tours they were made welcome by the Commanders who were honoured to receive the Grand Master at their Temple Lodges. The Party reached Poitiers without incident with hopes that the outcome of the discussions would result in the Order being safe from its critics. Gilles looked forward to visiting his family for he would only be two days ride from Mallyrand but during the discussions the mood of the Papal negotiators had begun to turn against the Order and the Guardians were put on alert.

The Pope had suggested that as the Order was no longer able to fulfil its obligations in the Holy Lands escorting Pilgrims to Jerusalem it should now be combined with the Knights of the Order of St John or as they were commonly known the Hospitallers. The first whispers of this union had reached the ears of the Grand Master Jacques de Molay during the previous year. To make the view of the Order clear to the Pope he had submitted a long treatise suggesting that a union between the two Orders was directly opposed to the wishes of the Church of Rome for the Hospitallers gave precedence to the charitable functions of the Church while the Templars were the Military arm of the Church protecting the poor and needy. As separate institutions he thought that they would be more effective.

During the negotiations Gilles and several other Guardians were able to witness the discussions. The Grand Master said he had explained in his letter to the Pope that the Order saw no advantage by combining with the Hospitallers because it was they who would gain nothing from this union while the Hospitallers stood to gain much. The Pope however gave a stark warning that certain charges had been brought by ex-members of the Order that gross impropriety was taking place within the ranks of the Order therefore it would be better for all if a union between the Templars and the Hospitallers took place to quell any fears of further action being taken. He had gone on to say that if these charges were proven the likely outcome would be excommunication of the Order and its members.

So the meeting ended in stalemate and the Guardians were told to have a care and be alert for there was great concern for the safety of the Grand Master during the journey back to Paris. However, the journey passed without incident and as the following weeks passed it was thought that the crisis had blown over.

Before long however, the Grand Master received a warning from a member of the French Court that King Philip was hatching a plot to bring charges against the Order. During the month of September 1306 rumours began to circulate throughout Paris that Guillaume De Nogaret one of the King's henchmen had been summoned by the King of France to seek out evidence of blasphemy and heresy against the Order. De Nogaret had been involved in the denunciation of the previous Pope Boniface VIII providing a way for Pope Clement to be elected,

The King was in serious debt to the Templars and a recent loan of 200,000 florins had led to an order by the Grand Master to the Templar Treasurer Jean de la Tour not to loan any more to the Court. This move angered King Philip and made him more determined to extract revenge. Now firm reports began to arrive from the Court that De Nogaret had obtained confessions extracted by torture from several ex-members of the Templar Order who had been earlier dismissed for unethical behaviour. These confessions had been shown to the King who ordered that they should be passed as evidence to the Pope who after some persuasion issued a decree instructing the Inquisition to investigate these charges and make arrests.

In anticipation of their arrests and on the instructions of the Grand Master, the Treasurer Jean de la Tour and the Preceptor of Normandy, Geoffrey de Charney had arranged to move the Templar Treasury and that part of the Library containing the sacred scrolls to a safe place.

The Guardians could do nothing but await the fateful day for it was inevitable that the Inquisition would arrive at the Temple. By a stroke of good fortune Gilles and some of his fellow Guardians would survive the catharsis. Thirty Guardian Knights including my grandfather were selected by ballot to escort the wagons containing the precious cargo to the port of La Rochelle where a group of ships from the Templar fleet were moored. The remaining Guardians would stay and protect the Grand Master.

William of Paris the Grand Inquisitor of France was given the task to carry out the investigation and if the charges were proven the Inquisition would be empowered to take steps to eradicate the Order of the Poor Knights of the Temple of Jerusalem forever.. On Friday 13th October, the

Inquisition brought charges of suspected heresy and lewd acts against the Templar Order and the arrests began. The Inquisitor was thorough in his investigation and the confessions extracted by torture from those arrested proved the basis for a greater purge. During the next few weeks 600 Templars including Alain de la Croix were arrested and their lands confiscated.

A great sadness overwhelmed Gilles for he had feared for the family in Mallyrand. In the position he was in now he could do nothing but pray that they might be spared the purges that were taking place and if not that God would watch over them always.

In the harbour of La Rochelle the black and white chequered Beausant, the Templar flag, flew conspicuously at the masthead of the fleet commander. The remaining vessels flew their battle flag the "skull and crossbones" pennant, marking the Templar ships out among the rest. As soon as the Treasury and sacred Library arrived and were safely loaded aboard ship, the fleet sailed and only when the news of this reached Paris did De la Tour and De Charney give themselves up to the Inquisition.

Once the ships were at sea the Captains executed an order to avoid capture by ships of King Phillip by splitting the fleet into two flotillas. The Treasury ship and its escort had been ordered to make for Scotland where many Templar families had already taken refuge. The remainder headed for Nazare in Portugal close to the Templar fortress of Tomar. Before long both flotillas ran into a great storm which split the groups up. Most ships survived the storm and made it to Portugal and Scotland but several stragglers were blown far out to sea and were never seen again. After an arduous sea journey, the ships arrived off the East Coast of Scotland putting into the harbour of Mussleborough where the precious cargo was unloaded.

Sir Henry St Clair of Roslin, a Scottish Knight whose forebear was related by marriage to the first Grand Master of the Order was chosen to take the Treasury and Library into his safekeeping. He was also obliged in accordance with tradition to give succour to the survivors in a secret arrangement made after the Poitiers negotiations when the Grand Master Jacques de Molay feared for the survival of the Order.

Sir Henry St Clair was fiercely nationalist and being the hereditary Guardian of the Scottish throne he was mindful of Papal interference in Scottish politics. Showing his defiance to this puppet Pope, he had allowed the Templar rituals to continue in the nearby Commanderie at Haddington and new Knights to be raised into the Order. Before long news arrived that the Grand Master had been released after confessing and was under house arrest. When de Molay some seven years later retracted his confession he was imprisoned once again and burnt at the stake. When he died he did so with the knowledge that the Templar traditions would not perish but would remain in perpetuity under the protection of the St Clair family.

The refugee knights repaid their debt to Scotland by joining the cause against the English in the regular border skirmishes that would flare up. Together with Sir Henry's son, Sir William St Clair, the Knights fought with true chivalry on the side of Robert the Bruce at Bannockburn and were instrumental in defeating the English army.

After Bannockburn, so as to conceal the identities of the Knights Templar Robert the Bruce created the Royal Sovereign Order of Scotland and also appointed Sir William St Clair as the Grand Master of Crafts and Guilds of Scotland. A meeting place was set up at Balantrodoch fifteen miles from Roslin for most of the Knights had now settled temporarily in that area. Land to settle on was always a problem for these exiles and some even went northwest to settle in the highlands and islands of Scotland.

My great grandfather was fortunate that he had been appointed by Sir William as Stable Master at Roslin Castle and so now established at Roslin would later married Gyslaine, daughter of Henry de Niort a fellow Templar. Shortly after the marriage Gyslaine had given birth to my grandfather who they named Guilluame after William the son of the Lord of Roslin.

In 1330, an ageing Gilles rode out from Roslin with Sir Henry' son, Sir William St Clair together with several other Knights forming an escort of Templars accompanying the heart of Robert the Bruce, which young Sir William and Sir James Douglas had pledged to take to the Holy Land for burial. As they passed through Andulusia a large force of Moors attacked them and the Knights fought a savage battle fighting bravely and killing many of their foes, both the young Sir William St Clair and Gilles de La Croix were slain. In a final gesture of defiance, Sir James Douglas charged into the midst of the attacking force throwing the heart of Robert the Bruce at the enemy. He was finally surrounded and cut down. The Muslim leader was so taken with the courage of the Templar Knights that he preserved the life of the survivors. The Knights were allowed to return to Scotland with the heart of Robert the Bruce, which was later buried at Melrose Abbey.

Gilles' orphaned son, my grandfather Guilluame de La Croix was raised to be a Templar Knight. He married Rosalind younger daughter of Sir John Neil of Hawick who bore him a son my father. They had him named Gilles after his grandfather.

Guilluame remained at Roslin where he served Sir William St Clair, but in 1358 Guillaume joined Sir William St Clair of Roslin and other Knights on a Holy Crusade in Eastern Europe. It was he that had brought back the news that the Lord of Roslin had been killed. Just two days later Guilluame de La Croix died from the effects of the wounds he had received in the same battle.

My father was eighteen years old when his father died and had grown up in Roslin Castle with heir to Roslin, Henry St Clair. Although grief overtook both families the whole retinue at Roslin Castle assembled to see thirteen-year-old Henry St Clair succeed to the title and the responsibility it carried.

At the beginning of 1365 Henry and several of his Knights including Gilles joined a new Crusade to recapture the Holy Land. King Peter of Cyprus was in Venice assembling a fleet of ships and Sir Henry had joined him there. When the ships reached Rhodes, King Peter revealed his plans, they would attack and capture the port of Alexandria in Egypt there he would bargain with the Mamluks to exchange Alexandria for

Jerusalem. The crusaders succeeded in capturing and sacking Alexandria but within one week were forced to withdraw when many of King Peter's followers laden with booty from the City deserted him.

After the withdrawal Gilles accompanied Henry on a pilgrimage to Jerusalem having obtained safe conduct from the Saracen occupiers. The Prince returned with his followers to Roslin in 1366. It was his twenty-first year and Henry received the honour of a knighthood. Through his mother's lineage, she being the third daughter of Malise Sparre, Earl of Orkney he now laid claim to the Earldom.

In these intervening years my father Gilles had become a trusted member of the St Clair inner circle. In 1378 Gilles had married Margaret Jardine the fifteen-year-old daughter of Sir Robert Jardine, of Westruther. It was his second marriage, his first wife having died childless in 1370. Soon the fair Margaret was pregnant and no one was happier than Gilles.

Chapter Three.
The Castle of Roslin.

In the early hours of the cold spring morning of the Twelfth Day of April in the year of 1379, I was born in the castle of Roslin. The last sounds ever heard by my mother were the birth cries of her infant son, for at that point she surrendered her young life to the aftermath of a cruel labour. I was taken away and suckled by a wet nurse until I was able to take solid food. For a time Kirsty the wet nurse became my surrogate mother.

It was in that same year I was born that Haakon, King of Norway finally agreed to Sir Henry's claim to be Earl of the Orkneys that he would take the title Prince Henry. It had taken years of requests and argument by Sir Henry St Clair's mother Isobel who through her birthright had first made claim to the title of Earl when Henry was seventeen. The Prince now twenty four years old in taking the title would be obliged to show fealty to both the King of Scotland and the King of Norway and would be forced to spend more and more time away from Roslin.

Because of these long absences I rarely saw my father but for a few brief periods each year, the remainder of the time he would be away with Prince Henry and the other Knights subduing the northern islanders and securing his Earldom of Orkney. My early recollection of my father was when he returned on occasions from Orkney he was a tall, heavily built man with a dark beard who would lift me up onto his broad shoulders and stride around the castle courtyard shouting orders to his men at arms. When we were alone together he would enthral me with the stories that his father had passed to him which have forever remained in my memory.

Roslin Castle was situated high up on the edge of a valley overlooking the River Eske. There were two main buildings the Keep and the Great Hall. Surrounding these were the stable blocks, kitchens, the blacksmith and sword smith forges, carpenters shops and great storage barns for horse fodder and carts and all kinds of farming implements.

When my father was away with the Earl I would hang around the blacksmiths forge watching the blacksmith making the shoes for the horses and all kinds of metalwork for farming implements. Using the same forge was the sword smith who produced weapons with such skill, hammering together layers of metal to make swords of high quality.

The two artisans took me under their wing and I soon learned that the blacksmiths name was Fergus and the sword smith Martin. As they worked they would explain the skills of smelting making iron stone rocks into metal and using it to forge all kinds of implements. On many occasions I would go with them to the forest to collect charcoal from the charcoal burners who produced the fuel for the furnaces.

Whenever the Lord returned to Roslin a great Tourney would be held. I would sit in the stand with the ladies of the castle overlooking the tilts and watch the Knights jousting, earnestly wishing that I was old enough to take part. Occasionally a Knight would be seriously injured but most of the time only their pride was hurt. In the evenings and I was sent to rest I could hear the sounds of merry making and feasting as the day's events were recalled. Later the Knights and ladies would dance in the Great Hall of the castle to the sound of bagpipes, tambour, reed pipe, fiddle and lute. When the ladies had retired the old Templar songs would continue into the small hours sung by the Minstrel to the court.

On one of these return visits my father had been riding in a Tourney at Roslin. Having won the first two tilts he was about to ride a third when his charger took a fit and started to rear. He was clad in heavy chain mail and armour. Struggling vainly to control the horse he was violently unseated and struck the trunk of a nearby tree breaking his neck. It was unbelievable my father had fought many battles and survived and by sheer chance a fall from his horse had killed him. I was an orphan what could I do now I had no one to support me and I had just turned eight years old.

Prince Henry hearing of my plight took pity and welcomed me into his household and as we were the same age he said that I would make an excellent companion to Prince Henry's son and heir, young Henry and his ten brothers and sisters. Henry and I were placed under the guidance of Prior James a tall middle aged monk with a tonsured head breaking through a circle of red hair, bright blue eyes and a brusque manner that hid a sense of humour that would occasionally reveal itself. Prior James had travelled widely he had been on pilgrimages to the Holy City and to Santa Iago del Compostella in Spain.

We normally conversed in Erse but under his firm tutelage we learned to read, speak and write Latin and the Norman French. We acquired court manners and etiquette, became proficient at formal dancing and of course learnt the traditional Templar songs.

On my twelfth birthday as a treat Prior James took me to see the Great Library, which was situated in the tower of Roslin castle. He had been so impressed with my Latin reading that he gave me permission to visit one afternoon when young Henry was out hunting with his father. Up until now books and scrolls had always been brought to Prince Henry's quarters by the Prior and taken away after our lessons so this was for

me a great treat. Prior James explained that in
this library was the accumulated knowledge of
mankind.

As I grew older the Library became a wondrous
source of knowledge for me and I asked
permission to visit once a week whenever Henry
went hunting. Although they were deemed heretic
works by the Papacy among the many illuminated
books housed there I found and read Latin
translations of both the Koran of Islam and the
Jewish Torah. I realised that there was little
difference in these works from the basic Christian
teachings and it seemed that we all worshiped the
same God. It made me wonder why so many lives
had been lost in the cause of religion but thinking
perhaps these were blasphemous thoughts I kept
them to myself.

To this day I thank God with all my heart for the
guidance of Prior James, may his soul rest in
peace, for he introduced me to many works and
gave me access to the writings of Plato, Socrates,
Homer, Virgil, Ovid, Pliny the Elder and Seneca
and the mathematics of Euclid and Pythagoras,
the science of Ktevious and Heron of Alexandria,

The astronomical charts of Ptolemy and of the Saracen astronomers. I learned about castle defences and the order of battle, about the great wars of the past and how they were won.

Prior James had noticed that I had taken a keen interest in an ornate iron chest which stood at the centre of the library among the great volumes. It had an air of mystery about it and embossed on the lid was a shield with the chequered design and another with an engrailed cross. Set in between the two shields was skull and crossbones which surmounted the lock. He allayed my curiosity by explaining that this was where the sacred scrolls were kept. Only Templar Knights who had passed through the ritual could access them. Very few soldier Knights had the skills of reading or writing, so the texts had to be read to them. Brother Clerics would travel from far and wide to see them and because of the keen interest, several copies had been made and were kept in the library allowing the original scrolls to be preserved.

I remembered the stories passed down to me about my great grandfather and how he was chosen as one of the Guardians escorting the Templar Treasure and library in the escape from France during the purges against the Templar Order. I asked Brother James whether this was the chest that my great grandfather had escorted. Brother James said that this chest had been commissioned by Sir Henry's grandfather to house the scrolls when they arrived in Scotland and with all the objects that they had to bring a great iron chest such as this would have been far too heavy for the Guardians to carry.

Every now and then Prior James would have to go to the Scriptorium at Balantrodoch which was situated nearby to take or collect manuscripts for the library. One day he asked me if I would like to accompany him I eagerly accepted. On our arrival we were greeted by the large rotund figure of Prior called Gilbert who was in charge of the Scriptorium. I found it to be a large room with several windows room where several Priors and craftsmen were engaged producing and maintaining the books and manuscripts I had seen on the vast shelves of the Prince Henry's library. I watched fascinated as several brothers supervised the craftsmen working on elaborate manuscripts. While some were setting down translations from scrolls in Greek to Latin text, others were creating the beautifully illuminated texts which on completion were passed to the safekeeping of the librarian Brother James who would visit the manufactory to collect the repaired volumes and new translations.

I was so keen to visit the Scriptorium again that I spent many days pleading with Prior James to take me whenever he had to go back there. He said that he would think about it but the very next time I was allowed to company him and did so thereafter. It was during one of these visits that I was allowed to copy some of the illuminations and gradually developed a talent for drawing. Prior Gregory said I had a natural skill and showed me how to copy out texts and illustrate them.

As I have said Latin and Erse were the common languages in the Castle in addition Prior James helped me to improve my knowledge of the Norwegian and the Orcadian dialect because I might find them useful in the future. Now and then I would find scrolls in the library with very different text written in a particular way almost like illustrations. Prior James said this was the Arabic text of the Moors and the scrolls had been brought back from Spain when he made his pilgrimage to St Iago del Compostella many years ago. I was keen to study how this language worked for it was completely different from the Latin I was used to and was surprised to find that Prior James through his visit to the Holy Land had gained some knowledge of the spoken and written text. I asked the old Prior if it was possible to learn Arabic and he set about teaching me what he knew. Because I seemed to have a natural ear for languages the Prior felt that I should be entered for the scholastic life rather than waste my time training to be a Knight. However, I wanted to follow the traditions of my forebears and could not be convinced to do otherwise.

On the days when Prior James was away and the young Henry was with his father, I would wander round the grounds of the castle. I made another friend one of the castle masons called Roderick who looked after the fabric of the castle. He spent time showing me his skills and by carefully examining the surface of different stone he was able to create beautiful patterns and statuary. He would lend me his tools and watch me create something out of the cast pieces of stone and soon I found it was a skill to my liking.

On these occasions I would chat to him while he worked and he would show me the different types of chisel that he laid to the stone from the rough hewing to the finest detail hammering ceaselessly in a natural rhythm. I watched him as he carved a Sinclair crest on a piece of stone. Each chisel formed a different pattern on the stone as the image of a ship which had been outlined in charcoal gradually appeared out of the rough hewn face. The crest gave me inspiration and I was once again anxious to try my hand at the work. He showed me where he wanted the stone worked and I set about the task. Just as I had mastered the sword and lance I found as easy to use a mallet and chisel as if I had been born with them.

I wanted to try to produce something out of stone myself so I persuaded the Fergus the blacksmith who had been one of my father's former Men at Arms, to manufacture a set of chisels for me and with them he gave me a mallet he had scrounged from one of the carpenters which didn't weigh as heavy as those the masons used. From the Mason's workshop and was able to cadge a piece of stone to practice on. At first I made a copy of a drawing from a book in the library and set to work on the piece of block producing an engrailed cross. Later I managed to find stone that had been discarded by the masons and soon I had mastered my own style by creating effigies of animals and other subjects. One of a Knight on horseback resembling the Earl was given to my companion, the young Henry St Clair and was noticed by Prince Henry himself who then encouraged me to continue the craft.

Life in the castle was governed by the Seasons. The dull days of winter had passed and spring burst forth in a profusion of buds and new growth. The Spring Equinox was welcomed with a huge banquet to celebrate this day an ox was selected from the herd and slain. It was then hung, cleaned and prepared by the cooks and was carried with ceremony into the Great Hall pierced with a spit iron, it was raised on the spit irons set up at either side of the fire that burned on the raised hearth under the kitchen chimneys.

It was a busy time for the vassals for the Ox roasting began in the early hours and a large tray had been placed under the spit to catch the fat. The Ox was turned slowly against the fire which, had been fed with logs on one side and as the hot embers built up these were raked towards the spit. The cooking went on into the evening and from time to time the Ox was basted by the cooks until the delicious smell of roasting flesh that permeated the castle was so overpowering that the assembled guests began to yell at the cooks for a taste of the mouth-watering meat.

When the Prince and his family entered the Great Hall the crowd was silenced. The Earl clapped his hands and visitors were amazed as from a platform began to rise from the kitchens through a hole in the floor containing huge dishes of meat and vegetables. As soon as the platform stopped the food was removed and swiftly distributed amongst the assembled crowd and placed on trencher boards which had previously been set on the tables by the servants and squires. When everyone from the humble servant to Lord had ate their fill it was time to make merry and the Great Hall echoed with the sound of fiddles, harps, rebecs, flutes and oboes bagpipes and drums played by red coated musicians music and laughter.

Ancient traditions were kept up like searing the cattle against murrain. On the first of May we all rode out after supper to the hills to see the bonfires lit and to watch the cattle being driven between the fires to make them immune against the pestilence that attacked the cattle.

Summer arrived and everyone welcomed the season of the Tourney. On the occasions when the Jarl returned with his Knights to Roslin from forays with the English or from his domains in the Orkneys the Knights would show their mettle at the joust trying with little success, to unseat the Jarl's champion. During the long summer evenings the younger Knights spent their free time in trysts with the unattached women of the Court where they would strive to advance their courting skills in the vain hope of capturing a young lady's heart.

Autumn was a time for conserving the produce of the summer. Cattle and sheep would be slain and the meat preserved and salted for winter food. The household kitchens buzzed with the sound of cooks and vassals collecting and preparing the produce for winter storage, brining, drying, pickling, salting and smoking. Fish caught in the Firth and bought in the fish market at Mussleborough were dried and smoked over oak chippings in a shed in the courtyard. As winter approached the cattle were corralled close to the castle to protect them from the winter snows.

Winters were usually spent within the confines of the castle. The huge tapestries in the Great Hall were moved over the window ports and the whole place was lit with the glow of fluttering torches. In the centre the huge log fire tended by the vassals on a raised hearth was kept alight during the colder days and the court ladies would huddle together around the fire to keep warm. The occasional feast to celebrate a Saints day would lighten the atmosphere and make the company forget the dull winter days.

One of the highlights of wintertime was celebrating the shortest day the sound of wassailing filled the castle as garlanded singers accompanied by bagpipes and tambour went through every part of the household finally arriving at the Great Hall. Once there they would entertain the Jarl and his Lady until it was the turn of tumblers and jugglers. The celebrations would continue with trials of strength into the early hours until everyone was too exhausted or too full of ale. It would be the last celebration before the coming of the New Year, for now began the days of preparation leading to the celebration of the Holy Mothers confinement and the anniversary of Christ our Lord's birth. Priors and clerics assembled in the great hall and would spend the day in prayer, thanksgiving and singing watched over by members of the Court all celebrating Christ's Mass.

It was in this atmosphere of traditional pursuits and study that I grew into manhood but manhood had to be earned before it was recognised by the Earl and his Knights. One way of recognising this was to go on the now regular border skirmishes against the English.

After Bannockburn a letter was sent to the Pope with a declaration that from now on in Scotland; "We will never submit ourselves to the domination of the English; for it is not glory, it is not riches, neither is it honour but is it liberty alone that we fight for and contend for, which no honest man will lose but with his life." The Earl's great grandfather had been one of the signatories of this letter, a copy of which I had seen in the library.

Since my early years a burly Knight Sir Malcolm Donald had schooled us Pages in the arts of war and as Pages it was important that we were taught horsemanship. The horses we used were Palfreys and Amblers (small ponies) later we would advance to a Destrier (a horse similar to the modern Hunter), but a Knight would always wish that he could afford a Courser (a heavy muscled battle horse). We practiced the use the bow, dagger and sword, lance and shield also learned to wear small but heavy chain mail smocks, helmets and armorial attachments which at first I found to be most uncomfortable but it was necessary in order to be able to fight in the junior tourneys and gain experience tilting our lances. We would spend hours riding a wooden horse on wheels and pulled along by the other pages we would learn to couch our lance by holding it close to the body and across the wooden horse's head and to try to strike at a target.

In later years as we reached our fourteen summers we would begin to learn to use the heavy battle weapons such as the two handed sword, battle axe and mace, but for now Sir Malcolm was rigorous in his instruction and when training with a wooden sword I received many a blow to the body and head through dropping my guard. We would climb on each other's backs and fight with our wooden swords and shields to learn to keep our balance when in mounted combat.

As we approached our fourteen summers we looked forward to becoming Squires but we found that the training became more aggressive we would now be using heavy weapons. A high level of fitness was required now for we would engage with sword and shield, quarterstaffs and maces. When we were mounted we would use the Quintain which was a dummy with a shield attached suspended from a swinging pole which when hit would swing round. It was our task to avoid the heavy dummy after it was hit for it would rotate and knock the unwary squire out of his saddle and off his horse. Many a time I found myself sprawled in the dusty earth until I got the measure of the Quintain. Another game of skill was called ringing or running the rings, we would take a lance and ride full tilt at a series of rings strung along a course with the object of taking as many as we could. I was becoming quite proficient in the fighting arts as now we moved to the next stage of our training Siege warfare.

This was a common occurrence for the English had been fighting for possession of Scotland for the last hundred years and castles changed hands many times. I was to learn that sieges were carried out in a chivalric manner and rules of conduct were strict. A truce or settlement was always offered and only at the last resort would siege warfare commence so we were taught the options when defending a castle. The weapons used in a siege were large and unwieldy and on these occasions which were rare for we were taught the majority of sieges ended with surrender through starvation. However the long sieges were generally brought to a climax by using the Trebuchet, Ballista, Mangonel, Battering Ram, Siege Tower and scaling ladders. In a general assault we were taught to avoid boiling water and fat which could be poured down on the attackers from the battlements by covering our heads with our shields. I became very interested in the design of the defences of a castle and would spend time in the castle library pouring over the manuals on this subject.

Before we were to be accepted for knighthood we had to prove that we were brave, resolute, and honourable and could withstand all manner of trials that might befall us such as hunger, cold and heat and above all we needed the confirmation from Sir Malcolm that we were ready. Then only would we be allowed to engage in warfare.

I was nearly seventeen summers when I went on my first border raid as part of a group that raided the town of Coldstream. It was the day of the cattle market there and a chance for us to gain some extra cattle for the Earl. What we didn't know was that the town had been recently garrisoned by troops from the city of York. Luckily our scouts had gone forward to check the town and reported back with the news. The senior Knight Sir Malcolm Innes decided that we would split our forces and one section led by him would draw off the troops while the other section raided the town. I found myself in the section which would draw off the troops.

Our section of Knights and Men at Arms made ourselves obvious to the town guards and before long English troops were pouring out of the town in hot pursuit. We drew the troops away from the town towards a nearby valley so that they would be out of sight of the rest of the town's population. The townsfolk went about their business as if nothing had happened content in the knowledge that the troops would pursue the raiders and deal them a heavy blow. Our second party by this time had reached the outskirts of the town.

The townsfolk mistakenly thought our party were some of the soldiers returning from the pursuit and seemed more concerned with what was happening in the market place than a troop of soldiers entering the town. Only when our raiding party reached the cattle market did they show their true colours and set about releasing the cattle from holding pens and driving them out of the town towards the border to the amazement the local landowners and townsfolk.

Meanwhile our raiding party had split into two and were driving up both sides of the valley. As we crested the hills on either side the English troops were entering the valley. At a signal from the senior Knight we swung back and drove down attacking the troops from both sides. We fought fiercely showing no quarter and soon those English troops still alive were being chased back towards the town were finally cut down. Two of our men at Arms were dead and most of us had received sword cuts from the fierce encounter. Although we would eventually recover they would be a constant reminder of the battle fought which would last for the rest of our lives.

We returned in triumph to Roslin with about fifty head of cattle and Prince Henry rode out to greet us congratulating us on the success of our raid. From that time forward I joined several similar raids all with a degree of success. Eventually as the English placed huge garrisons of troops in the border towns our raids became less frequent.

During my eighteenth summer I became very attached to a lady of the court called Margaret, the fourteen year old daughter of Sir Robert Lindsay Preceptor of Haddington. Lady Margaret was a member of the Earl's household and served as a young companion to Janet the Lady of Roslin. I was joyful when she responded to my courteous advances and before long we were making secret trysts.

I quickly learned that the custom of courtship was to prove my love by some heroic deed or by pleasing the Lady with amorous verse. My fighting skills in the regular border skirmishes with the English were commended by the Prince. I was a brave opponent in the Tourney and I was respected for this so I thought I would try the other approach. Recalling the love poems of Ovid from my studies I became very proficient at composing amorous verses. My meetings with the Lady Margaret became more and more frequent.

We would seek out dark corners of the castle away from prying eyes and her chaperon and once alone I would read out my latest verse and in response she would allow me kisses. Before long I was smitten and lovelorn and in due course our behaviour became more and more reckless almost to the point of making love.

My foolhardiness was to be my undoing for whilst walking in the castle corridor one of the Ladies in Waiting found a piece of verse intended only for my Lady Margaret's eyes which my Lady had unwittingly dropped. The Lady in Waiting saw my signature beneath the verse and being quite enthralled with my poetry passed the verse around. The piece of verse became for a time a popular subject for discussion by the ladies of the Court I still remember it. It went like this:

I look for beauty in a face
A smile that has a glow
But beauty just means form and grace
When deeper I should go
Real beauty comes from inside
From a heart that's filled with love
The rest is all aesthetic

The body's like a glove
Just a protective outer shell
That eventually wears away
But love remains forever
Our love is here to stay.

It soon became common knowledge that we had been meeting secretly and eventually Lady Janet was and passed the knowledge on to Lady Margaret's father thinking I might be a good match for her. Sadly, Lady Margaret had already been promised to Sir John Maxwell, a wealthy landowner from the borders and her father was not impressed with my conduct. He was furious and I was brought before the Prince with a slight smile reprimanded me for he knew the rigours of courtship. Lady Margaret was immediately ordered back to her father's house and told she was never to see me again.

The day she left the castle I felt heartbroken, I knew I had lost her forever. Many months passed before I could console myself of the fact. Even then I never forgot the beautiful Margaret and would for some time after ignore the advances of the ladies of the court.

As I approached my twenty first summer, I was summoned to take instruction in preparation for becoming a Templar knight. As soon as I had learnt the ritual to the satisfaction of my Brother tutor, the initiation ceremony was arranged. Since the dissolution of the Order in 1307 there had been a continuation of the rituals which were held in secrecy. For some time prior to the Papal intervention the strict rules of celibacy had been dropped as part of a devout Christian worship. It was now common among the Knights initiated into the Order that they take a wife and only the Priors were confined to strict monastic lives as before. The virtues that had been the foundation of the Order, a strong faith, helping the poor and needy, charity, chivalry and honour in battle and a sense of brotherhood remained.

On the night prior to the ceremony I was made to stand vigil at the statue of the Virgin in the castle chapel. As the hours went by I found my eyes getting heavier and heavier, my head started to fall and the jolt would wake me up again. I spent the rest of the night fighting this sensation and praying to the Virgin to give me the strength to remain awake. I was glad when the first rays of sunlight crept in through the windows of the chapel knowing that soon my initiation would begin.

Later that morning I was taken blindfolded to a room specially prepared in the Castle and there was initiated as a Templar Knight by Prince Henry, the Grand Prior and two Knight Wardens. When my blindfold was lifted I stood before the Prince and was told I had to repeat after him the Oath of a Knight when I had finished I was slapped across my face so that I would remember it. From that day onward I would understand the meaning of Templar songs that I had known since childhood, of the strange artefacts I had seen in the castle and why Templar knights would congregate together in secret ceremonies at certain times of the year and now for the rest of my life I would follow the path of a Templar Knight as Sir Guillaume de la Croix.

Prince Henry had returned to the Orkneys in 1397 to make repairs to his fortifications and because of the recent death of his Master mason, had need of an Overseer to supervise the works at the castle of Kirkwall. He had been made aware of my skill and knowledge of fortification and masonry so Earl sent a message with the flag ship "Roslin" for me to join him there.

It was with great sadness that I bade farewell to the Lady Janet St Clair and the rest of the family I had grown up with. Roslin had been my life until now and Lady Jane had been like a second mother to me. On behalf of my surrogate family, Prince Henry's four sons and six daughters, the young Henry presented me with a pair of silver spurs. In turn I gave Henry a carved St Clair crest in polished granite that I had made and so we said farewell and I took horse to Mussleborough where I would join the Prince's ship Roslin.

**Chapter Four.
The Noble Venetian.**

Thus with a heavy heart I took my leave and made for the port of Mussleborough. The "Roslin", the Jarl's flagship was moored in the harbour. Leaving my horse with a groom to be ridden back to the castle I took a small rowing boat and was rowed out to board the flagship of the Prince's fleet. It was my first time on board a ship and I was alarmed at the prospect of sailing out into that vast sea.

We waited for high tide and with the great sail unfurled set off for the Isles of Orkeney. The flagship "Roslin" was one of two large ships the Earl had commissioned to be built on the lines of a Venetian galley. She was over sixty sword lengths long from stem to stern. The width was eighteen sword lengths amidships. There was one main mast with cross pieces made up of two spars spliced together supporting a huge square sail. There was a crew of a Captain and five sailors as the crew but when the Earl was aboard along the bulkhead were up to twenty-four rowing positions reserved for the Men at Arms who were capable of propelling the vessel along when there was no wind.

On the first day aboard I was introduced to the Captain of the Earl's Fleet, Antonio Zeno a native of the great seaport of Venice. I recognised in Antonio the manners and bearing of an aristocrat. Antonio told me that the Zen family were a noble family in Venice and occupied several palaces in that great city. His elder brother Carlo was Admiral of the Venetian fleet and his other brother Nicolo was Prince Henry's previous Captain of the fleet until his death in 1394.

I noticed that whenever Antonio went about the ship he was accompanied by a tall, well built black man who he would address as Jeruba who remained silently at Antonio's side and never speaking a word, I felt that hidden deep behind his somewhat sad facial expression was a man searching for a way to express himself fully. The man fascinated me, he was the first black man I had ever seen and I wanted to know more about his background.

Antonio on the other hand was a small man of slight build. He was sharp featured with an intelligent brow and the aquiline nose which I had read somewhere featured predominantly in the Italian aristocracy. Although at first meeting he seemed very serious I found that after conversing with him I found him to have a friendly personality to which I could not fail to be attracted. I was anxious to know more about this

Antonio Zen and wondered how he came to be so far from his native land. As the days of the passage passed I spent more and more of my days on the high deck in his company and was able to piece together the story of how Antonio came to be the Captain of the Earl's fleet.

When he had some time away from running the ship Antonio told me his story.
'Some years before, his elder brother Nicolo had been sent by the Doge and the Council of Venice to open new trade routes in the north. Whilst sailing around Britain, with other Venetian trading ships his ship had run into a storm and foundered on the shores of the remote Fer Island, (Fair Isle), which happened to be part of the Earl's domain. By the greatest of luck Prince Henry had been negotiating with the natives on Fer Island when Nicolo Zeno's ship foundered there. The islanders became hostile to these shipwrecked strangers for they heard them speak to each other in a strange tongue. They had heard rumours from local fishermen that it was these people from strange lands that had brought the plague to the land many years before. Fearing they might carry the disease they had surrounded

the survivors and were about to dispatch them while others on the beach began to carry away the salvaged cargo. It was at that moment that Prince Henry and his Knights arrived at the beach and intervened. Antonio said that his brother Nicolo had stepped forward and introduced himself in Latin hoping that just as in other places throughout the world it would be commonly spoken. Practiced the Latin tongue, the Prince was able to establish where the survivors had come from. His brother Nicolo told the Prince that they had sailed from Venice to trade with the northern lands. After conversing with Nicolo for a while the Prince realised that while in Venice on the way to Crusade in Egypt, he had met their elder brother Carlo Zeno the Admiral of the Venetian Fleet. Carlo Zeno was feted for repelling a sea borne attack by the Genovese fleet at Chioggia. He had inflicted a deadly blow on the Genovese destroying most of their ships and had saved Venice. Now he knew who this stranger was and where he had come from the Prince welcomed him to his Jarldom and asked him to accept his protection. Nicolo and the survivors had little option but to accept. The captain and his crew were given sanctuary by the Jarl and told that as they had no ship for the time being they would remain in his service. A tall well built African with skin as black as ebony had stepped forward with the captain. He only acknowledged the captain when the name Jeruba was mentioned so the Jarl asked who the giant Nubian was and how he had come to find him. His brother had explained that whilst his ship was sailing off the North African coast they had been attacked by Levantine pirates. His ship had come off better in the battle and the Levantine ship had been sunk. The Nubian Jeruba had been a slave oarsman in the Levantine ship and was below chained to one of the oars when Nicolo's ship attacked. Not realising there were slaves locked in the hold the Pirate ship had been sunk using the ships high deck cannon. Jeruba had somehow survived the explosion but had lost consciousness, when he came to he was floating in the sea still chained to a piece of the bulkhead which he had clung on to until he was finally rescued. The Nubian spoke in a strange tongue and occasionally in a language he recognised from his time in the North African ports as Arabic but with he had little knowledge of the languages and could not converse with him. A Venetian merchant on board the ship had a better knowledge of the dialects of Nubia and had translated what the Nubian was trying to say. He told the Merchant that his name was Jeruba and explained that he had been one of the oarsmen in the ship that had been sunk. He had been sold into slavery then bought by Arab traders who sold him on to the Levantine pirate ship captain as an oarsman. Hearing this story my brother had told him that anyone who had survived such an ordeal should be a free man and from that day forward he would be free. Jeruba was so indebted to my brother for saving his life that he had become his shadow and would not leave him. Antonio explained that his brother had eventually accepted this willingness to guard him and Jeruba had remained with him ever since and asked that Jeruba should remain with him. The Jarl said he could and although the other survivors would eventually be sent home to Venice when a ship became available my brother was asked to remain in his service as his navigator. Because my brother's life had been saved by the Jarl he felt it was his duty to remain with him.'

The Venetian explained that his brother was to become of great assistance to the Jarl using all his experience of naval and military tactics, He showed the Jarl the art of casting the Venetian style bound cannon and the Venetian method of ship building. He was adept at navigation and sailing skills and was instrumental in subduing the savage Shetlanders and repelling attacks on the fleet by the Baltic pirates. The Jarl had recognised Nicolo's unique abilities and within a year he had appointed him Captain of his fleet. Knowing that he would now have to remain in the Prince Henry's service he appealed to the Jarl that he might send for his younger brother Antonio to join him.

Antonio laughed at this. 'The Jarl had granted my brother's request and was delighted at the acquisition for I proved to be a better navigator and mapmaker than my brother.'

Antonio later told me that he was twenty-four years old when he arrived in the Orkneys and had been in the Jarl's service for five years. During this time his brother Nicolo had set about building up the Jarl's fleet and had been involved in designing this flagship "Roslin".

Whilst engaged in one of our many conversations on the upper deck Antonio told me that his brother had been commanded by the Prince to take three ships from the fleet and to escort the Bishop of Orkney to Greenland. The Bishop had received a Papal dictate to exchange his post with the Bishop of Greenland. The Jarl felt it was a great opportunity to explore the coast of Greenland and ordered Nicolo to carry out a survey and make maps of the coastline.

Antonio had afterwards read Nicolo's log of the journey he learned that his brother had visited a wondrous monastery on Greenland called St Thomas run by the Preaching Friars, monks who had travelled from Iceland. He was amazed to find that the whole building was heated with the boiling water from nearby volcanic springs. Vegetables and herbs were grown in the heated soil. Bread was baked in dry caldrons set over the boiling waters. Nicolo could not believe how well the monks lived in such a hostile environment surrounded by great ice fields.

Antonio said that his brother had recorded that while he was mapping the coastline, he had met natives who fished from boats made of animal skins, shaped like a weaving shuttle, (kayaks). They went out fishing in all weathers in these boats and when the seas were high they would pull a cover made from animal skin over their heads. If water came in they had a method of expelling it by using a funnelling system made from the same skin. The native fishermen had told him about the coastline to the West Side of Greenland.

Having mapped the whole of the East Coast Nicolo Zeno now rounded the South Cape and surveyed part of the West Coast to where a great ice flow known as a glacier flowed slowly into the sea discharging huge islands of ice. As he could make no further progress up the coast because of ice the ship returned to the Faeroes.

Antonio said the two years of icy weather in treacherous seas, with little or no protection had impaired Nicolo's health. On landing there he had suddenly became ill and within days he was dead, he was sixty years old. Antonio had been utterly devastated by his brother's death and asked the Jarl to be relieved of his duties and be allowed to return to Venice. The Jarl had refused saying he needed Antonio more than ever to replace his brother as Captain of his Fleet.

I noticed certain sadness in the eyes of both companions, one that could not be assuaged by the occasional laughter that would come out of our conversations on the high deck. I had penetrated their world but could only imagine their inner grief at being exiled far from the land, family and friends. I had known loss as a young boy but with the help of the Jarl's family had time to adjust to my life as an orphan but now I too had been separated from the family I had grown up with. I felt that we all had something in common and that Antonio and his constant silent companion Jeruba would make long lasting friends.

The talk of new lands had given me an appetite for exploration for I had been confined to the small world of Roslin and the Border country too long. It also made the journey to the Orkneys a pleasant distraction from the sadness I had felt on leaving Roslin. Eventually we arrived at Kirkwall, entered the main harbour and moored up alongside the quay. The harbour was dominated by two great buildings the church of St Magnus and the new castle built on the remains of the old Viking one,

At the quay I picked up the leather sack containing my belongings, said my farewells to Antonio and Jeruba and was escorted to the castle by a burly Man at Arms. On my arrival I was summoned to the Jarl's chamber and he gave me a great welcome then explained the work I would be undertaking. I took my leave and bade a servant to take me to my quarters where I found I was to share a cold bleak room in the tower with four other Knights. I noticed that the Knights referred to Earl as Jarl the Norse title so from that day forth I made a point of using this form rather than the one I was used to in Roslin.

I quickly settled in and began to explore the new castle that Henry had built it was much smaller than Roslin and I quickly had the measure of it. The castle had gradually expanded from the original Nordic fort and I was to supervise further expansion. In the first week I was able to get out and visit the countryside surrounding Kirkwall. Orkney was a strange and ancient Island of bald hills swept bare by the gales from the both the North and Western Seas. Unlike Scotland it had very few trees and those that survived were bent by the winds. The small dwellings that housed the residents had thick stone walls and roofs of turf to withstand the gales.

Kirkwall was mainly a fishing community and its inhabitants rarely ventured into the countryside. The more affluent islanders lived in crofts scratching a living from the poor soil and keeping sheep which provided meat for the table and wool for their clothes and a few dishevelled cows for milk. Others were engaged in cutting peat for the fires. The Orcadian women amongst all the other household duties wove fine woollen material on small cottage looms which they later sold in the market at Kirkwall.

And so within a month of my arrival, I now was fully engaged supervising the building of those additional fortifications around the old Nordic castle site at Kirkwall. I found that the main fortress had been started some years before I arrived and was complete but in addition to the fortress the Jarl wanted to make a secure base for his knights and his fleet. My job was to supervise the construction of a ship building and repair yard alongside the fortress, following the tradition of the Norsemen. I found myself totally occupied with this tasks and it was almost a year before all the work had been completed. The year had passed quickly and I began to make crossings to the surrounding islands to do were general repairs to the fabric of the fortresses or brocks dotted around the islands. I found that little maintenance was needed as most of them were merely a single tower.

Part of my time was spent travelling around the main island checking the outlying fortifications and I used as my mode of transport a small sturdy pony native to the island who I named Steadfast. We became quite attached to each other on the long days journeying, he wanted for nothing scrapping off turf flattened by the wind and drinking from the streams and pools. He never seemed tired and just plodded on at a steady pace until we reached our daily objective.

Although Orkney had little to provide for the islanders comfort, people had certainly settled there for generations getting a living from the sparse land and the bountiful sea. The links to their past were marked by strange and fascinating standing stones and huge mounds from ancient times past which the natives of the islands had built. These were said to be ancient burial mounds inhabited by spirits of their forbears and the natives kept well away from them. I decided that if I had time I would come back and explore them. Soon my tour of inspection was complete and Steadfast and I were heading back to Kirkwall to make my report to the Jarl. By the time

I arrived back at Kirkwall and had reported the state of the fortifications to the Jarl, I realised that supervision wasn't needed anymore for the repair dock and extra fortifications for which I had been responsible. These were now completed and the several masons employed by the Jarl were capable of carrying out the tasks of cutting and replacing stone blocks as and when they were required. Most of the other knights now spent long periods away with the Jarl as he extended his rule over his domain or visited his estates in Pentland. I soon found myself with nothing to do and becoming bored with my lack of employment at Kirkwall I needed something else to occupy my time.

First I tried to spend the long hours of inactivity travelling back around the island with Steadfast to inspect more closely the standing stones erected by some ancient race that once lived there and the strange mounds that were dotted about the fields of the island. When tired of travelling around I set my mind to improving my local Orcadian by spending time with the fishermen down at the harbour listening to tales about their adventures at sea. I met fishermen from Norway the Low Countries and Brittany and we would try to converse with each and although I knew some French dialects our conversation often was mainly with gestures.

One day by chance I was wandering about the castle and found myself in what seemed to be a small library. There I found the elaborate copies

of the Templar teaching scrolls, which the Jarl
had ordered to be copied from texts in the sacred
Templar scrolls. Being an initiate of the Order I
could now read the texts and was curious to
know more about them. I found that Prior
Ragnold was the Templar cleric in charge of the
small library and asked him if there was copy I
could read. The cleric thought this request
unusual because many of the Templar Knights in
the castle were illiterate and showed little interest,
nevertheless he agreed.

Curious about this strange Knight, the Prior
made enquiries of the cleric that had travelled
with me on the "Roslin" and found out that I had
been brought up with the Jarls heir and had
shown great merit in my studies. Therefore each
time I visited the library the cleric would present
me with a page of text from the scrolls. These
were Latin texts copied from the original Hebrew
texts found long ago under the remains of the
Temple in the Holy City and I spent long hours
poring over them.

One day by chance I happened to be reading a
text about the search for God's kingdom on earth

and discovered a passage about a bounteous land which would be found under a star in the western sky called Merica. At first I thought this must be a place in the imagination of the writer but evidence that I began to gather while talking to the fishermen in Kirkwall harbour would soon change my ideas. The discovery of the text began to consume my waking hours. I became obsessed by thoughts that there were lands to be discovered across the Western Sea and whenever I met with fishermen and sailors down at the harbour I would quiz them about land to the west.

One story in particular fascinated me, it was about a fisherman called Johanson who recounted stories about a crossing he made to the far western waters and by accident came ashore on an island covered in a great forest with coastal waters that had fish so abundant they leapt into the nets. Johanson had suddenly arrived at the port after ten years away with stories of how he had been captured by natives in the land across the Western Sea who had kept him prisoner until after many years he had managed to escape. Many of the fishermen I took these stories as a fishermen's yarn but in my heart I felt they might have an element of truth. I made my mind up to discuss the matter with Antonio Zeno. After all, his late brother Nicolas had brought back the charts he had made of Greenland and may have heard these rumours there. Antonio certainly validated the stories. He had told me that while on his voyage from Venice he heard many references to islands in the Western Sea from fishermen in ports along the Breton Coast. Whilst in one of the Breton ports he had spoken to local fishermen who frequently sailed westwards close to what they called the "Isle of Mists" where they had found fish in abundance. His brother Nicolo had made references in his log that whilst surveying the western part Greenland the native Inuit people had spoken of islands that lay to the south. They told of natives coming from an island in the southwest to trade with the Greenlanders. I was now becoming more and more convinced there was some truth in the texts. I spent hours reading to find other references to the star Merica but there were none. Soon an opportunity came for me to air the matter with Prince Henry.

One day the Jarl came into the library and found me pouring over the texts and asked me what was of so much interest that I couldn't acknowledge his presence. I got up from my seat, bowed low and apologised for my indiscretion explaining that I had discovered a reference to a star called Merica which would lead to lands in the west and explained that I had spoken with fishermen in Kirkwall who had told stories of lands to the west which could well be same place. I also repeated the conversation with Sir Antonio of the log that Nicolo Zeno had recorded whilst in Greenland.

The Jarl treated my enthusiasm with certain coolness. Although he was aware of the reference in the Templar texts, he considered it just as a parable about Paradise. He certainly knew of the tales and songs of the Orcadian fishermen telling of great sea voyages to the west but he had passed the off as fishermen's tales and had never really linked the two facts. However later that day the Jarl summoned Antonio Zeno and asked him what he had heard. The Captain of his fleet confirmed the stories of the fishermen his brother had said it was common knowledge among the native Inuit that there were lands to the Southwest of Greenland. He repeated the story about fishermen from the Scottish islands and the French coast who often spoke of sailing southwest to an island where they said, the fishing grounds were so plentiful, that the nets were sometimes too full to be raised into the boats. They said parts of the island were covered in forestland that stretched for miles and where fresh water was abundant.

The Jarl was beginning to feel there might be some truth in the stories. Land was growing sparse in the Orkneys and the Shetlands and the population had doubled since the last great visitation of the Black Death. If the islands to the west were as the fishermen had described he considered that they might support settlements and with the timber available the settlers would be able to build more ships and thus increase his fleet. Perhaps this might be a unique opportunity to extend his Jarldom. Eventually he decided that it might be beneficial to him to mount a small expedition to find these islands and lay claim to them.

Rumours spread among the seamen about the expedition. Some of them came to me and said that that the old fisherman Johansson, who had told the story of his journey across the Western Sea and his capture and escape, still lived just outside the harbour. Seeing an opportunity for making this voyage of exploration slipping away, I passed this news on to Prince Henry. The Jarl ordered me to find the fisherman and bring him to the castle where he would speak with him. I went into Kirkwall and sought out the fisherman but found him to be an old man in no fit state to undertake any journey. The years of captivity and life at sea had taken a toll and the man was riddled with rheumatics and nowadays he lived ashore permanently. I told him that the Jarl required his presence and arranged for a cart to bring him to the Castle and a litter to carry him as he was unable to walk more than a few steps, thus the fisherman was brought before the Jarl.

The old man was so frail that he was barely able to bow before the Jarl. The Jarl asked his name and speaking in Orcadian patois he said that his name was Olafur Johansson. The Jarl not able to fully understand asked for an interpreter so I stepped forward and translated. While I continued to translate the Jarl explained his intent to sail to these western shores and asked the old fisherman whether he had been there.

The old man explained that as a young man he had regularly sailed across the western sea to fish there. Depending on the weather and winds it took between twenty and twenty five days. On the last occasion he had set sail for the island the ship was blown south by a squall and the crew was forced onto a strange coastline many miles south of the island of mists. Whilst searching for a place to land and get food and water the ship hit a reef and sunk leaving only six survivors who struggled ashore. They managed to light a fire with a flint striker and while they were occupied constructing a shelter a group of natives appeared and became hostile. The fishermen naturally were in fear of their lives were taken captive and brought before what appeared to be the headman. By a series of hand gestures they demonstrated how they fished with nets and showed that many fish could be caught this way. On hearing this, the Chief ordered them to make nets from gut the natives had taken from slain animals. For a week they had toiled making a large net with this material but knowing that in water the gut would stretch they all agreed to make the net with a very fine mesh. As soon as it was finished the chief took two of the fisherman away and they were put into a small canoe escorted by two natives. They were taken to sea and dipped the nets over board and paddled the canoe around in a circle. After a while they withdrew the nets and to their astonishment found they had captured number of large fish. Their fishing techniques made an impression on the Chief and he spared their lives. By teaching their fishing skills to different tribes of natives along the coastline they realised they could avoid being put to death.

Several years passed as they were forced to go from one tribe to another moving steadily south along the coastline of this great land.
After they had been five years in captivity they were sold to a great tribe, which lived in huge cities made of stone. Great temples rose from a broad base to a point high above the earth. The old man explained that these natives in the southern lands were devils in disguise and

sacrificed men to their Gods on the tops of these great temples in a bloody ritual. He soon realised that if the fishing became sparse the Chief would use it as an excuse to sacrifice them and had begged his colleagues to join him in an escape. The fish were plentiful, they could not believe their lives were in danger and they refused.

One day he took out a small boat he had rigged with a sail and had stored it secretly on the boat. A native guard accompanied him and they set off to fish a bay further up the coast as usual. When they had been at sea for some time and were ready to haul in the net, he persuaded the guard to help him haul it in. While the native was leaning over the side he had dispatched him with a blow to the head and pushed him into the sea. He recovered a sail that he had hidden on the boat and managed to escape by sailing north.

After several days at sea he was forced to find water and eventually located an island where he felt safe remaining there for two years with a friendly chief. One-day some Breton ships appeared in the bay and although he was unable to speak their language he was overjoyed that at last he was united with other fishermen from the east. He spent two more years trading with the fishermen until they were able to take him back to Kirkwall. By this time he had been away for more than ten years.

Johansson said he was too frail to accompany the Jarl but there were two other fishermen in Kirkwall who were crew on the ship when he had returned from Brittany to Kirkwall they had been across the Western Sea many times. He said that if he was forced to go and the Jarl's ships ventured south of the western island, he would not go ashore but it was clear that man could not survive another sea journey so the Jarl dismissed him.

Three days later the old sailor, who had related so vividly his experience of the western lands, died suddenly. The Jarl commanded that the other two fishermen who had sailed to the western waters be found and brought to him and after several days scouring the port they were found. At first they were reluctant to make another journey across the western sea but after some persuasion by the Jarl who agreed that they would be given a grant of land on Orkney if they would guide his ships to the western lands. Only now did the Jarl begin to make preparations for this great undertaking.

I now took this opportunity to ask the Jarl to take me along as the translator. I could speak the local dialect fluently and could be the interpreter between the fishermen and the Jarl. I gave other reasons to go, when they reached the land to the west the Jarl would need someone to design sturdy shelters and fortifications and I had the skill to design and build them and if necessary I could fight as well as any of the other Knights should I be required to do so.

The Jarl considered my request for a long time. He had always treated me as a second son and initially he was reluctant to allow me to go but he could see the merit in taking me with him and in the end gave way.

Chapter Five.
The Unforgiving Sea.

The Jarl summoned a council of his Knights to consider mounting an expedition although by now he had already made his decision to go so there was no opposition. The Jarl decided that the main fleet would remain at Orkney under the command of his steward Sir Erik Ragnussen and he would leave sixteen of the Knights to guard the castle with three hundred men at arms and they would remain ready to defend the Orkneys should it be required.

At the end of April 1398, the Roslin, the three Drakkars, the Haggar, the Kral and the Kreland and six Galleys and the three Cogs, the Help and the Hold named after two famous St Clair dogs

and the Haakon, were provisioned and made
ready to sail from Kirkwall. Knowing the dangers
that might face them on such a voyage before
leaving Prince Henry made certain dispositions of
his lands to his brothers, John and David. To his
eldest daughter, Elizabeth, who married Sir John
Drummond of Cargill, he left his lands in
Norway, if he should die without a male heir.

His Captain of the Fleet would travel with him in
the "Roslin" to navigate and draw maps in
addition two of his Knights, Sir Hugh Douglas
and Sir Guy de Blanchefort would sail each with
fifty Men at Arms in the Galleys together with the
captains and crew together with the Priors and
craftsmen. Two of the Cogs the Help and the
Hold would carry more provisions, chandlery,
tools, ropes and sailcloth and barrels of fresh
water and the third the Haakon was chosen to be
fitted out with stalls to accommodate the horses
and the Knight's squires in attendance with
enough fodder for several weeks.   .

The Jarl, Sir James Gunn, the Grand Prior and
Antonio Jeruba and myself were each given a
small space in the aft of the Roslin under the high

deck. Three clerics would be quartered along the ship sides together with the two fishermen guides, twelve seamen and twenty Men at Arms who made up the Jarl's escort found accommodation where they could. A cook took an area in the centre of the ship where a large iron plate with folded edges on which a fire could be lit had been placed on two heavy beams. The cooking would be carried out in a large cauldron hung over the fire on three heavy chains from a crossbar. One of the forward sail hatches would contain the food and water for the cook to use on the journey. Sailcloth, tar, tackle, gunpowder and ropes would be stored in the others and any remaining ropes, blocks and tackle would be stored in the prow. There were two banded cannons assembled by Nicolo Zeno a few years before which had been mounted on swivels on the high deck. The ship was steered with a huge sternpost rudder and tiller which required two men to operate in rough sea. "Roslin" was truly a fine ship and the Jarl was proud of her.

.

On the day the fleet prepared to sail on the morning tide, Antonio Zeno stood ready with the

others on the main deck of the flagship.
Wherever Antonio went Jeruba shadowed him,
never uttering a word. He appeared to take these
duties very seriously and the crew kept well away.
They rowed out of the harbour, hoisted the sails
and began to move into the open sea and heading
northwest the ships made good progress.

On the third day at sea we reached the Faeroe
Islands and as soon as we had taken on food and
water we set sail once more. After a further two
days at sea we reached a large island and with the
intention of taking on kindling wood and more
water put boats ashore. The two fishermen
accompanied the party ashore to speak to the
islanders. The Jarl had commanded the shore
party to show good will to the islanders and to
find out where we might find a safe harbour and
provisions. Having seen a large fleet approaching
the island and thinking they had arrived to take
possession of their island home, the islanders
became hostile and soon a large group assembled
brandishing spears and bows and arrows. The
shore party was ordered back to the ships and we
sailed round to the eastern side of the island and
located what appeared to be a harbour.

We made a landing and were successful in obtaining a few supplies. However the islanders that we had seen previously appeared in numbers and again became hostile. They attacked the men still ashore and in the retreat to the boats, a battle ensued. In the melee the two fishermen guides, three of the Sir James Gunn's men were killed and two others were wounded as they fought a rearguard while the rest of the party clambered aboard the boats. The Jarl, frustrated by the encounter, decided to leave the island as soon as everyone was safely on board.

As the fleet sailed away it encountered dangerous shoals around the island and soundings were taken and lookouts were posted to assist the passage, the infuriated islanders followed our progress by running along the cliff tops howling and shouting and occasionally shooting arrows which dropped harmlessly into the sea. All the ships made it through the shoals and soon we had left this God forsaken hostile land far behind. The Jarl commanded Antonio to head for Iceland to find a safe harbour and signalled the rest of the fleet to do the same. There we hoped to obtain the remainder of the supplies needed but alas it was not to be for by that evening the fleet ran headlong into a storm.

For three days the seas pounded the flotilla. On the "Roslin" the sails were reefed, the huge tiller was lashed in a central position, a sea anchor was cast over the side and the ship was left to ride out the storm as best it could. It was hoped that captains of the other ships in the fleet had the foresight to follow the same practice. Every now and then a huge wave would burst over the prow drenching everyone and everything. All un-essential crew were confined below the gunwales exposed to the elements, using anything they could find for shelter.

As the days went by the lurching ship began taking on a lot of seawater and both sailors and men at arms worked frantically with wooden buckets to bail it out. Although I volunteered to assist I was told to stay below the high deck and leave it to the men. So I crept back into the small confined space but at least while I remained there I was dry. Throughout the turmoil and fury of the raging storm I lay with my cloak wrapped around me listening to the shouts of the men as the ship creaked and groaned around me. Along the deck Men at Arms huddled together trying to protect themselves from the surges of spray and seawater invading the ship while Antonio and Jeruba also wrapped in their cloaks spent hours on the quarterdeck searching for a break in the weather.

For sustenance we were forced to eat dried fish, there was little else for the storm had prevented the fire normally burning in a metal fire box with a great cauldron swinging over it from being lit. When the storm finally ceased a light wind allowed us to light the fire once again, make repairs and to reduce the level of sea water that had entered the bilges.

The fleet had separated in the storm and the Jarl ordered a search to locate the others. After two days searching the horizon only five of the six Galleys and a Drakkar had been accounted for, so a wider search was commenced. Eventually the wreck of a Cog Haakon was sighted and several horses and men were found floating in the sea.

Shortly afterwards the two other Drakkars and the Cogs Help and Hold were finally sighted and once again joined the fleet.

At the end of a very long day searching this vast ocean the missing ships were declared lost with all hands. The Jarl mourned the loss of the men and his favourite horse which had been lost with the Haakon as were all of the Knight's horses and their accompanying Squires. The mood on board ship was low after this for many of the squires had served the Knights for years. The Head Prior led prayers for the souls of those lost at sea.

With the two fishermen gone Antonio had no one to guide him in his navigation and had to make the best of his experience. After the storm he noted the ships heading had moved round from northwest to due west and although he had tried desperately to keep on course for Iceland, he could do nothing but inform the Jarl that the strong winds and changing currents during the storm had driven the ships way off course.

Not knowing how far landfall would be to the west it seemed foolhardy to sail on westwards without essential supplies Antonio argued that to try and retrace their previous route to the north could be just as bad. The Jarl decided however that we would continue westwards and pray we would reach land before supplies were depleted. When the remaining ships were signalled and told of the decision some of the soldiers began murmuring about the decision for they believed that world was flat and they would sail off the end if they went too far west.

The wind freshened during the next two days and the ships were able to make headway. The storm had turned the "Roslin" into a cramped and stinking space below the main deck but at least we had survived all that the storm could throw at us. I now cherished every moment of time spent above deck and each day I would awaken at first light, leave my hammock and go to the high-deck. Following the fashion of the other sailors I would take a wooden bucket tied to a rope, throw it over the side and haul seawater back in order to drench my body. The cold sea water revived me and helped to rid me of the lice that had invaded my body. Afterwards I would consume some of my daily ration of food and water and then wander up to the high deck to join Antonio who spent most of his days bent over the at the navigation table noting the changes in the weather and the currents.

Apart from my time on the main deck with Antonio and Jeruba, I spent the days walking back and forward along the deck thwarts in order to stay fit and most of the time I spent in the company of Sir James Gunn. We were about the same age and had both been initiated as Templar Knights in the same year.
Sir James Gunn of Clyth was the son of one of the Knights who managed the Jarl's Pentland estates. A giant of a man, he stood head and shoulders above most of his men. He had a large square jawed face with piercing blue eyes, a roman nose and a shock of red hair with a beard to match. Well skilled in the fighting arts he could wield a sword with accuracy. It was he and his men at arms who had managed to stave off the attack by the hostile islanders allowing everyone to get back to the boats. He was a cheery soul and would make me roar with laughter at his jests.

On one occasion whilst taking my daily ablutions, I asked him to re-fill my water pail. James, who was standing behind me, dipped the bucket and line into the sea and hauled it out but at the last moment had swapped it with one left by the gunnels by the cook containing the slops from the deck kitchen. I was still soaked from the previous drenching and picked it up and without noticing the contents pouring it all over myself. I retaliated by drenching James with the contents of the real water pail only to be caught in the act by the Jarl who seemed displeased at our antics.

I realised that James had been taught well by the variety and depth of his conversation. For a knight used to battle he was enlightened in Latin and Greek and well versed in ancient history. We would pass our time discussing family history and the kind of land we would find to the west, considering whether it would be the promised paradise that the star Merica would guide us to and as time went by we struck up a firm friendship.

I also spent a lot of time on the high deck with Antonio as the voyage progressed. I was there one day when Jeruba caught his foot on a block lying on the deck. The huge man let out a yell and a stream of words that I recognised immediately as Arabic. I decided that I would try to converse with the silent Jeruba in the little Arabic I had learnt as a boy at Roslin to see whether he would respond. I addressed the tall African by his name and asked him where he had come from. The African suddenly became animated his eyes lit up and excitedly he replied.

"I am Jeruba, a warrior of the Dinka tribe. I come from a land beyond Egypt; my village is in southern Nubia. In my language my village is called Nyala".

I asked him to slow down and repeat what he had said so that I could get used to Jeruba's form of the language. Once I had mastered the African's style I asked Jeruba how he had been taken from his home.

"We were at war with the Shilluk tribe. Shilluk warriors raided my village. I received a spear wound in the leg and could not run."

The Nubian pointed to the long scar on his right thigh.

"I was taken prisoner with several others and eventually sold to Arab slavers. They took me down the great river to their City of Al Misr (Cairo) and sold me to a dealer. From there I was taken to Alexandria and eventually sold to a Levantine captain as an oarsman. I spent the next six years on the ship until Sir Nicolo the brother of Antonio saved me from the sea and for this I owed him my life. It is good to hear the sound of my own voice I have had difficulty understanding your language so I have kept silent since Sir Nicolo died."

Antonio, who knew no Arabic, was surprised by Jeruba's animated conversation and was eager to know what had been said. As each day progressed I became more fluent remembering many of the words that I had been taught by Prior James. Each day Jeruba told me more about life in his small village. I would translate all Jeruba said for Antonio and before long an account of the previous life of the big Nubian began to emerge. He spoke of a country where there were great droughts when even the village wells would dry up. On these occasions his mother and sisters would have to walk miles to seek water.

When Jeruba was twelve he was among several boys who were taken away from the village to a secret place. There they had gone through training for initiation by the village Shaman and some of the older warriors. He was taught the finer arts of hunting and preparing meat. His teachers explained how warriors would drive deer into traps set in the ground in order to provide food and clothing for the village. He learned about poisons and curatives, which could be found in the roots of plants in the Nubian Desert. When certain berries were crushed and placed on the tips of arrows they had the strength to kill a lion. The training ended with a ritual ceremony of circumcision and so by the time he returned to his village he had left his childhood behind and had become a man.

I learned how Jeruba had become skilled with the bow and spear and had killed his first lion when he was sixteen summers and when he had returned triumphantly to the village with his kill, the Shaman had cut into a vein in the lion's neck and drawn blood into a dish which Jeruba was offered to drink to take on the strength of the lion. The village elder presented with a necklace made up of the of the dead lion's teeth as a trophy to his skill as a hunter. From that moment he would be accepted a warrior thereafter join the village hunting parties and would spend weeks with them in the desert seeking game.

He said that every return of the hunting party heralded a great feast. The women of the tribe would sing songs of praise to the hunters as they prepared the food. Following the feast the warriors would dance into the night, mimicking their encounters with the prey. Jeruba demonstrated how the dance went by making a great leap in the air then a small jump then another great leap. He repeated this over and over again humming a strange rhythmic chant.

This had been a happy time for him and he was ready to take a wife. Soon his village would hold a huge celebration where all the surrounding villages would come together for a choosing ceremony and the young girls from the villages would dance with the young men culminating in the choosing of brides. It was nearing this time and while the women prepared the young men went off to hunt for the food for the feast. While they were away from the village disaster struck for they found on their return Shilluk warriors had invaded their village and were rounding up the women. A fight ensued during which several of the hunting party were killed. Jeruba had been badly wounded in the thigh and couldn't avoid capture. He was herded with the rest of the survivors to a place outside the village and watched while it was burned to the ground. All their treasured cattle were rounded up and they were taken together with the cattle to the Shilluk where they were held awaiting the arrival of Arab slave traders. They men were eventually sold to these Arab slavers and the woman were taken as wives by the Shilluk. He was just eighteen summers.

Jeruba went silent as memories of his days with his people flooded back and remembering his family his eyes glistened with tears. I was quick to realise his loss for I understood the pain of losing loved ones so I laid my hand on the giant's shoulder and speaking in Arabic said softly.

"You have a new family now Jeruba and from this moment on we will pledge to defend each other against any danger that may befall us if and when we reach the new lands."

The giant smiled briefly but not even this could quell his sadness.
Now that Jeruba could converse with us the bond between us became closer and Antonio and I formed a greater respect for the Nubian knowing his background. Jeruba was anxious to learn more about both our lives expressed a wish to learn our common language Latin so that he could converse with Antonio. So while Antonio was engaged with the navigation of the ship, I spent time teaching Jeruba. The Nubian learned quickly and very soon he was able to make up short sentences. Antonio was amazed at his progress at last could converse with a man who had been his silent but constant companion since his brother died.

By the fifteenth day at sea the whole mood on the ship had changed from optimism to unease. There were still no signs of the land the fishermen had promised would appear although the Jarl seemed outwardly calm behind the mask, he too was worried. We were now down to the last of the provisions carried on board, the salted meat had finished some time ago and what was left of the fresh vegetables and fruit had rotted away and had been thrown overboard ten days before. We were living wholly on any fish caught each day and now of the four large water barrels that we carried all but one were empty and the last barrel had enough water for five days sailing.

The Jarl feared that the ships were sailing too far south and had expressed his thoughts to Antonio some days before. By now Antonio was having difficulty convincing the Jarl that this was not the case. The crew perceived the disquiet in our leader and once again there were murmurings of discontent which soon spread throughout the rest of the ship. The Jarl was quick to dispel the rumour and forbade anyone to spread such talk under the penalty of punishment.

It was now the twentieth day since we had left the Orkneys. Antonio was on the quarterdeck, carrying out his daily routine making compass checks and desperately searching the horizon for some sign that they were nearing land. The ever faithful Jeruba stood by his side. It was around midday that Antonio noticed towards the west on the far distant horizon there were, cloud formations. There were certain clouds, which he knew from past experience, could only be associated with land. However he kept these things to himself until he had proof then in the middle of the afternoon several gulls descended on the jettisoned scraps trailing behind the ship. Antonio was no convinced that we would make landfall within the next two days and passed his observations to the Jarl. The Jarl immediately ordered a lookout to the masthead and one to the bow.

However on the twenty fifth day at sea a great fog descended and the ships were becalmed. The Jarl ordered the ships to close up and lines were passed to connect them together. Prince Henry's ship took the lead while the others lay astern. The fog made everyone jittery. There were legends of

great sea monsters rising out of these fogs and swamping ships. A sullen mood seemed to affect the whole company who went about their duties in silence and trepidation.
Our progress became very slow, there was no wind and the men at arms had taken to the oars.

As the fog lifted it signalled a noticeable lifting of spirits before long we had caught a light wind and were making good progress. Just after sunrise on the twenty ninth day since our departure from Kirkwall, a great shout came from the masthead lookout.

"Land Ho! Off the starboard quarter!"

Everyone on board looked to starboard, systematically searching the horizon. I joined the Jarl, Antonio and Jeruba on the high deck. My heart was pounding with excitement. There on the horizon I could make out the dark shape of land. The shouts had caused the nearby ships to send up lookouts and they too joined in the celebration. Tedious routine surrendered to spirited activity as the Jarl began to shout orders and Antonio set a course for the distant shore.

The sailors now went into the routine of trimming the sail to get the best of the wind. The excitement I had experienced now to spread throughout the fleet as we sped towards our first dry land for nearly two months.

Chapter Six.
The Land below the Western Star.

Next morning as the small flotilla of ships was approaching the uncharted coastline the Jarl warned both the lookouts at the masthead and the prow to be on their guard for submerged rocks. He passed the order to the other ships and they followed suit coming about in line astern. The landfall seemed to be a continuous formation of tall impenetrable cliffs and small rocky offshore islands.

Antonio intent on finding a suitable place to make a landfall set about making a chart but which ever direction he looked tall cliffs dominated the shore, stretching uncompromisingly to the distant horizon. To the south however, he noticed a slight break in the cliffs and felt it should be investigated. He approached the Jarl and suggested we tack southwards following the coastline. The Jarl agreed and the rest of the fleet was signalled.

For a night and half a day we tacked steadily southwards keeping close to the shore. Antonio had been right in his assumption the cliffs appeared to be reducing in this direction but even so, every inlet we passed seemed inaccessible.

It was now almost two days since we had first sighted land. Everyone on board was eager to get ashore after enduring such a long time at sea. Antonio was busy at his post mapping the coastline that we were passing. At mid-day we rounded a tall headland and saw an expanse of open water with what looked like two large islands rising out of the distant cloud. Antonio ordered the ship to be steered well away from the islands keeping them away on the starboard beam for fear of hitting submerged rocks.

The Roslin was now heading south across open water and the other ships followed in line astern. Everyone looking towards this new land could make out on the horizon what appeared to be a line of green hills. As the ships ran towards the shoreline the green hills resolved into thick lush virgin forest covering the land as far as the eye could see. Far away to the west rising above this forestland was a bald grey mountain.

The ships stayed in line behind the Roslin making progress alongside a bank of raised gravel that fell away to the shore making Antonio almost miss seeing the narrow entrance to what appeared to be a fine natural harbour which seemed suitable to afford protection from the open sea.

I stood on the prow with the Jarl who was staring thoughtfully at the shoreline above the gravel bank which was thick lush virgin forestland as far as the eye could see.

"Observe that fine stack of trees Guillaume." He mused. "What a fleet we can build from those!"

"It is all that the texts promised the land beneath the star Merica would be Sire." I replied.

"Your researches proved right my son. We must praise God, the great Architect of the Universe for guiding us on our safe passage." The Jarl placed his hand on my shoulder. "We have discovered a fine land."

Standing close by to the men at the edge of the high deck a seaman leant over the side of the ship swinging a knotted line to which a lead weight was attached each knot was tied at where the outstretched arms of a man was. Each time the line touched bottom he would retrieve it, count the knots and shout out the depth to Antonio who was on the high deck plotting them on his map of the coastline. Guillaume was keen to know what the seaman was doing and why the line had knots tied at varying distances and while the seaman continued his task he explained that each knot was tied at the width of a man outstretched arms and that distance was called a fathom. The seaman pulled the rope up checking the line where the water came to and shouted.

"By the mark four fathom!" He shouted and again. "By the mark four fathom...."

At this point Antonio made a mark on his chart showing the water depth along this stretch of the coastline. The ever-vigilant Jeruba stood close by, his huge arms folded, staring thoughtfully at the shoreline. The ships were now sailing into the estuary of a river and the count continued.

"By the mark three fathom... By the mark three fathom!"

The estuary bottom was coming up quickly now so when the depth reached two fathom Antonio reported it to the Jarl. The Jarl ordered a seaman to signal the other ships to heave to and the stone anchor to be lowered.

One of the ships four rowboats was lifted from the deck and lowered over the port side of the ship. A messenger was dispatched to row to the other ships and pass the command that all

Knights join the Jarl on the "Roslin" next morning to make arrangements for the first shore party.

As the morning mist cleared small rowboats began to arrive bringing the Knights to the flagship where they assembled on the high deck. The muffled conversation and laughter around the ship ceased as the Jarl appeared on the high deck to address them.

"Gentlemen knights, we have travelled far, overcome savages, great storms and treacherous seas which by the grace of God we have survived and at last we have reached a new land. Truly this is the land that was confirmed in the Templar texts, the earthly paradise set below the star Merica".

A great cheer went up. The Jarl held up his hand.

"At first light tomorrow Sir Guillaume de la Croix, Sir James Gunn, Sir John Douglas and Sir Guy de Blanchefort and their men at arms will accompany me ashore. Sir Guillaume and the Prior will travel with me and the rest of the knights and their men will follow and together we will carry out a survey of the immediate area."

The red bearded Sir James stepped forward.

"And should we encounter savages as we did on that accursed island my Lord?"

"If we encounter any savages Sir James we will show them respect and that we come in peace." The Jarl replied. "Do not provoke them unless you are threatened. Our prime task is to find water and fresh food for we must restock our water barrels and find game to hunt."

"It will be done as you command my Lord." Bowing slightly the Knight stepped back to the circle.

The Jarl resumed.

"The rest of our company will be allowed ashore as soon as we have established that we can survive independently here. My aim is to explore this land and if we find fresh water and a source of sustenance here to build settlements for my people."

He pointed towards a small sandy beach set between two rocky out crops.

"We will assemble around the flagship in our boats at dawn and make for that inlet. It appears a good place to land."

He turned once again to the assembled company.

"So my Knights leave me now and go forth to make preparations to set foot on this new land we will muster once again on the morrow."

The knights broke up into groups and made ready to disperse to their awaiting boats. The air of expectancy had now given ground to the enlivened chatter of conversation. I joined James Gunn on the high deck.

"To be the first of our party ashore in this New World," I said excitedly, "what good fortune."

"Your fortune might change if we meet hostile savages like those we last encountered." chortled James.

By the time the Knights had returned their ships the sun was sinking behind the trees. I joined the Jarl and Antonio to eat a last meal of dried fish washed down the wine from the Jarl's one remaining barrel. The Jarl, in a somewhat ebullient mood, praised Antonio for his skill in navigating the fleet across the great sea. Soon in the small deckhouse, the conversation had lapsed into an atmosphere of heightened anticipation, which could only be suppressed by sleep and one by one we bade the Jarl good night and returned to our cramped quarters, leaving the Jarl alone with his thoughts. Although desperately tired after all the excitement of the day, I lay in the darkness thinking about the coming day but soothed by the gentle rocking of the ship I soon lapsed into a deep sleep.

**Chapter Seven.
An Earthly Paradise.**

I woke to the sound of shouting and went up on deck the men were scurrying about preparing for the shore party; sailors were busy preparing and lowering the two rowing boats over the side. As I reached the high deck the sun was just peeking over the horizon. Antonio was already supervising the disembarkation I greeted him cheerily as my body took my usual bucket of refreshing seawater. It washed the sleep from me and brought me back to life.

Returning below I got dressed putting on my leather doublet, hose and shoes and fastening my sword belt around my waist. Finally I positioned my metal head guard and returned to the high deck. Antonio stepped away from the chart table and approached me.

"My friend this is a great day, I wish I could share in your joy at landing but as Fleet Commander I must remain with the ships. However, I have asked Jeruba to accompany you whenever you go ashore and he has agreed."

The tall Nubian stepped forward.

"I will be happy to watch over you just as I have safeguarded my friend Antonio and his brother before him."

"Thank you Jeruba, I am glad to have such a warrior protecting me." And turning to Antonio

I said. "I am sorry that you cannot be with us Antonio but my return I will recount our adventures in the new land."

I shook Antonio's hand and bade him a fond farewell for who could know what fate would have in store for us once we were ashore.

The sailors still seemed to be hurrying about. Men at Arms were assembled under the command of Sir James and despite what the Jarl had said about not provoking the natives some were armed with shields and lances others with long bows and quivers of arrows. After our previous encounter with hostile natives they didn't have the appearance of a foraging party instead they appeared ready to take on the meanest foe. Only when the Jarl appeared would the order to board the waiting craft be given.

The Jarl stepped from his quarters under the high deck. He was dressed in a long brown studded leather smock on which were emblazoned the arms of the Jarldom of Orkney depicting a red mythological beast rising out of a silver crowned helmet surmounting a silver shield on which was a black scalloped cross. The smock was drawn at the middle by a wide belt with an ornate buckle from which hung his sword and dagger and set on his head was helmet with a circlet of engraved gold. He walked over to where Jeruba and Sir James and I were waiting.

"It seems you have a shadow now Sir Guillaume." He said noticing Jeruba at my side. "Sir James, I will take a Sergeant and five of your men with Sir Guillaume the Prior and Jeruba. The remainder will go with you in the other two rowboats. We will meet the other parties on the small beach and there we will hold a service to thank God for our safe arrival. Sir Guillaume fetch my Standard and let us to the boats."

The Jarl climbed down the rope ladder at the side of the ship and was helped into the boat by the accompanying sailors. I followed carefully carrying the Jarl's Standard which consisted of an oblong shaped pennant with the Jarl's Arms embroidered on it. The Men at Arms who were beginning board other rowboats, cheered at the sight of the Standard.

The sailors and accompanying Men at Arms rowed the boats towards the shore. The Jarl took the Standard from me and now remained still and pensive in the prow of the boat. He appeared determined to be the first to set foot in this new country and as he boat scraped shore he leaped from the bows clutching his Standard and ran through the shallow water to the beach. Dropping down on his left knee he took the Standard and pushed it firmly into the sand.

"On this day the 1st June in the year of Our Lord 1398 by the mercy of God, I, Prince Henry St Clair of Roslin, Jarl of the Orkneys, take this land unto the protection of the St Clair family and its forebears and name it West Scotland.

He raised himself up just as we began to arrive ashore followed by the other Men at Arms who gathered round the Jarl. He commanded that as many of the party as possible were to come ashore leaving a skeleton crew aboard the ships. Soon boats were scurrying from ship to shore landing Men at Arms, the small company of Priors and craftsmen and a few of the seamen and by the time the last boat had returned from the ships there were over sixty men on the beach.

The Jarl bade his Knights form up their Men at Arms into three sides of a square and he stood with his back to the sea with Jeruba and myself at his side and addressed the assembled party.

"Grand Prior, Gentlemen Knights, Serving Brother Clerics and Craftsmen, Men at Arms and ship's crew, I salute you all. We have suffered the worst that the great sea could bring forth but we have survived to discover this new land. Some of you witnessed earlier that I have called this land West Scotland and so it shall remain for all eternity. Now Grand Prior we will hold prayers to thank God for the safe deliverance."

Three dark green-mantled clerics came forward. At their centre was the bearded Prior Bernard carrying the Holy Book. He bade us kneel then led us in prayers for our salvation, prayers for the Jarl's house and lineage and the souls of those who had succumbed on the journey. After a short period of silent prayer he bade us all rise and with the other two clerics returned to the group and the Jarl stepped forward once again.

"Sir Robert Melrose this day you will take your men to the west following the line of the river. You will seek game and fresh water. Sir Guillaume de la Croix with the Nubian Jeruba and Sir James Gunn and his Men at Arms will accompany me to the south to search there for game and be sure that all parties are returned to this shore before sundown. The clerics and craftsmen will remain here with Sir Hugh Douglas and the rest of his men to obtain a store of wood and to make fires. God grant you all good luck in your enterprise."

The Jarl's party headed into the forest leaving the shore far behind. After being confined so long on board the ship, the thick green canopy rich in insects and an abundance of birds made me feel wonderfully alive. Everywhere around me the forest echoed with strange chirruping sounds and shrieks. It dawned on me that even the trees seemed different to those in my native Scotland many were of great girth and age and had stood there for hundreds of years. I was filled with awe at this bounteous land it truly was all that had been described in the scripts.

The sun rarely penetrated through this canopy of thick leaves and branches and gave the men a sense of foreboding, raising the spectre of strange monsters lurking in the depths. So when the party came upon large natural clearings and broke out of the gloom into warm sunlight, there was a sense of relief and wellbeing. Jeruba had also appeared unsettled since leaving the beach, all the time looking left, right and to the rear of the column and seeing his unease I asked him what ailed him.

"We are being watched Guillaume and have been since we entered the forest." He replied.

"Are you sure Jeruba, I have seen no one, apart from our party, since we left the beach. Who is watching us?"

"I have only seen shadowy figures. So far I have counted three up ahead of us and there are three more trailing us at the rear."

"Are they armed Jeruba?"

"They don't appear to be but I cannot swear to it."

"Then I feel I should warn the Jarl."

I ran up ahead and approached Prince Henry.

"Sire, might I speak with you?"

"Of course Sir Guillaume walk at my side."

I joined the Jarl and we walked together.

"Now what ails thee?"

"My Lord, since we left the beach, Jeruba has tracked six figures travelling with us. He has seen three men up ahead and three men behind us but cannot say whether they are armed."

"Is Jeruba sure about this? Forest shadows can play tricks with the eyes."

"Sire Jeruba is a warrior of the Dinka tribe of Nubia. He is trained in the arts of tracking and hunting. He would not say anything unless he was sure."

"Very well we will proceed with caution. Bid Sir James and his Sergeant at Arms to come to me when next we take our rest".

"At once my Lord."

I made my way back along the line of men to Sir James and passed on the Jarl's request.

After about a two-hour march we were approaching the top of a steep hill and soon came out of the trees onto the summit. From the top, we could see the harbour and the coastline and far away towards the mountain where smoke was rising from what seemed like a forest fire. The Jarl called a halt and bidding the men rest he sat down on the trunk of an uprooted tree.

The Men at Arms settled close by and the water skins were passed around. Sir James spoke to his Senior Sergeant of Arms, a grizzled veteran of many crusades, the man rose and together they went to the Jarl. They bowed before him and were made at ease.

The Jarl looked up at the grizzled Sergeant at Arms. "Ah tis, Bernard of Thirsk".

"Yes my Lord. I fought with you at Alexandria."

The Jarl smiled. "The years have slipped by since those great days. We have both lost our youth."

"That we have my Lord but we still remain a match for most men."

The Jarl acquainted Sir James and the veteran with what Jeruba had seen. He told Sir James and the Sergeant to instruct the Men at Arms to be on their guard but they should show no concern if natives appeared and above all should not provoke a fight unless attacked first. The Sergeant at Arms bowed and returned to tell his men and the chatter that resulted signified that they had received the news with interest but it was soon to quieten down. We had been warned and for the moment it was sufficient for us just to be cautious.

When rested, we continued the trek southward. After forcing our way through dense trackless forestland for an hour we halted close to the edge of a ravine through which foaming water surged. The rocky sides were so steep it was impossible for anyone to reach the riverbank. We could go no further in this direction so the Jarl directed we would continue to the west along the edge and seek a suitable place where we could replenish our water skins.

We continued along the side of the gorge staying as close to the edge as safety would permit. We seemed to be climbing further and further away from the river but occasionally we would catch a faint glimpse of the rushing torrent in the depths below. From this distance it was a ribbon of white foam cutting its way through the rocks.

Since the last halt Jeruba and I had brought up the rear of the column. I was totally engrossed in my impressions of the new land. The thought that I was one of the first men from the east to set foot on this virgin land inspired me. More and more West Scotland seemed truly to fulfil the description of the Garden of Paradise that the text promised the land below the great star La Merica would be. There were hundreds and hundreds of acres of forestland still waiting to be explored.

I was feeling such contentment as I strolled along that it was only when I turned round to convey these feelings to Jeruba that I noticed that the Nubian had disappeared. This alarmed me greatly for the Jarl had commanded that we should stay together. Jeruba was only armed with a large skinning knife that was given to him by Nicolo Zeno. Who knew what the Nubian would do if he encountered any natives?

I began searching the tree line for sight of the Nubian and had dropped back from the party. Just as I was beginning to give up hope, Jeruba appeared carrying a large animal on his back, his face displaying a broad smile. I had been unaware that Jeruba had been less than one hundred paces away. He told me on his return that as the party mounted the last ridge he had noticed a young deer like animal grazing under the cover of nearby trees and had approached silently keeping up wind of the beast. The animal had continued grazing as he made his approach and he had been within a few feet so with one enormous leap he grasped the neck of the beast and had thrust his knife into the base of the animal's skull. The beast had raised its head up startled as the knife penetrated its cortex then quivered for a few moments and died. Jeruba had lifted the dead animal across his broad shoulders and had stridden back to the edge of the gorge.

"Jeruba." I shouted angrily. "I thought you had been taken by a wild animal or savages but I see I was wrong. Come, we must return quickly before we are missed."

"The "savages" as you call them have disappeared into the forest my friend." The tall Nubian replied. "I followed their trail for a while but I haven't seen them since our last rest stop. I thought that it was time we had some fresh meat."

We set off climbing along the edge of the gorge. Way up ahead we could see the rest of the party had already halted and were scanning the forest for our return. The Jarl was scowling as we approached and I was expecting a rebuke, but on seeing the fresh meat his attitude changed.

"So Sir Guillaume since you are unable to control your Nubian friend perhaps he would be more useful if you take the lead and scout ahead. He certainly has the hunter's blood in him and by his worth we shall eat fresh meat tonight. Sir James bid your men cut a pole to carry the beast. Make haste for we must continue, it is past the suns zenith, we must return to the beach before dusk."

The ground rose steeply towards a tall rocky outcrop. The unbroken noise from the river rushing far below through the gorge had now increased to a tumultuous roar. The two of us were the first to reach the crest. I couldn't contain myself by what I saw and let out a loud yell.

"My Lord come quickly I bid you look at this." I shouted excitedly.

Not knowing what to expect the Jarl climbed to the top of the rocks but as he reached the top it became clear. Stretching away to the west was a small freshwater lake and immediately below them water poured from the lake through a huge gap in the rocks creating a waterfall that plunged over a hundred feet into a bubbling cauldron of foam. The sunlight on the spray caused a profusion of multi-coloured lights and I had never witnessed anything so remarkable in my life. Soon the rest of the party came alongside me and were taking in this amazing sight. A shout from the Jarl soon brought them all to their senses.

"We must make for the shore of the lake and fill our water skins. We have little time to rest before we have to start back for the beach".

The party made their way down to where the lake flowed down a narrow flat gully leading towards the waterfall. The Sergeant at Arms who had already tested the water and found it to be sweet and clear bade the men fill their water skins. The Jarl took a silver cup from the pouch at his waist and his manservant filled it for him. The manservant tasted it and passed it to the Jarl who quenched his thirst. By now the water skins were being passed around the men. Jeruba brought one over to me and bade me drink by now I was thirsty and took a long draught of water from the skin.

"Do not be too hasty my friend." Jeruba warned. "Too much water will make you ill."

I heeded his warning and passed the skin back to the Nubian.
The rest of the party refilled their water skins and moved on to the shore of the lake staying but a short while for our presence seemed to attract swarms of aggressive flies which bit with a ferocity unmatched by anything we had seen in our own lands. The Jarl checked the position of the sun and confirmed a route towards the northeast. The party formed up once again and marched into the forest.

The trees were not so thickly grouped here and there were numerous rocky outcrops which had displaced them or prevented the growth. After marching for an hour the ground started to slope sharply and very soon we had re-entered dense forestland and were glad when eventually we emerged from the cold darkness into a wide area of bald rocks. Here there was little or no vegetation just lichen attached to the rock face and the surrounding forest now blocked our view towards the sea and we were unaware of what lay ahead. The Jarl called for a short rest then our party began the march back under the forest mantle.

It seemed a long time since we left the lake. The Jarl knew that we should have reached the seashore by now. Before us lay endless forest and by now he was beginning to doubt whether we were travelling in the right direction so at the next rest stop he sent Jeruba and me ahead to scout the route.

After trekking for a while through virgin forest Jeruba called out. When I reached the Nubian I found he was on the banks of another wide river. I waited there while Jeruba ran back to fetch the rest of the party and they soon appeared through the trees. I had an idea that this might be the river that emerged close to where the ships were

moored and offered my thoughts to the Jarl. The
Jarl agreed and said that if we now followed the
course of the river we would eventually reach the
sea and so we marched on. The river became
wider and wider until finally we could see an
estuary opening into the sea.

At first no one could recognise the terrain but on
rounding a headland there were the ships moored
off the shore. Below them, the wide beach from
which we had started was now almost submerged
by the tide. Two large fires had been lit on the
high shore well away from the water edge. A
great heap of dead wood had been collected ready
to feed onto the fires. Some sail canvas had been
brought from the ship and a temporary marquee
had been erected and the Jarl's chair placed
beneath it. Men standing round the blazing fires
suddenly spotted the returning group and began
to shout. We returned the greeting as we made
their way down to the shore. At the sight of the
fresh meat, the waiting men ran forward to gaze
in awe at the strange beast, half deer, and half
horse. The Jarl enquired after the other group
but was told that they had not yet returned.

The sun was beginning to set over the bay as the cooks in the party prepared the feast. They set to work cleaning and preparing the meat for cooking. Although it had no time to hang the animal that Jeruba had caught had been skinned, gutted and cut into quarters. It was mounted on a long iron skewer with a handle at the end ready to hoist on two trestles set either side of the fires. The fire had been built up until and was now glowing with huge red embers. The four quarters of the deer were then lifted onto the spit and as they were turned over and over by the cooks were basted with hot animal fat collected in pans underneath. The scent of the roasting meat drifted across and as we hadn't tasted meat for over a month I found the smell tantalising.

Suddenly a shout rang out from the headland and the other group appeared carrying two deer. On their arrival the deer were passed to the cooks and quickly skinned, cleaned, gutted and quartered. Some of the meat was salted and stored in barrels the rest was prepared for the spit.

That evening was set aside for merry making as the men ate their fill of the fresh meat. The Jarl felt they had something to celebrate they had achieved all they had set out to do. Here was a new land that had the promise of being richer than the land they had left.

The Jarl ordered all unessential men from the ships to come ashore and celebrate and to bring with them the remains of the last barrel of wine. Large pieces of roast meat were sent to those who remained on the ships. The evening was to be spent rejoicing their safe arrival.

The boats began to arrive on the shore and as the men came ashore we were re-united with Antonio and told him of our adventures in the forest. Eager to hear everything that had happened he asked numerous questions about the land, the animals and birds. He told them that he had spent his time on board taking sightings to finish the maps he had been making. Now he was keen to see the country and was hoping the Jarl would give him the opportunity.

The Jarl summoned the Knights around him giving a brief report of his expedition. Then he asked the others for their report and Sir Guy de Blanchefort spoke for their group. He said that they had managed to cross the shallows of the river and follow the north side of the riverbank towards the west for about three hours. After climbing steadily through forestland they reached a boggy plain which stretched across to the slopes of the high mountain that they had first spotted far out at sea. From this location they could see signs of smoke rising from the base of the mountain. After resting they turned north, across the wetland and continued through dense forestland. Here they had come upon a herd of deer grazing in an open glade. They managed to kill two stragglers from among a group and these they had brought back for fresh meat. Sir Hugh Douglas and his men had remained with the dead animals to prepare them for transportation back to the beach while he had continued on with his men. They marched on climbing a steep forested hill. On reaching the top they found they were looking down on a river estuary flowing out into a huge bay from the other side of the mountain and directly below them was another beach.

Across the bay to the north Sir Guy made out a tall headland and to the east in the distance were the large islands they had sailed past shrouded in mist. Far to the west he could see another wide, river estuary enclosed with several small islands forming a natural harbour. So far they had found sufficient sources of fresh water and the country was teeming with game. The river estuary was worth further exploration.

On their way back , Sir Guy and his men had encountered a party of about eight natives two of the party were carrying a strange looking deer like animal on a pole. The natives had skirted them in silence and continued into the forest. Sir Guy said they had shown no sign of hostility. The Jarl was well pleased with the expedition for it proved that this rich new land would be capable of supporting several settlements.

Rather than returning to the ships the men rested close to the fires for the night. We found a soft area of turf and settled there. It had been a tiring but exhilarating day for us all and I was soon fast asleep with the knowledge that the tall Nubian would be close by keeping watch against any dangers of the night.

**Chapter Eight.
A First Encounter and a Meeting of Equals.**

On the morning of the second day after their arrival, shouting awakened me. I quickly came to, sat up and looked around Jeruba was nowhere to be seen. Sir James was gesturing animatedly towards the headland. Lined up along the top were half a dozen unarmed natives. All but one were carrying baskets on their heads.

Antonio sitting alongside me spoke in a hushed tone.

"Now we shall test the nature of the inhabitants and it will be by this meeting that they will test us." He said.

We rose and joined the rest of the company.

The Jarl rose to his feet and placing his helmet with the gold circlet on his head bade his knights to line up their men.

"Let these people come forward in peace. We will greet them as we would any friends. There will be no hostile moves. Sir Guy, bid them welcome and bring them to me."

The Knight walked slowly towards the headland and beckoned the natives forward. As they came closer he could see the baskets contained freshly caught sea fish. He beckoned them once again and turned and walked back towards the Jarl.

Their leader was tall, broad shouldered and powerfully built. His clean-shaven countenance was bronzed and dominated by a hooked nose and a large cleft in his chin. It was covered in a greasy substance, as were his hands and part of his exposed chest. The narrow brown eyes were set deep above prominent cheekbones but they revealed little of what he was thinking. However, they showed an intelligence far above that which the Jarl had expected.

He was dressed in a buckskin smock and trousers with leather fringes sewn together with sinew. Both the smock and trousers had been intricately decorated with zigzag patterns. On his feet he wore shoes that had been constructed from pieces of buckskin also sewn together with sinew. His black shiny hair was crowned with a hide band that echoed the complex woven pattern of his dress. It was decorated extravagantly with bird feathers. Two plaits hung down each side of his face and tied in a zigzag manner with thin strips of leather.

The rest of the group appeared shorter in height, lean and sinewy and their long dark shining hair, though parted in the middle hung loose around their faces and was held in place by a small leather coronet with a bird feather stuck in the back. Their exposed flesh was also covered in a greasy substance. They seemed accustomed to wearing nothing but a small buckskin apron tied about their waist and leather leggings. Sun and wind had weathered their upper bodies. All wore the same soft buckskin shoes as their leader.

The Jarl stood alone in the centre of the company and signed the leader to come forward. The natives followed behind until they reached the edge of the square. The tall native signalled the others to remain where they were and stepping forward began to speak. At first the words sounded strange but among the words the Jarl thought he recognised the Orcadian dialect. He called for me to come forward and translate.

I greeted the native in Orcadian, which I tried to pronounce slowly and clearly. The native lifted his right arm palm facing them and replied in short sentences in a strange sounding Orcadian tongue. At first I was able to translate the word "peace" and "gifts" then, as I got used to this new pronunciation of common Orcadian words they became easier to translate for the Prince.

"My name is "Deer who runs swiftly". My father is Chief "Bear that stands tall". We are Mikm'aq of the Pectougawak clan. Our hunting parties informed us of your arrival. My father welcomes you to his summer lodge it is at the place called Pectou."

Running Deer then rendered Pectou into the Orcadian language as "bay that is shut-in",

"We are two days march from here on the other side of the mountain that smokes. We bring you peace offerings of fish freshly caught."

I translated these words.

The Jarl replied. "Sir Guillaume, tell them who I am and where we have come from and that I welcome them in Peace. I accept their gifts with gratitude."

He undid his belt, slid a handsome dagger on a tooled leather sheath from it and passed it to Guillaume.

"This is a gift from me to his father the Chief and I look forward to meeting him at his lodge..."

"Give this as a gift to your father the Chief." I translated and passed the dagger to Running Deer.

Running Deer, the leader, acknowledging the gesture, turned to the rest of the natives and spoke in their strange dialect, displaying the dagger. They began to smile and raise their left hands in the same greeting as the spokesman. I was about to explain who the Jarl was and where they had sailed from when Jeruba stepped from the cover of the trees carrying another strange deer like animal across his shoulders. On seeing him the natives became alarmed and started to back away I could see the situation deteriorating before my eyes I shouted in Orcadian.

"Do not be afraid this is my friend Jeruba. He is a warrior of the Dinka tribe from a country many miles beyond the great sea."

The leader translated the words and they became calm again. He turned to me and spoke once more.

"I am sad that we showed fear at the sight of your friend but we have never seen such a tall man with skin burnt so black by the sun. We thought that you had brought a strange spirit with you.' Then he turned to the Prince and said. 'I thank "Great Kuloscap" on behalf of my father for this precious gift."

I asked Running Deer why he called the Jarl "Kuloscap"? He replied it referred to the Jarl's helmet he had never seen a shining hat like the Great Chief wore and to his tribe this was a symbol of wisdom and greatness. I passed this on to the Jarl who gave a courtly bow towards the Chief's son. The Jarl was interested how Running

Deer knew Orcadian, so I asked him how he had learned the language. He explained.

"When I was a small boy, a man was washed up on our shores and was taken to our village he was cared for and came to live with us. He was from a land called "Orkeni". Although he has now passed over to the spirit world the wisdom he gave to us lives on, for he showed us many things. He taught us to fish with nets instead of spears and to gain a better understanding my father insisted that he taught me his language."

I noticed they had the greasy substance on their skin and was curious to know why. Running Deer explained that when the sun was high there were many biting insects in the forest and the grease of the Bear gave protection. The tall native then turned to his followers and spoke to them in their own language possibly explaining to them what had been said between us. Eventually he turned back to me and said.

"Now we must return to my father's lodge for it is more than two day's march from here. Let us meet in peace there in three suns."

This I translated for the Jarl who passed his greetings on to the Chief and agreed that he would visit the village in three days. Running Deer turned again and made a signal to the rest of the group and the natives placed the baskets of fish on the sand in front of the Jarl, bowed and walked away towards the headland waving all the time until they were out of sight. As soon as they had disappeared from sight everyone on the beach began to talk about the visit. The babble of conversation was soon halted by a shout from the Jarl.

"Sir Knights, Priors, Craft masons, Sergeants at arms and Serving brothers I command your attention. Our first contact has been in peace and for that we should be thankful. This is the way we shall continue for if we once show any malice to these people our discovery of this earthly paradise will count for nothing. We will show them respect and that our ways are just, honest and we will act with dignity. We will learn their ways too, for peace is the only path to follow if we are to succeed in settling this place. Pass this my command to everyone and mark this, should I hear of anyone who disobeys this decree, he shall suffer severe punishment. Now disperse to your duties".

As the groups of men broke up, I went forward to examine the baskets more closely. Each held four reasonable size fish and were fabricated by using thin shaved branches from a tree, several of which had been tied between a larger branch bent into an oval shape and the ends secured together. The branches formed the framework through which strips of tree bark had been spliced to form a very rigid carrying basket. I was impressed by the skill in which the baskets had been made but as the men began to take the fish to the waiting boats my attention was suddenly diverted, the Jarl was calling me over.

"Sir Guillaume I bid you come and sit at my side."

The Jarl was seated under the awning on the sturdy wooden chair which had been brought ashore from the ship and had been placed on an area of grass above the beach, he was studying a chart, Antonio stood beside him.

I joined them and sat down on the grass beside the Jarl. Jeruba who had long since deposited the deer into a boat stood quietly behind them.

"We must search for more safe havens where we can establish our first settlements." Prince Henry began. "Although this harbour is ideal I fear that in winter this area would be much exposed. My opinion is that we should sail westwards round the headland and seek the more sheltered harbour that Sir Guy saw on the other side of the island. I opine that it should be no more than a day's sail from here. What say you?"

Antonio replied first.

"Sire, what you say is right this seems a protected anchorage at the moment because we are enjoying good weather and the winds are from the South. As soon as winter approaches this area will be at the mercy of fierce winds from across the bay to the North is it your wish that we take sail again and seek out a better anchorage?"

"Yes it is my wish but first I will speak of our move to another location with the other Knights." The Jarl stood up and pointed to the headland in the far distance. "I bid you navigate around that headland on the morrow and we will seek out this sheltered anchorage that will withstand the worst of storms."

The Jarl then spoke to me asking me to accompany him on a walk for a while before returning to the Roslin. Leaving Antonio and Jeruba behind we strode along the beach towards the headland. Pausing by a large rock the Jarl spoke.

"I've been thinking about the settlement here in West Scotland. Amongst your many talents my son, your knowledge of the craft of the mason would be of great assistance here. Therefore you will remain with me here with the other Knights, their companies of Master at Arms our clerics and craftsmen. We will keep two Drakkars and two rowboats, three galleys and a Cog here for I intend to explore this land in detail, the Drakkars will be easier to haul if the need arises.

Before winter, the Sir Antonio and the other captains will take the rest of the fleet back to Kirkwall. So my son we will need to complete those shelters before the first winter snows. I wished to convey these, my wishes to you before I tell the men who will remain here because they will need to know they will be sheltered and safe from the dangers of this land. It is important that I am clear in what you would propose for the shelters so I command you give me your thoughts. What think you that we should erect for our first settlers?"

"I think they should be sturdy. Perhaps with a surrounding stonewall built to a height of a sword length from local stone. Each shelter should have a single entrance to withstand weather and wild animals. If we drive several short pickets into the earth on the inside of the oval base we can use these to support timbers for the roof. The central roof structure can be a square made up of spars supported by four poles set in the ground two-sword lengths apart. One moment my Lord I will find a stick."

"I think that something like this would make a fine permanent settlement."

I took a stick and began to sketch the plans for the settlement in the sand. I started with a large oval building, which would serve as the Jarl's quarters.

"This will be the Langhalla and your quarters my Lord."

Adjacent to this I drew a similar building they could use for a central refectory.

"Another two similar sized buildings would quarter the Men at arms, clerics and a workshop for the craftsmen and six smaller shelters would be used for storage of food and quarters the Knights and their Esquires."

The Jarl studied the sketches in the sand.

"What about the roof covering? It must be able to protect us from all that the heavens send."

"I was intrigued the baskets the natives brought the fish in. They make use of strips of bark from the birch tree. It makes a strong lining. I believe that we can weave the birch bark in the same manner as we would weave wattle boards. These firmly attached between the main roof timbers would support sods of turf placed on the top. The sods will grow to form a natural cover which should protect us against the worst of the elements. We can set our fires between the four poles leaving the central part of the roof open to carry off the smoke. They can also be used to support the spit rods for roasting our meat and holding our pots."

"Then let it be so my son." Said the Jarl, he seemed well pleased with what I had drawn up. "Prepare your plans on vellum. It is my intention to meet the native clan Chief before the settlement is built so that there is no misunderstanding."

Come we will return to the company."

The two men walked back along the beach. When they reached the awning the Jarl called for everyone to attend him. He made known his intention to find a safer haven and establish a settlement before winter set in. An undercurrent of anxiety spread among the sailors on shore for they had hoped to return to the Orkneys and their families before winter set in. However Prince Henry's mind was made up, the sailors from the Drakkars would remain.

"It is my intention to find the bay that Sir Robert saw. Return to your ships and make your preparations to sail on the dawn tide."

Everyone moved away and started to clear the beach. By midday the men and equipment had returned to the ships. The beach was deserted but for the Jarl and Guillaume. A single rowboat stood by on the beach. Four sailors stood alongside waiting for their return.

The Jarl followed me aboard and we were rowed back to the "Roslin". As we left the shore I gazed back at the small beach now completely deserted; the only indication of our brief tenancy was the black scarring where the great fires had been laid.

2.

By mid morning the ships had rounded the headland and passing a small island to their larboard quarter they sailed into a narrow passage that sliced through tall cliffs. It reminded the Jarl of the fjords he had seen in Norway. As there was little or no wind to fill their sails, so the ships were rowed through the passage.

After about two hours the ships reached the end of the channel and entered a large bay. In the distance was a tall headland and the Jarl decided to make for it. Tacking straight across the open water they came upon the first inlet, which was as Sir Robert had described.

Seeing that it was very exposed to the open waters of the bay, the Jarl decided to sail on. It was late afternoon by the time they had rounded the second headland and soon they were running down a rocky coast, which gradually merged, into a tree-lined shore. By dusk they came upon a second narrow inlet, which the Roslin explored followed by the other ships. It led them into a natural harbour with a large sandbank splitting the estuary of a great river. The narrow entrance gave them complete protection from open sea.

The three ships hove to in the eastern part of the estuary and dropped anchor. On the far distant shore close to the western estuary Antonio pointed out a group of strange conical dwellings with smoke rising from the tops. The Jarl came up from below deck to see. I stepped forward pointing towards the dwellings.

"Sire I think that must be the place known as Pectou, summer camp of the native Chief."

"Aye, Sir Guillaume." said the Jarl. "Should we remain here I will make contact with them straightway." He turned to the Captain.

"Sir Antonio make signal to the other ships tell them that we go ashore on the morrow and explore the surrounding area for a suitable site to make a permanent camp."

Antonio bowed. "As you command my Lord."

As the dawn light spread over the bay lighting up the lush green forestland I climbed up from my quarters to the high deck to stretch my aching muscles and looked around. The ships were standing off a sandy beach. On the shore side of the "Roslin" the dense forestland spread away towards the foothills of the great mountain the slopes from which black smoke was rising. When I crossed over to the other side of the ship I could see a large bay where the rest of the ships were moored. A range of tall cliffs extended across the bay broken only by the entrance channel it appeared that this harbour would afford protection against the worst of winter weather that would come from the open sea to the North.

The Jarl had ordered that one of the banded cannons should be taken ashore together with ammunition and gunpowder and as I stood two Seamen were dismantling it using a rope and pulleys. As they began to lift the cannon from its swivel mounting the cannon suddenly slipped its ropes and plunged into the water below.

The Jarl appeared at my side he was angry and shouted all manner of curses at the men. He said they should be lashed for such incompetence. He told them to get out of his sight or he would wreak more havoc on them for the fools that they were. They scurried away if only to get away from the blasts of anger coming from the Jarl.

When they had gone the Jarl turned to me and said quietly.

"Perhaps it was God's will that we should not bring such weapons into this new land and thus it was lost."

My Lord I am sure you are right if this is to be the paradise that was promised then it is better that we come in peace and not with a weapon of war such as the cannon."

The Jarl nodded and turned his attention to the shore.

"This place has the making of a permanent settlement does it not Sir Guillaume."

"Indeed my Lord."

The men came ashore and the two Drakkars were drawn up high above the waterline dis-masted and turned over. All the spare canvas sail cloth was made available from the ships and stretched across poles to form an area of temporary shelters for the men and stores coming ashore. They would at least provide some protection for the men while the settlement was being built.

In a long stream the men passed the stores and provisions together with the craft tools required by the masons, carpenters, and blacksmiths. The Priors carefully brought ashore their own jars filled with herbal remedies for every ailment and soon a large area of canvas shelters had been erected to store them. Hunting parties were sent out to provide fresh meat and soon the shore line at the eastern estuary became a temporary settlement.

**Chapter Nine.
A Delicate Alliance.**

Two days after their arrival at the harbour the Jarl dressed in the ceremonial clothes and coronet he wore when he first landed, had his first meeting with Chief Standing Bear at Pectou. I had earlier accompanied the Jarl and Sir James Gunn together with his men at arms to the native village. Jeruba stayed behind on this occasion with Antonio.

Some distance from the village Running Deer had suddenly came out of the trees escorted by two braves. He had greeted them as honoured guests and led them forward into the village. The village was made up of large conical structures constructed by placing several stout poles upright in a circle together securing them leaving an opening at the top and covering them with strips of bark from a birch tree. Running Deer explained these were called "wikoum" in his language and they made a warm and secure dwelling.

He led the party through the village to the Chief's wikoum. It was about three times bigger than the rest of the others and was decorated with coloured symbols of animals, birds and strange zigzag patterns. I noticed a large skull set above the entrance. I had never seen anything like it although it closely resembled the skull of a horse. Being curious I asked Running Deer if the skull was from a horse. Running Deer looked puzzled and said he did not know what a horse was. This he said this was the head of a Caribou a word he translated as "The one that pushes snow". During a hunt, this particular animal had charged and killed his younger brother. Running Deer said that it was their belief that the Caribou had taken on the form of his brother and that the skull reminded his father of his lost son.

As they approached the Chief came out raising his right hand in a sign of peace. He was followed by five elders of the tribe wearing leather aprons round their waist tied over leggings, leather bands on their arms all richly decorated with similar zigzag patterns, as were the moccasins on their feet and a band of leather round their heads with a circlet of multi coloured feathers. Running Deer explained that these were kill feathers a sign that they had hunted the larger wild animals and made a kill. They were all covered with a kind of grease, which had been spread evenly over their arms legs and body. I observed that it gave off a quite pungent smell.

One elder stood out from the rest, wearing a decorated conical cap he was rather resplendently dressed in a buckskin cape decorated with zig-zag lines and different bird feathers. He carried in one hand the claw of a bird in the other a rattle covered with feathers. The Chief introduced the resplendently dressed elder as the Shaman, and then one by one he invited the Jarl to meet the elders.

I noticed that there were few women in the village and Running Deer explained that they were in the forest gathering berries and tending to the traps. As he spoke the animal skin flap of the wikoum opened and a woman wearing a long decorated buskin dress and moccasins came out. Her shining black hair showing signs of grey was bound in plaits, which fell either side of her slender bronzed face and neck around which was an intricate necklace of small coloured shells. On her head she wore a conical decorated leather hat. She was carrying a half-finished decorated woven basket. The Chief introduced the woman as Tetees the mother of Running Deer and indicated that she should sit at the entrance of the wigwam. Running Deer explained that his mother's name translated as Blue Jay. When all these formalities had ended the Chief bade them sit with him beside his wikoum.

The Jarl and the Chief were of similar age, but the harshness of living in this wild place had taken its toll on the Chief and his people. Guillaume noticed his bronzed face was extremely lined and gaunt. The long black hair flecked with silver was surmounted with a large conical head-dress covered in bird feathers. He was dressed in a fringed buckskin smock, which came down to his knees; trousers and shoes all lavishly decorated with porcupine quills. Around his neck was the Jarl's gift attached to leather plaited cord. The Chief spoke in his native tongue while first Running Deer and then I translated.

"I am Chief Standing Bear, my tribe the Pectougawak are part of a larger family of Micmac who have hunted these lands for many generations. So this is the great Chief Kuloscap of the white faces who sailed the seas on the backs of great whales to come to this land I welcome you to my lodge and I thank him for his gift."

Chief Standing Bear said he had had a vision about the Jarl's coming and had summoned his Shaman to help him to take the vision quest. The Great Spirit had spoken to him during the vision of a mighty chief that would come riding on a big whale from where the sun rose who would bring wisdom to the Micmac peoples. He had summoned the elders of his tribe for counsel and they decided that he should welcome the arrival of the great Chief Kuloscap and his tribe. He said that the lands the Micmac hunted stretched as far as the eye could see and it would take more than three moons to cross. The Micmac had been in these lands since the Great Spirit passed this land into their keeping. He said his people had been taught by the Great Spirit to be a peace-loving nation. Hunting was plentiful in the forests and there were many fish in the rivers and great waters to help his people survive the season of snows.

The Jarl explained through me that they had come in peace across the Great Sea from a land where the sun rose called Orkney. They would like to remain here and live in peace with their neighbours the Micmac. It was their intention to build and enclosure with some shelters close to the eastern river estuary and he asked whether the Chief had any objections. The old Chief gazed steadily into the Jarl's eyes for what seemed like an age then he turned and addressed the elders in his native tongue.

"I find truth and wisdom in the eyes of the great Chief Kuloscap and my heart tells me that our friendship will be long and bring many rewards. If it is the wish of the elders that the Great Kuloscap build his shelters and live in peace with the Micmac then it will be so".

Some of the elders commented loudly on the hearing the Chief's words. The Chief remained silent as the debate continued to and fro between them. After several minutes the Chief raised his hand and asked each elder for his answer and one by one they nodded their approval until finally all had agreed. Again he addressed the Jarl and his party.

"The elders of the tribe have spoken and we welcome the Great Chief Kuloscap and his tribe to live together in peace with the Micmac".

The Jarl said that he respected the wisdom of the Chief and while his tribe remained with the Micmac peoples he would ensure that they would keep the peace, exchange ideas and learn their ways. He spoke of many things that they could exchange knowledge about, survival in the winter, their skill at crafts, methods of hunting, what the forest plants and trees could provide as food and the Micmac use of healing plants.

While the talks had continued the wife of the Chief had sat silently listening to what was being said while her skilful hands worked away at the decorated basket. It appeared similar to those that I had seen on the first day of their meeting with the Micmac, however this particular basket had the start of an intricate diagonal pattern woven into the design which I thought very pleasing to the eye.

Chief Standing Bear led the party into the wikoum and invited them to sit around the central hearth. The elders followed them one by one and sat cross-legged behind them. His wife offered them water in cups made of carved whalebone and some dried deer meat they called Pemmican, which the visitors gratefully accepted. At first I found the meat was hard to chew but had a pleasant smoky taste.

Following the refreshment the Chief was handed a narrow wooden stick by the Medicine Man which had a small bowl close to the end. The stick was covered in carvings and decorated with dyes. He then took some dried brown vegetation from a covered pot and pushed it tightly in the bowl at the end. Lighting a taper of wood in the fire the Chief lit the end and began to suck the smoke through. He blew the smoke out slowly, fanning it towards his face. Running Deer explained that it was the custom to smoke the sacred pipe to seal the agreement that had been made between our peoples and the act of drawing smoke from the sacred pipe showed that they accepted the responsibility they had undertaken in these discussions for the whole of his life. He said that everyone would be called upon to be a pipe bearer.

The Shaman who carried the pipe for the Chief was practised in the pipe ceremonies it was a great responsibility and with great dignity he carried the pipe until the time came for him to pass it to the next bearer. The sacred pipe belonged to the tribe as a whole and gave the Shaman certain powers of sight as well as an ability to heal and purify. But if he should become deceitful or lie and cheat, the pipe would quickly repossess these gifts and the possibility of misfortune would befall him. The substance that the Shaman placed in the bowl was a leaf called to-bacco and grew in certain places in the forest only known by the Shaman who collected the leaves and laid them in the sun to dry until they were ready for the pipe.

The Chief now passed the pipe to the Jarl who sucked some of the smoke into his mouth and immediately started to cough. The Chief smiled and through his son said that the Great Kuloscap would one day, get used to the smoke that purified. Now it was my turn, as I took the pipe I noticed that there were seven animals carefully carved and beautifully coloured along the stem. I placed the stem in my mouth and sucked. The smoke tasted sweet but I was unable to hold it in and coughed it out to the amusement of both the Chief and his son. The pipe continued to be passed from one elder to the other until all had partaken. When the ceremony was over the Chief stood up and invited the Jarl and his party to tour the village. The Jarl said it would please him greatly and together they walked down a wide strip of grass between the wigwams.

Running Deer explained that the Chief's summer lodge consisted of ninety-five "wikoums" or shelters each containing a family group. By now the women had returned from the forest and the camp was busy as they went about preparing the food for storage. Close to each wikoum frames had been erected made from two parallel branches supported by two stout branches driven into the earth. These were tied together with strips of hide to form a standing frame. Tied in rows to the frames, fish, which had been gutted earlier, were drying in the sun. Some of the women were busy scraping buckskins, which had been tied to similar frames. In front of each wikoum a small circle of stones had been laid where a fire had been lit. Here and there more women were preparing the berries and what appeared to be a fruit covered in green leaves. As the leaves were peeled back they revealed a head covered in yellow seeds which they scraped with a piece of bone loosening the seeds so that they fell onto a piece of buckskin laid out on the ground. Running Deer explained that this was maize a basic food that was planted each year in plots cleared by the women in the forest and harvested. The maize could be used for cooking with the meat or roasted and eaten and if the crop was plentiful the excess would be stored for use in the winter months.

Passing by the women they came upon a group of children playing a game using sticks and a leather ball. It seemed that the aim was to strike the ball against a decorated pole which had been set into ground. They screamed with laughter as they attempted to take over the ball and drive it against their opponents using all their guile to get the ball and some would use their sticks to trip their opponents up.

The party approached the shore where several upturned boats lay made from stripped branches covered in birch bark. Running Deer described these as Ca-noos, used for fishing they were very stable in the open sea. About six sword lengths long by one wide, the Ca-noos were pointed at each end with a rounded prow and stern. The sides of the craft were rounded and at the centre of the boat the keel took on a humped shape. The ca-noos were decorated with crude but brightly coloured symbols and animal forms.

Noticing that the Jarl was interested in the boats the old Chief commanded two of the braves in attendance to take one out on the water, once launched they moved the Ca-noo through the water by using short broad bladed oars. To the delight of the visitors they demonstrated that they could steer the boat, turn it in a circle and stop it in a short distance by skilfully manipulating the oars. There were several types of ca-noo pulled up onto the shore including two very long ones, which would take a crew of four braves. Another two-man ca-noo was covered in a protective skirt made of hide, which stopped water entering the boat. Running Deer said that this was for fishing on the great salt waters and offered protection to the braves if the weather changed. As they watched the crew showed off their skill manoeuvring the boat. The Jarl was extremely impressed and remarked that on his next visit to the Chief he would like to learn how to row the Ca-noo.

The Jarl and the Chief exchanged information through myself and Running Deer and talked about their families but all too soon the sun was dipping over the horizon and it was time to say farewell and make our way back to their encampment. The Jarl asked that the Chief visit his camp soon and Running Deer passed on the invitation. The Chief said that it would please him to visit the lodge of the Great Kuloscap.

Over the next few weeks I was totally absorbed in planning and supervising the building of the settlement and by now a large area had been cleared in the forest about a mile from where they had first landed. Stones were selected from the shoreline and teams of Men at Arms hauled them from the shore to the clearing where the three craft masons had begun to preparations to build the foundations.

The first building erected was the quarters for the Jarl and his body servants this was the Langhalla, a long hut. The large stones were built up to form a sturdy foundation and timber that had been felled to make the clearing was stripped of its bark and used for the main roof supports. Smaller branches had been cut into suitable lengths and fixed in lines between the main roof timbers. The salvaged strips of bark were woven between these to form a strong base for the roof. Finally the roof was finished off with grass sods. I felt that the lodges would give them reasonable protection from the worst of weather.

By the end of May the building of quarters had been completed and when everyone had moved into the respective lodges an air of permanence settled over the community. The final part of the protecting wall around the settlement had been completed and the Jarl was well pleased praising me for the speed at which the work had been carried out which I passed on to those who had worked so hard to complete the task.

Regular contact with the Micmac had begun with that first visit by the Jarl to their village and soon it was the turn of Chief Standing Bear to visit our settlement. He was greatly impressed by the lodges and the Langhalla where the Jarl held court but he said it would be difficult to move when the time came to go to the winter lodges. The Jarl laughed at this and said that these lodges would protect them in any kind of weather. With a shake of his head the Chief shrugged his shoulders and smiled. The visits became a regular ritual during which ideas were exchanged about food gathering, native medicines, hunting, fishing and the dangerous animals that lived in the forest.

The Jarl continued to send parties out exploring the land and reporting back to him as well as hunting for fresh meat some of which was sent to the Micmac village. In exchange the Micmac women brought maize and berries to the settlement. It was inevitable that the peace should be tested. Some of the Men at Arms seeing the young Micmac women bringing produce from the native village were regularly reminded that they had not had contact with the opposite sex since leaving Orkney.

One day, an angry Running Deer came to the settlement and on behalf of the Chief complained that the day before a young woman had been taken by two of Kuloscap's men repeatedly raped and left for dead. The Jarl was furious he said he would assemble the Men at Arms and asked Running Deer to for his help to identify the men who had brought dishonour to the settlement. Running Deer said that after the attack the men had taken to the forest so the Jarl immediately ordered Sir James Gunn to take a party of men and bring them back. The next day the men were brought back to the settlement under escort to stand trial I was dispatched to summon Chief Standing Bear to witness the proceedings.

The next day Chief Standing Bear arrived in solemn procession accompanied by some of the elders and the Shaman. He was wearing his full head-dress of feathers, another beautiful suit of buckskin which had intricate diagonal designs woven into the jacket. In his left hand he carried an eagle feather and in the right a carved wooden staff. Running Deer and several warriors and their Squaws and a lone warrior who was the husband of the victim also attended him.

They were escorted into the Langhalla and to accommodate he assembly benches had been set out in the main part of the hall. The Jarl sat in a chair at the far end of the Hall and another chair had been placed alongside the Jarl. The Jarl bowed and formally greeted the Chief summoning him to sit by his side he bade the rest of the party to sit on the benches provided. The Knights entered the Langhalla and sat on the left-hand side of the hall. I took my place on a bench set behind the Jarl and Running Deer behind his father.
I interpreted as the Jarl told the Chief of his dismay in learning what had happened and said the men responsible would shortly stand trial.

The two miscreants shuffled into the hall their feet and hands shackled the escort led them to the centre of the hall where they were stood in front of the Jarl and the Micmac Chief. The Jarl signalled that the trial commence and while Running Deer translated for the Chief, Sir James Gunn, from whose own Men at Arms the accused had been, read out the charges.

I translated as the Jarl asked the Chief if there were any witnesses to the crime. He signalled for one of the women to come forward and explained that because the victim was too ill to attend a woman who had accompanied the victim on the day of the rape would tell her story. The woman came forward visibly shaken looking all the time at the floor of the Langhalla and in a quiet voice that sometimes gave way to tears she related what had happened. They had been collecting berries in the forest when the men had come up on them and grabbed them both forcing their attentions on them. She had felt ashamed and humiliated and after a struggle in which she received cuts to her arm from a knife wielded by one of the men, she managed to break free and ran for help. When she returned with some warriors from the village they found the girl lying bleeding, on the ground she told them that she

had been repeatedly raped and beaten by the men adding that they had run off into the forest.
The next witness was the victim's husband he said he first heard the news when one of the women had run screaming into the village bringing news of the assault. Accompanied by several warriors he was taken by the woman to where his wife lay. She was covered in blood and moaning and as he knelt by her side she told him two of Kuloscap's men had come out of the forest and attacked her knocking her to the ground repeatedly raping her. At that point she had lost consciousness and while the other warriors searched for the man he had carried her to their wigwam where she was treated by the Medicine Man. She was recovering from her wounds but he said she was not the same woman he knew as his wife for her mind had been affected by the ordeal.
There were no more Micmac witnesses so Sir James Gunn then rose came forward and said that he had been ordered by the Jarl to find the accused men and had led a party into the forest. The Micmac warriors had already found them and taken them to their village and Running Deer

had handed them over to the custody of the Knight.

As there were no witnesses for the accused the Jarl asked them men if they had anything to say in answer to the charges made against them but they just stood with their heads bowed. He asked them once more if they had anything to say but they remained silent. The Jarl through Guillaume invited the Chief to decide whether the men were guilty or innocent.

Chief Standing Bear sat quietly for a moment then said.

"The wounds on the body of our little daughter of the tribe will heal as suns rise and fall but the wound in her mind will never recover. These men show what is in their heart for they speak no words to counter the words spoken by those who saw our daughter. They fled like startled deer into the forest to hide from the truth and when caught they showed no care for the misery they caused our daughter and for our people. While two suns have passed I have spent time with the Shaman casting the seven stones and passing through the healing smoke trying to find a reason for this attack but the Great Spirit is silent and cannot help me search for pity in my heart for these men. There has been much talk today of the guilt of these white men but nothing to show their innocence therefore my heart tells me these men are guilty".

The Jarl stood up and bowed to the Chief and in a grave voice pronounced the sentence.

"Take heed all who are assembled here as I pass sentence and may this reckoning be an example to all that the carnal desires of men have to be confronted, for this day I shall reveal to you the dire consequences".

He then addressed the accused men.

"After trial you both have been found Guilty and it is my duty as your Jarl to pronounce sentence. By your actions you men have brought dishonour on my family, your colleagues and our Holy Order you have all but destroyed the life of one of our friends the Micmac. Therefore at sunrise tomorrow in front of the assembled Men at Arms you will be taken out and hung by the neck, your bodies will be cut down alive and you will be castrated and dis-embowelled. Your remains will be taken into the forest and left to be devoured by the wild animals. May God show the mercy on your souls that you failed to show to your victim. Take them away and guard them closely".

The men were taken out and Chief Standing Bear stood up and addressed the members of his tribe.

"You have seen with you own eyes the wisdom and justice of the Great Kuloscap. Running Deer and the husband of the victim will stay to witness the white men's fate at the return of the morning sun".

The Jarl led the Chief out of the Langhalla and escorted him to the gate of the settlement. As he bade them farewell the Chief turned and said. "I say to the Great Kuloscap when two suns have passed, come to my wigwam and we will smoke a pipe and let this sadness pass away between our two peoples".

Both myself and Running Deer translated as the Jarl said he was grateful to the Chief for his understanding and wisdom and would be honoured to visit the wigwam of Chief Standing Bear. They said farewell and Running Deer with the husband of the victim remained behind and were taken to quarters to wait for the next sunrise.

A makeshift scaffold had been erected overnight as the guilty men prepared for their last day on earth. At sunrise, in front of the Jarl, Running Deer and the brave, the Knights and assembled company of Sergeants and Men at Arms, the men accompanied by the Prior were led to the scaffold.

I recognised the executioner by his long stride it was the same Bernard of Thirsk the grizzled veteran who led Sir James' Men at Arms. He was wearing a leather doublet and hose with the brown Templar over-mantle on his hands were large leather gauntlets and his head was covered with a black hood with holes cut in it for his eyes to see. He led the escort of Men at Arms surrounding the prisoners walking slowly with sword drawn and carried raised.

The Prior who led the procession suddenly broke the silence his thin high-pitched voice chanting a prayer for their souls. As they reached the scaffold he finished with a loud "Amen" then stood to one side while the executioner led the prisoners up the steps. His duty finished the Prior made the sign of the cross in front of each man, turned slowly away from the scaffold and withdrew to stand behind the Jarl.
The executioner offered each man a blindfold, one man accepted and his eyes were covered the other shook his head and stood passively with his head bowed. The executioner placed a noose around each man's neck securing it tightly. He then stood back to await the signal from the Jarl.

The Prince drew his sword and raised it above his head. As if smiting the guilty the sun glinted on the blade casting a broad beam of light across the scaffold and the guilty men. A gasp rose from the assembled men as they witnessed this strange phenomenon, some thought it was a sign from heaven branding the accused. The assembled company waited and in the brief pause that followed the drawing of the Jarl's sword the man with the blindfold pissed himself. The urine began to trickle through the raised platform onto the men waiting below to release the chocks holding the trap doors.

The Jarl lowered his sword in a sweeping movement, the chocks were knocked away from the hatches and the two men fell, their feet kicking the air frantically searching for some invisible surface that would stop the pressure on their necks. After a few minutes they were cut down and their bodies taken to a bench specially prepared where the next part of the sentence, castration and disembowelment was carried out swiftly by the old Sergeant at Arms. This was the first execution that I had witnessed and I felt shocked and sickened by the sight. The bodies and parts were placed on a hand litter, dragged away through the gates of the settlement by four Men at Arms who disappeared into the forest. The mood of the men in the settlement was cowed over the next few days they had seen the results of the Jarl's fury and knew now that any transgression against his orders would be swift justice and terrible retribution for the guilty.

And so it followed that two days later the Jarl visited the Chief and the differences between the two camps were settled by smoking the sacred pipe. Thereafter the daily routine of the Micmac women bringing corn and fruits of the forest to the settlement continued as if nothing had happened.

**Chapter Ten.
A Sad Farewell.**

The Jarl felt that it was now time for him to send the remainder of his fleet back to the Orkneys with news of their safe arrival and maybe attract more settlers to make the journey. Summoning a council of the Knights and ship captains to the Langhalla, the Jarl set out the plans he had in mind. He would remain in West Scotland for one year together with the Knights, Men at Arms, craftsmen and priests and explore the surrounding lands.

Antonio and the captains and crews of the "Roslin", three of the Galleys and the Drakkar 'Kreland' back to the Orkneys leaving two Drakkars the Haggar and the Kral with crews and four rowboats for exploration and the two Galleys and the remaining Cog, the Help would remain in the bay close to the settlement at Pictou until the Jarl returned from his exploration of the area. Should none of the ships return after one year then the Jarl would return to Orkney with those who remained and spread the news of their discovery.

Word of the Jarl's decree spread throughout the camp the only dissenters were the sailors who had to remain with the ships not returning for their hopes to get back to Orkney before the winter set in had been dashed. They wandered about the camp with sour faces resigned to their fate, quietly mumbling their disapproval out of earshot of their captains.

Soon the day arrived when the Roslin and the other ships were ready to depart. I accompanied the Jarl on board to say farewell to Antonio and Jeruba. It was to be a sad parting for we had forged a firm friendship and being aware of the dangers they might meet on the return voyage I wondered if we might ever see each other again. Antonio and Jeruba were waiting for us on the lower deck and greeted us warmly. As if he had seized the moment, Jeruba suddenly stepped forward and stood alongside me.

"Sir Antonio I promised Sir Nicolo that I would guard over you and keep you safe and I have done this faithfully. Now I wish to be relieved of this duty even though I swore fealty to you as I did to your brother. For the first time since I was taken from my homeland I feel free, I have found a country where I have the same freedom to roam that I had in the place of my birth. Grant me release of my obligation to you and allow me to remain with Guillaume and I will protect him as I have protected you."

Antonio took Jeruba's arm.

"My friend you have been my strength and my shadow but you are a free man and must do what is right for you. I gladly discharge you from your obligation but that is not to say that I will miss your friendship deeply."

With tears in his eyes and a heavy heart Antonio stepped forward still holding Jeruba, he pulled me towards him and we hugged each other.

"My dear friends, until we meet again, both of you will remain in my heart."

Then suddenly, as if to use his duties as an excuse to palliate the pain of this parting, he released us both turned to the Jarl and said.

"Now my Lord we must talk before I make preparations to sail for the tide is turning and soon you must return ashore."

With a final gesture of his hand he turned to Jeruba and me.

"Goodbye my friends may God go with you." He said

He turned and strode with the Jarl towards the high deck.

The Jarl gave his final orders and we were rowed back to the shore. With heavy hearts we stood on the beach and watched the to-ing and fro-ing as the ship made ready. At last the sails were hoisted and the "Roslin" began to move slowly out of the harbour followed by the other two Galleys. Having escorted the Jarl back to the settlement we ran to the cliff top from where we could see the ships entering the bay. There we remained waving until the ships became a speck on the horizon. Only then did we break contact and return to the settlement both struck dumb by our own thoughts about a friend that we would sorely miss.

Chapter Eleven.
Learning the Ways of the Micmaq.

With the "Roslin" and the other Galleys gone, the Jarl set about completing final plans for an expedition to explore the northwest of the island. Jeruba and I would spend our free days at the native village in the company of Running Deer. Anxious to learn the Micmac language, Running Deer would translate and give me everyday words to learn this way I was able to gain knowledge of much about the customs of the Micmac. Jeruba was happy now because for the first time since his capture he would be once again in his natural environment as a hunter.

As time went by Running Deer told me how Creation stories had been passed down through each generation. He spoke of the gathering of the Great Council where these stories would be recounted. The seven Chiefs from the surrounding Districts would sit inside a sweat lodge and smoke the pipe and burn sweet grass. Water would be poured over seven then fourteen then twenty-one heated rocks to create the hot steam. A cleansing or purification would take place together with a symbolic re-birth and the Chiefs would give thanks to the Gisoolg, Spirit Creator, Nisgam, the Sun and Ootsitgamoo, the Earth. I noticed some striking similarities between some Templar ritual and that of the Micmac and it made me eager to know more.

Running Deer taught us the ways of the forest and the names of the animals. The dogs roaming about the summer lodge he said were Imuj but the wild dog or wolf was Paqtism. The great black bear or Muwin was to be feared for although they would seem to walk about in a calm manner they could attack at a moment's notice and tear a brave to pieces. I asked what the women decorated the clothes and headdress with Running Deer explained these were the quills from the Matuwes (Porcupine). When hunting we would come across animals and Running Deer would point them out, the fleet footed hare was called Aplikmuj, the great antlered Moose was Tiyam, the bald headed Eagle, Kitpu, a bird Sisip and a serpent Mteskm and in this way I gradually built up my knowledge of the animal names. I discovered like Jeruba and his culture the Micmac had great respect for nature and only killed animals for food and materials. They treated all animals as their brothers and sisters and when a creature was killed would pray for their safe conduct to the realm of the Great Spirit. Running Deer was an admirable guide to the ways of the forest we learned about the different trees or Nebookt. He showed me those best used for ca-noo building, others for harvesting for food supplies and importantly those that provided curative and remedial properties. I spent much time mastering the intricacies of the Ca-noo, the use of native bow and arrow and to use the fishing pole to spear fish.

We spent many days in the village sharing Running Deer's lodge. One day he said the women of the village would erect a new wikoum for us to stay in when we spent time in the village. We watched fascinated as the women of the village began this task by choosing five spruce poles. They lashed them together with split spruce root and raised them up spreading them out evenly. Shorter poles were then lashed horizontally to the five supporting poles to provide support for the covering. From the forest they collected birch bark and laid it over the top like shingle on a roof starting from the bottom and overlapping each piece as they worked towards the top. The top was left open for the fire smoke to escape. A gap was left in the side to allow access and Running Deer pointed to a large animal skin and said it would be used to cover to entrance and in the extremes of winter an extra cover of birch bark could be pulled over the top. More poles were laid against the birch bark to hold it down. The floor inside was then covered in fir twigs and moss woven mats and animal skins and the wikoum was ready. I was greatly surprised how quickly they had put the wikoum together and was quick to praise them but they lowered their eyes and went away chattering and laughing among themselves.

As the days passed I felt that I should show Running Deer the way we used the sword and lance. The Micmac had never seen metal knifes and swords until the arrival of the Jarl's fleet, for they had always used animal and whalebone to fashion knives, arrow points, scrapers and clubs and tools made of stone. Running Deer though impressed by my broadsword and belt, chainmail coif (over mantle) and helmet, hauberk and chausses (suit of chainmail); felt it was too heavy to fight in. We discussed how we both would tackle an opponent in a fight I explained that in the lands to the east the chainmail was worn to save life. Battles were fought facing the opponent and wearing armour would often prevent an arrow with a head made from the same material as the Chiefs dagger from penetrating the body. Running Deer thought it better to copy the ways of his brothers the animals and seek the cover of the forest to overcome an opponent and Jeruba was quick to agree for there he could move swiftly and silently on an opponent just as he would track an animal and when he was in close range and only then use the bow and arrow with accuracy to make a kill. In close quarter combat I learned how the Micmac could wrestle and defeat an opponent and asked who were the Micmac's enemies? Running Deer explained that occasionally raiding parties would come from the north west and would take away Micmac women for their squaws but where they were situated there would be plenty of warning of a raid and none had ever reached Pectou.

During my time with Running Deer and the tribe both Jeruba and I grew to admire the Micmac ways and we gradually became more and more proficient in their language and customs. All their clothing was made from the skins of animals, birds and the bones of large fish the skins were tanned using a mixture of bird livers and oils and animal brains. It was a long process but the results were skins of beautiful fur and soft leather. Awls made of fish bone were used to make holes in the leather for sewing animal sinew which had been separated and served as thread, I watched and learnt fascinated that these people existed by using natures provisions. There was a code of behaviour among these people where they shared everything and stealing another's goods was unheard of, they existed in harmony with one another allowing any small disputes to be settled by the Chief.

The Chief heard about my keen interest in the ways of the Micmac and summoned me to his lodge. There he told me that the L'nuk his term for the Micmac had dwelt in these lands since they were created. He said that now there were seven districts each of which had a Chief and every winters end when the snows had melted, they attended a Grand Council of Chiefs to discuss any problems that had occurred over the past seasons.

The village was close to the sea shore which provided all types of shellfish and seaweed to add to their diet. When the winter weather broke the men would take their ca-noos out to sea and fish for Cod, Herring and the occasional small whale. As soon as the signs of winter were upon them the Micmac would move from the village to winter quarters in the forest inland close to a river where they prepared for winter hunting. They hunted Elk, Caribou, Bear, Moose, Beaver and Porcupine. The winters were fierce and they travelled around in special snowshoes and train their dogs to pull 'tabagan' to bring back the animals killed. In the warm weather the women would go out into the forest to tend their plots and plant maize seeds, then when they had matured they would gather a harvest of maize, berries, plants and tree bark. In the snows they would remain in the wigwam sewing clothes and repairing the cooking implements as well as making sure the dried fish and other winter stored were kept dry ready for use. The Chief added many things about the tribal customs and I began to realise these people weren't the poor souls that we had first encountered. They had established a unique way of life by living on Mother Earth's bountiful provision.

One day we were called to the Chief's lodge he told us that he was happy that I had taken to the ways of the Micmac and said that he was going to make us members of his tribe. He called the elders and the Shaman to his lodge asked them one by one if they objected to us being made Micmac brothers. They unanimously agreed and in a short ceremony inducted Jeruba and I as his brothers. He presented us each with a suit of buckskin consisting of a long sleeved smock, a loincloth of soft skin and leggings all beautifully sewn with beaded zigzag patterns and depictions of animals and birds. With it we were given hunting bows decorated with pieces of fur and bird feathers and a sheaf of arrows together with moccasin boots. I was presented with a bear's tooth attached to a medicine pouch set on a beaded necklace and was given the tribal name

"Ntutem" (friend from another land). Jeruba was given the name Maqtewek Muwin (Black Bear).

From that day I took to wearing the native dress, which I found more comfortable in the forest environment. With the leather moccasins I could move swiftly and silently and became adept at hunting the native way and I could now understood why Jeruba was such a skilled hunter and told him so. He just laughed and said that the people of the northern lands had lost the old ways and perhaps I would realise that they had been handed down for generations to both his people and the tribe that they now were a part of.ach time we returned to the settlement I would relate to the Jarl everything I had learned. The Jarl was greatly impressed by their culture and the way they could survive in such a hostile environment with such primitive tools.

One day as we entered the compound on our return from the Micmac village I was summoned to the Langhalla, where Prince Henry held court. As I entered the Jarl beckoned me over to where a rough-hewn wood table had been set before him.

"Attend me Sir Guilluame".

I joined the other Knights and saw that spread across the table was a copy of the map made by the Venetian. The Jarl turned and addressed me.

"Sir Guilluame I crave use of your skill at drawing. Are you able to make maps like the Venetian?"

"I would feign try my Lord, though I doubt it would be as accurate as the Venetian might make it."

"Then I bid you try, for in ten days I intend to set out on an exploration of the coastline to the northwest. Sir James, Sir Robert and their men at arms will be my escort. I will take two brother priors for our spiritual welfare and the remainder of the party will be cooks, craftsmen, man servants and seamen to man the Drakkar s. You will accompany me to make maps. I pray we will discover new lands for my people to settle. Sir Hugh, Sir Guy and their men will remain here to await the return of our ships from Orkney.

Should misfortune befall us and we do not return within one year then those remaining here will set sail for Orkney and pass the news to our loved ones."

The discussions carried on well into the afternoon and when plans for the journey had been finalised, the Jarl dismissed the Knights but not before asking me to remain. He waited until the rest of the Knights had left the Langhalla the Jarl spoke.

"I have another task for you my son. I wish you to attend the lodge of Chief Standing Bear and inquire whether I could have the presence of Running Deer and a few of his men and ca-noos to accompany us on our expedition. It would be a great favour and assist us when we reach unexplored territory."

"I will attend to your request on the morrow my lord and return with the Chief's decision."

Before leaving I took this opportunity to ask if Jeruba could accompany me on the expedition.

The Jarl thought for a moment and replied.

"The Nubian has skills that will also be useful in unexplored territory and he has earned the right to accompany you as your squire. So be it".

I left the Langhalla bursting with anticipation I had imagined that my fate would be to remain in the settlement I could not contain my excitement at the prospect of the journey ahead. I hurried in to tell Jeruba who was sitting cross-legged by the lodge. The tall Nubian stood up as I arrived.

"I have heard the rumours around the camp and I hope we will not be left to rot here while the others go exploring this new land Guillaume my friend."

"I have dreamed of exploring a land such as this and wherever I go you will accompany me. I promised Antonio and I will keep my promise. It is the Jarl's command that you go with me on the expedition as my squire".

The Nubian couldn't contain his composure and began to jump in the air higher and higher grinning from ear to ear in a ritual dance from another time until finally he had to be restrained and when he finally came to rest he hugged me tightly shouting.

"Then my friend our fate is written where you go so will I and I shall be your shadow and your protector."

As the next day dawned dressed in the buckskin suit and moccasins I accompanied Jeruba in similar dress and we set out for the summer lodge of Chief Standing Bear. We were greeted at the edge of the village by Running Deer who welcomed us as we walked towards the assembled lodges I explained the Jarl's request and straightway he lead us to Chief Standing Bear's wigwam. Running Deer was exited at the prospect but cautioned me that his father would not consider this request lightly.

I greeted the old Chief warmly and he invited me into the lodge while Jeruba stayed outside with Running Deer. We entered, sat down by the fire, the Chief listened respectfully to what I had to say then after a long silence he spoke.

"Ntutem what the great Chief Kuloscap asks fills my heart with sadness Running Deer is my only surviving son. It is he who will lead this tribe when I have gone to the spirit world. I am happy to allow three of my braves to accompany you but whether one of them will be Running Deer that decision I can only make after long contemplation with the Spirits. The great Chief Kuloscap will have my decision in three days if I am in favour of his request it with be brought to your lodge by Running Deer if I am against it will be brought by one of the braves I have told to accompany you".

I understood the old Chief's dilemma. I stood up and made a sign of peace. "Chief Standing Bear I thank you for receiving me and I will carry your message to the great Chief Kuloscap. May the Great Spirit guide you well, ease your heartache and guide you to a just decision.

The old Chief stood up and walked with me through the open door of the wigwam.

"May the Great Spirit also guide the great Chief Kuloscap". He made the sign of peace by raising his right hand. "Farewell Ntutem".

The old Chief returned inside his wigwam and Running Deer accompanied us to the edge of the village where I grasped Running Deer's forearm in a gesture of farewell.

"Goodbye my brother. May the decision of your father the Chief be filled with the great wisdom that comes with age."

Running Deer held my arm tightly. "We must hope that the Spirits of his ancestors will guide him to a just solution Ntutem my brother. Go in Peace."

On the third day after my meeting with the Chief I waited with the Jarl for the answer that was expected. Much depended upon the decision for the Jarl felt that the rank of Running Deer was important when contact was made with other tribes of the Nation. Being the son of a Micmac Chief carried high status and would command the respect of other Chiefs. It was late in the afternoon when figures were spotted heading towards the stockade. I went out to greet them and immediately recognised Running Deer with three braves. I ran forward overjoyed to see the group and brought them into the settlement to where the Jarl waited in the Langhalla.

"My father sends greetings to the Great Kuloscap and asks me to bring you his answer."

The news however was not quite what the Jarl was expecting. The Chief had made his decision Running Deer would accompany the expedition but he would remain with the party only as far as the limits of the lands of the Micmac Nation. Running Deer took out a piece of buckskin from his jacket and opened it up, it was covered in symbols. As he spread it open on the wooden table they could see that it was a crude map showing landmarks such as their summer and winter quarters the smoking mountain, rivers, lakes and the coastline.

"Great Kuloscap." Running Deer said addressing the Jarl. "My father the Chief of the Pectougawak has spoken and these are his words. My son and two braves will take three can-oos to navigate the rivers and guide the Great Chief to the farthest limits of the Micmac tribal lands." He pointed to a curving red line. "This is the boundary between the Micmac Tribal lands and the rest of the Algonquin Nation and it is at this point that we will return to my father's lodge."

From what I could make out from the crude map, the Micmac lands stretched many days march to the west and to the south the limit of the Micmac lands stretched over a great sea and I passed these observations to the Jarl.

Satisfied with the outcome the Jarl addressed Running Deer and the Micmac braves.

"Please convey my thanks to your father the great Chief of the Pectougawak for his wise counsel. We know that he has made a great sacrifice by allowing you to guide us on our expedition and while you and your braves remain with us you will all be under my protection. We will decide on an auspicious day to leave and Sir Guillaume will summon you. Go now in peace. "

With that I led Running Deer and his braves out of the stockade and bade them farewell. I knew it would not be long before I would return to their Lodge to tell Running Deer to prepare to leave on the expedition.

Chapter Twelve.
In Search of New Lands.

On the tenth day of July 1398, the Drakkar Ships Haggar and Kral sailed out of the harbour leaving the Kreland and the remaining ships under the command of Sir James Douglas and his Men at Arms, two Priors and several Craftsmen would also remain to maintain the settlement at Pectou until their return.

The Drakkars were fine vessels with shallow draughts and had been built in Denmark for the Jarl's fleet because he wanted long ships rather than the cargo carrying Kroll because they could be easily maneuvered both at sea and over land. They were about sixteen sword lengths long and five sword lengths across the beam and had six rowing positions on either side. The ships used one large rectangular sail with a crossbeam at the top set amidships which could be maneuvered easily to catch the wind. Although the Drakkars had been constructed as open boats at the aft end of each ship wattle enclosures had been added which housed supplies and on the Haggar was used as the resting place for the Jarl. Both the stem and the stern were raised by additions to the rugged but shallow keel to spread the buffeting of the waves and the hulls were sleek and light allowing the ships to travel smoothly through the water. The ships were of clinker construction that is to say that the boarding overlapped to form the main hull and were steered by side mounted rudder set to the starboard side of the stern.

Those on board the Haggar included Prince Henry, Sir James Gunn, and their Men at Arms, the Head Prior, three craftsmen, three man servants and four esquires including Jeruba and the Captain and six seamen and myself. On the Kral were Sir Robert Melrose, Sir Guy Blanchfort and their Men at Arms, a Prior and the captain and his seamen. Running Deer and his braves who he had introduced as Keskiaqasit (Husky

Dog), Sasqatu (Flying Squirrel) sailed on the Haggar with the Jarl, Jeruba and myself. Two can-oos were secured along the sides of the Haggar and the third to the side of the Kral.

Following the coastline towards the northwest, the ships made headway in the strong breeze. I stayed in the stern of the Haggar plotting the coastline. On the starboard lay the large island we had seen when we first entered the mooring at Pictou almost a year before. I noted another smaller island closer inshore and marked it on my chart. The captain set a course west around the smaller island and we were soon approaching a section of coastline which consisted of two adjacent bays divided by a huge rocky peninsular. We sailed closer to get a better look but noting the jagged rocks close to the shoreline we withdrew to a safe margin. After two hours the ships had left the islands and first bay to our stern and were following the line of a sparsely covered rocky shore. The shoreline ended in a small headland and beyond was another wide bay.

The sea remained choppy and the two ships made excellent progress as the breeze stiffened. From the stern of the Haggar I marked a huge inlet on my chart and noted that it would make an excellent mooring, I mentioned this to the Jarl but the Jarl decided to sail on. In another two hours we had crossed a smaller bay and were heading along another stretch of rocky barren coastline.

The shoreline ended abruptly and opened up into a channel. The Jarl thinking the channel would lead to another stretch of open water decided to enter and explore the land beyond. He ordered the Kral to be signaled to follow astern and the two ships made for the entrance. As we rounded the headland what was seen to be a channel turned out to be another inlet with two branches. The Jarl commanded the Captain to take the larboard inlet and the Kral followed. The ships sailed on until the inlet started to narrow and soon we found we were entering the mouth of a wide river. Light was failing so the Jarl signaled the Captains to anchor off the riverbank for the night.

I was rudely awakened by water showering down on my face and quickly realised it was raining hard. Suddenly there was much movement in the ship as the seaman scurried about fixing a rope line set up between the prow and the mainmast and throwing the spare canvas sail over it. Jeruba and I grabbed a part of the large sail and with the others succeeded in lifting it over the rope line. Once in place and secured to the sides of the Drakkar the party huddled underneath out of the rain and tried to catch up with their disturbed sleep.

After the deluge that had continued most of the night the morning broke fine and clear. The Jarl summoned me to the stern of the Haggar, Running Deer was already with the Jarl waiting there.

"Sir Guillaume I have given thought to send a scouting party out to see what obstacles lay ahead. I bid you go with Running Deer, Jeruba and the braves use the can-oos and follow and chart the river to its source. I will expect your return in three days. What say you my son?"

"I will prepare for the task straightway Sire for I am sure Running Deer will agree the earlier we start the more ground we will be able to cover."

"That is what I expected my son. There are many dangers in the forest so be on your guard. I will pray for your safe return."

I went forward to my allotted area and changed into my buckskins and moccasins. I chose to take with me a square buckskin-carrying pouch containing my drawing materials, my striking flint and for protection and hunting food my short dagger and the native bow and a sheaf of arrows that Running Deer had given to me. Jeruba joined me on my way to the stern and I told him of the Jarl's decision. Before long he had collected some dried fish and meat and had filled a water skin and with a huge grin on his face was ready to leave. Running Deer and the braves had detached the ca-noos from the ships and were waiting on the water. We climbed over the stern and slid into the ca-noo already occupied by Running Deer. The Jarl and the knights bade the party farewell and we set off up the river towards the forest.

The river at this point spanned about two hundred paces and meandered between high banks of virgin forest. Running Deer said that he had never hunted into this part of the Micmac tribal lands and seemed exited by the prospect. On several occasions I noticed deer taking water on the banks of the river seemingly unconcerned by the movement of the three ca-noos. Soon the river gradually began to narrow until it was some one hundred paces across and rocky outlets began to appear on the banks either side. Every now and then I would test the depth of the river to see whether it would be suitable to take the draft of the Drakkars.

After paddling for several hours against the flow of the river we reached a point where the river had narrowed to about fifty paces and suddenly became very shallow. Up ahead the river flowed out through a narrow gorge in a savage flurry of white water. I made a note on the chart I had drawn and we headed for the shore there being no way that we could navigate the river further. The ca-noos were drawn up onto a flat sandy bank where we rested and ate some Pemmican (Dried Meat) and assuaged our thirst.

Running Deer broke the silence.

"My brother the only trail now is over this hillock. We will take it in turns to carry the ca-noos and at the top follow the course of the river to its source."

I was lost in thought busy filling in the details of our journey on a chart and didn't hear asking him to repeat what he had said. He looked puzzled for a moment not fully understanding why I hadn't heard so I explained.

"I'm sorry I was spending a moment to finish charting this section of the river I will be ready to move soon."

Meanwhile the braves had prepared the ca-noos ready for carrying. The braves retrieved a leather sling from each ca-noo and tied the ends to the sides. The central wider part of the sling was fitted over the head enabling the ca-noo to be lifted and carried on the back while the other brave steadied it as they marched.

Jeruba volunteered to carry our ca-noo first. When the ca-noo was lifted onto his back he found it surprisingly comfortable but his forward vision was limited. Running Deer was able to guide him and we set off up the slope. In a short while we had reached the top of the hill and began to follow the cutting in the rocks where the river forced its way through. Although the trail continued to climb the going was reasonably easy for no trees grew on the rocky outlet. At this point I took my turn carrying the ca-noo. I soon got used to the gently swinging ca-noo as the head sling forced my body to take the whole weight. After about an hour Running Deer signaled us to stop. He had not uttered a word since the last stop but now he spoke.

"I think we should find a suitable place to rest. I will send Keskiaqasit and Sasqatu ahead to hunt food and seek out somewhere to cook it. Perhaps Jeruba would like to go with them?"

Jeruba happily nodded his approval and as Running Deer spoke to the braves Jeruba joined them and they ran off ahead and into the trees. This time Running Deer and I had no option but to carry the ca-noos and we prepared to move off.

We climbed steadily leaving the gorge behind following the course of the river through a birch forest of tall straight trees. The river was now all but a small tributary no more than fifteen paces across so we continued to follow its meandering passage until the sun was high up above the tree line. Then as if by some established signal Jeruba and Husky Dog came out of the trees and we exchanged greetings. They announced that a suitable clearing had been found up ahead and a fire prepared. They had caught and skinned two rabbits, which they had prepared for cooking and led us to a wide clearing. In the centre was a circle of stones where dry wood had been placed ready to be lit. Flying Squirrel was busy preparing several long sticks, which had been stripped of the bark and sharpened at one end.

Husky Dog collected the rabbits from where they had been stored in a nearby tree away from the reach of prowling animals and began to prepare them for cooking. He took them to a large stone and using a whalebone knife stripped off the fur, gutted them and quartered them ready for cooking. All the time he chanted a dedication to the rabbits praising their courage, strength and cunning during the hunt.

Meanwhile Running Deer gathered some dry moss and was about to use his fire stick to start the fire when I came forward and offered my flint and striker. After several blows the moss started to glow and was soon aflame catching the dry timbers in the circle of stones. We gathered around the fire each of us took a piece of rabbit and stuck it on the end of the stick over the smouldering embers. The smell of cooking flesh began to permeate the whole area.

As Husky Dog turned his piece of rabbit over it slipped off the stick and fell into the fire. Everyone roared with laughter as he tried to recover the rabbit just saving it before it was burnt to a crisp. We settled down to consume the meal and afterwards the braves began to relate stories about different hunting expeditions they had been on. I listened intently and translated for Jeruba as the stories became more exaggerated the chitchat became noisier. It took me back to times of celebration in the castle of

Roslin when the knights would boast of their deeds at the tilt and of their conquests with the fair ladies. I realized that apart from their primitive way of life there was little difference between this culture and that of my own for if we stripped away the trappings of our world I knew that basic human nature remained the same.

When we had eaten our victuals Running Deer ordered the two braves to clear the ground ready to move out. They set about dowsing the fire and clearing the circle of rocks and after a few minutes the area looked as if no one had disturbed it. Running Deer helped me lift the canoo onto my back and we set off,

It was late afternoon before we reached the source of the river. A natural spring gushed out of the side of a hill feeding a small rocky pool. After sating our thirst Jeruba filled the water skins while I climbed to the top of the ridge. I was immediately overwhelmed by the panorama that spread out before me.

Some fifty paces below me another rock pool fed a stream that poured down the hillside probably from the same spring. In the far distance I could make out a river, which snaked into a large inlet, beyond the inlet was open sea.

I noted the position of the sun in the sky and judged that the inlet and open sea were to the south-west. It was what the Jarl had hoped for, a route to the lands to the south, which he could explore. We had found a route south and it had not been difficult to traverse. With the men he had with him it would be quite easy for the Jarl to organize the portage of the two Drakkars across this short section of the forest.

I quickly made notes and a plan of the country ahead. Once again I was so
Involved with the task I didn't see Running Deer approach.

On hearing a rustle behind I was distracted for a moment and drew my dagger ready to ward off any danger.

"Hold Ntutem my brother it is only Running Deer."

"Running Deer you startled me, I was deep in thought and was suddenly aware of something behind me, and naturally I went on guard. For this my friend I am sorry." I pointed to the distant river. "Kuloscap must be told of this route to the south. Jeruba and I will return before nightfall to bring him the news. You my brother and your braves can scout the river to the south and find out what other hazards we face before we meet the great sea. We will meet here again in two suns."

"I know this part of my land the village of my mother is not far away. It lies close to where the river enters the great waters down there." He said softly pointing towards the wide river below. "We will be made welcome there so while you return and tell Kuluscap I will go with my braves and prepare them for your coming. "

Having finished the chart I collected my things together and went to find Jeruba. He arrived and in one great swoop lifted our ca-noo on his back.

We said our goodbyes and retraced the route
back through the trees.

As we reached the first waterfall we had
encountered on the way the sun now resembling
a reddish orb hovered fleetingly over the tops of
the trees lighting the forest in a breathtaking array
of golden hues before dipping below the horizon.
In the gloaming that followed we scrambled
down the slope. Jeruba lowered the ca-noo and
launched it into the river we climbed in and began
paddling downriver.

Very soon we came upon the two Drakkars
barely a quarter league from the cataract where
we had commenced their portage two days
before. They were moored close to an open area
of grassland surrounded by trees and thick forest
undergrowth. The men had taken advantage of
this excellent rest area and had made their various
camps at the edge of the tree line. A huge fire
burned in the centre where several Men at Arms
stood watch.

As we hauled the ca-noo out of the water Sir James Gunn approached with one of the Men at Arms. He hailed our safe return.

"Well you weren't eaten by some wild beast then." He said cheerily. "The Jarl bade the Captains move the ships as far upstream as they could to save us distance if we are to undertake any land crossing tomorrow. It saved you both a fair journey Guillaume. The Jarl is taking his rest and will hear your account of the journey in the morning. Go take your rest now."

We were both exhausted and lost no time in finding a soft place to bed down under the surrounding trees. There would be plenty of time to plan the route south in the morning. Within a short time I found myself drifting into sleep.

I woke to the sound of axes cutting timber, it seemed that many trees were being felled close by. Soft sunlight penetrated the green canopy above. I heard a sudden movement beside me and sat up.

"The Jarl commands your presence my friend."

Shielding my eyes from the light, I recognised immediately the familiar voice of Jeruba, it boomed out once again.

"The sun is already high and he is anxious to depart."

I raised his aching body from the pallet of soft turf and moss I had used for a cot, yawned, got to my feet and stretched. I strode towards the river and stripping off my buckskin jacket knelt at the riverbank, splashed the cold refreshing water over my face and upper body. I couldn't keep the Jarl waiting so I dressed again quickly, joined Jeruba and together we went to look for him.

A team of craftsmen were busy felling slender birch trees, stripping the branches with their axes and cutting the trunks into sections to use as rollers for the easy passage of the two Drakkars. A slipway of logs had already been laid close to the riverbank so that the ships could be dragged ashore.

Sailors were busy on board dismantling the masts and fixing them securely along the ships thwarts under which they had stowed the sails, provisions and personal belongings. Ropes now tightly secured to the bow and gunwales of the first of the Drakkars were thrown to men waiting on the bank in preparation for hauling the ship out of the river.

We found the Jarl speaking with Sir James Gunn's Sergeant at Arms whose men had already formed up into two lines ready to take up the ropes from the Haggar. Bernard of Thirsk bowed, left the Jarl and began to shout orders to the waiting men. The two teams of men spread out in a "V" formation either side of the slipway and the ropes were passed along the lines.

"Mark my words men, the sooner we get the boats out of the water the sooner we can get under way. Take up the str-a-a-a-in, heave and heave and heave..."

Slowly at first the Haggar started to move out of the water and onto the slipway. To the rhythm of the Sergeant at Arms command the ship began to shudder forward and as the slipway began to take its weight the whole ship began to slide along the supporting slipway at a steady rate. Men using poles on either side of the moving ship maintained its upright position while one man swinging a small keg of fish oil splashed the contents along the laid out timbers allowing the keel to glide more easily, the smell of the fish oil became overpowering. The bulk of the ship was on the slipway now and was being hauled towards the next line of timbers already set in place as a holding position along the riverbank.

Sir Robert Melrose' Sergeant at Arms, Dagmar Olafson now divided his men into two teams and set them to the task of hauling the second ship out of the water. Shouting orders Olafson bade them take up the strain on the ropes and begin to heave. Just as the first ship had done, the Kral slowly left the water in a series of small movements until it too was firmly settled on the slipway ready to be moved forward.

Jeruba and I approached the Jarl who was watching the progress of the moving ship.

"Good morrow my Lord. The day is set fair for the portage."

"It is my son. Come we will parley, the route has to be planned." He led us to a fallen tree trunk where the two ship Captains and Sir James Gunn stood waiting, shortly afterwards Sir Robert Melrose Joined us.

"This makes a goodly place to sit and confer. Sir Guillaume I bid you show me what lies ahead? "

I took out the buckskin chart and spread it out along the trunk revealing the crude map I had drawn. Pointing to my representation of the falls from where we had carried the ca-noos I described the route the portage of the two Drakkars would have to follow.

"We have found a course to a southern sea. We must traverse two rocky outcrops but once beyond we will meet another river that will take us there. I estimate the portage will take two days. The route between here and the hill measures about a two leagues Sire and a further two leagues to where the Drakkars can be launched on the other river. The trees for the most part are spread well although there may be some sections of the journey where we will have to fell trees that are growing close together. The two rocky outcrops with cataracts here and here," he pointed to the areas shown, "the source of both rivers lays near the top of the second cataract here we should show caution for the way down from the cataract is steep. I have arranged to meet Running Deer at the second cataract in two days; he and his men are presently scouting the easiest route to the navigable section of the other river at this place. Afterwards he said he would go to the village of his mother which lies close to the mouth of the river and prepare them for our coming."

"Sir James, Sir Robert and Captains as soon as both Drakkars are in a holding position straightway we will start the portage. At every turn of the large sand glass we will take rest for an equivalent time. Sir James, your squire will see that the sand glass is turned and call out the stops and starts. Sir Robert your squire will bring up the rear and with the Priors to ensure that anyone who is injured during the portage is cared for. Both your Sergeant at Arms will take charge of the hauling teams. We will need a few Men at Arms to form a team of axe men ready to fell any trees that bar our path. Captains you and your seamen will be responsible for the stability of the ships as they are drawn along. We must avoid at all costs any damage to the hulls for the ships are our life line. So men go to your duties."

The Jarl asked us to remain while the rest of the group dispersed.

"The scouting party has done well my son and for that you have my gratitude. You and Jeruba will accompany me on the portage. Now go take some refreshment and I will send for you when the Drakkars are ready."

The Kral was just being hauled into the holding position as we sought out some victuals. We ate some pemmican, drunk the clear river water and filled our skins ready for the journey. Then we sat watching the activity as the remains of the camp were cleared awaiting a summons. It wasn't long before the Jarl's manservant came running over and bade them attend the Jarl.

The Men at Arms had already started to take the logs away from the slipway on the bank and place them forward of the holding area forming a line along the bank of the river. Soon a narrow wooden slipway three times the length of both ships was ready. Both Drakkars were hauled onto this slipway and before the first had reached the end the Men at Arms and Seamen in attendance were taking the logs from the rear in a continuous line and placing them in the front making an uninterrupted runway for those hauling the ship. Thus the portage began, running smoothly for the first league with Sir James' squire calling the stops as the sand glass emptied and was turned over.

It was late afternoon, the first steep section close to the waterfall had been surmounted and the men were being rested. As the water flasks were passed around some of the men poured them over their heads. One of the cooks wearing the green habit of a serving brother passed among the men with dried fish and meat and berries from the forest. The Jarl pleased with the progress discussed the route ahead with me while Jeruba hovered like a silent sentinel.

"We need a place to make camp before nightfall. Have you a place in mind Guillaume."

"There are many clearings in the forest. If you will keep on this course with your approval I will go forward with Jeruba and find a suitable place to prepare for your arrival."

"Go to it my son." The Jarl replied.

Together we left the portage and walked into the forest. Soon we found a wide clearing where a rocky outcrop had prevented the growth of trees. I began to look for loose rocks to prepare a circle of stones to contain a fire. Jeruba left me and went off into the forest before long he had returned with a deer and a brace of Coney. The fire was already alight and I was collecting more dead wood and piling it close by.

Jeruba quickly skinned and gutted the meat and hung it in a tree then we went to meet the rest of the party. The grind of the Drakkar hulls against the wooden logs drew them to the point where the portage had reached. We approached the Jarl and told him that a clearing just about a hundred paces ahead had been prepared, a fire lit and a small amount of fresh meat prepared. The Jarl shouted to the cooks to go with Jeruba to the clearing.

The first party arrived hauling the Haggar into the clearing. When both ships had been dragged into the clearing they were gently turned over and laid on supports to provide shelter for the Jarl and the Knights. Jeruba meanwhile had been out hunting again and had caught three more fowl, which were soon prepared for the pot. The cooks had set up a roasting spit over the fire and were busy turning and basting the venison. The smell that met the nostrils of the exhausted men was overpowering.

It was some time before the cooks declared that the meat was ready. Some of the hungry men ate ravenously until all that was left was the carcass of the deer and an empty stew pot; others were so exhausted that they simply fell asleep where they lay with food still in their mouths.

By midday they had reached the source of the rivers and Running Deer and a large group of braves were waiting there. Running Deer came forward and greeted the Jarl he introduced his relations one by one and the Jarl patiently acknowledged them.

Running Deer then explained that the braves had scouted a route to where the river could take the draught of the two Drakkars. The Jarl anxious to get under way thanked Running Deer and shouted to his Knights to commence the next part of the portage.

Extra ropes were tied to the stern of each vessel to check their descent and thus Drakkars were manhandled down the rocky escarpment. The Kral was about a third of the way down the slope when suddenly one of the men slipped on some scree and lost his grip followed by a second and a third man. The vessel lurched to one side throwing all the Men at Arms on that side to the ground. There was a moment when it was thought that the men would lose control hold of the Kral and it would dash to pieces on the rocks below.

All was saved when Dagmar Olafson had the presence of mind to grab the loose end of the flaying rope and looped it twice round a nearby tree taking the full weight of that side of the Kral. Although the tree looked as if it would be uprooted the Kral steadied and slid to a halt. He shouted to the men on the other side of the vessel to hold their position while the fallen men recovered their ropes. Fortunately no one was seriously injured apart from a few bruises and the journey down the rest of the escarpment went smoothly. Soon the Drakkars were once again on the temporary slipway and the teams were making their way across level ground.

After two rest stops we had reached the river and in the distance could see smoke coming from the cooking fires around the wigwams of the Micmac village. Jeruba and I went ahead with Running Deer and the braves who were to show them where the river was deep enough to take the Drakkars.

We had travelled but half a league when Running Deer and one of the braves left the group. Shortly afterwards the brave came back and beckoned them towards the riverbank where we found Running Deer waiting in a grassy clearing leading to the river bank. At this point the river widened to about one hundred paces.

"The river from this point to the great water is as deep as the height of two men standing on each other's shoulders. Nokumaw (My Cousin) tells me there are no more dangers apart from the occasional submerged tree and they are usually found close to the bank. The great ca-noos of Kuloscap will have no trouble floating from here. I will send two braves back to Kuloscap to guide him here."

It was not long before the first of the ships being drawn across the wooden slipway shattered the natural sounds of the forest startling birds and other wild creatures that fled seeking refuge from this unusual disturbance to their habitat. Soon the Haggar came into sight followed by the Kral. As they neared the bank of the river the strain of the journey that was etched in the tired faces of the men at the ropes changed to one of relief as their part in the portage would be soon at an end. The captain and several seamen climbed into the deck and the Haggar was maneuvered into the river. The team holding fast onto the ropes watched as the Captain steered the Drakkar out of the main stream and back towards the river bank.

Soon the Haggar had been secured and the seamen set about restoring the rigging and getting it shipshape and ready for the next stage of our journey. A gangplank was lowered from the side of the ship to the river bank and soon everything was secured and ready for the waiting groups to board.

The Jarl and the rest of the men left the seamen to their tasks and remained ashore until the Kral had been launched and secured alongside the first. When we finally came aboard I informed the Jarl of the close proximity of the native village and said that Running Deer had gone ahead to make arrangements for the Jarl to meet his uncles the elders.

The Drakkars moved off down the river drifting with the slow current and soon they were approaching a village similar in size to the one in Pectou. Many of the people lined the banks of the river to see the great ca-noos approach shouted to each other in excited chitchat. I could make out some of the shouts.
"Look at the great ca-noos floating like big whales".
"I see the great Chief Kuloscap it is true his head dress shines like the sun". "Look how many warriors he has he is indeed a great Chief".

The Drakkars slowly neared the shore and found that just downstream of the village the water was deep enough for the Haggar to come up alongside the banks of the river and secure ropes at stem and stern to trunks of trees. Once the ship was secure the Kral came up alongside and was secured to the first. A gangplank was lowered from the deck to the shore and the Jarl together with Me Jeruba and Sir James Gunn and Sir Robert Melrose went ashore. There was a series of whoops and yells as we stepped ashore close to where a party of elders waited with Running Deer to greet us. One of the elders approached with Running Deer who introduced him as his uncle Chief Wape'k Kitpoo, which he translated as "the eagle that is white", Sagamaw of the Missaguash Clan of the Micmac Nation. The Micmac Chieftain said he welcomed the great Chief Kuloscap to his village saying he had known about the Jarls coming for it had been foretold that a great Chief would arrive from across the sea on the back of a great whale and bring peace and justice to his people. Presenting the Chief with a belt of tooled leather with an ornate buckle said that he was honoured to meet the uncle of Running Deer and thanked the Chief for the great welcome.

The Chief then invited the four of us to his teepee where food had been prepared in similar baskets to the ones that Running Deer had brought when they first met. Running Deer explained that there was the meat of a turkey cock, fresh cooked salmon which had been prepared with wild mint, sweet maize and round brown vegetables which grew in clumps underground which had been boiled until they were soft so that the skin could be peeled off. I found the food welcome and appetizing. When

we had eaten our fill a pipe was prepared by the
Shaman which was lit and passed to the Chief
who took several long draws and wafted the
smoke over him and passed the pipe to the Jarl,
The Jarl managed only one draw and quickly
passed it on. When the pipe had been passed full
circle the Shaman removed it from the Tepee.
The Jarl listened for a while as Chief White Eagle
told of the good hunting to be found in the local
forests and then asked me to explain why he and
his followers had come from across the great salt
waterway.

Through me the Jarl said he and his party would
like to explore the country and were seeking a
lodge where we could spend winter when the
time came. The Chief said there were many places
he could show the great Kuluscap but to build a
lodge sheltered from the great storms that came
with the snows he would need somewhere
enclosed with fresh water at hand. He pointed
across the bay to a spit of land rising up out of
the water. On the other side of this headland
called Chignecto was a place where there was a
sheltered inlet the great ca-noos could rest. Close
by was a piece of open ground with a fresh water

stream surrounded by the forest which would give shelter from the icy fingers of the Great Spirit Kjiniskam that came down from the north. His braves would lead them there when the great Chief was rested.

The following morning Chief White Eagle bade Running Deer to take six of his braves who would lead the party to the place he had mentioned it said it would be quicker to cross the bay in the great ca-noos. The Chief gave a stark warning of the winter snows to come and said that we should build shelters as soon as possible while the weather remained mild.

"The Shaman has foretold that in three moons the first snowfalls will begin and hunting will become difficult and meat will become scarce. The snows will get steadily worse then a great freeze will descend over the whole land and will remain for several moons until the great thaw starts".

He advised the Jarl to store plenty of firewood and food for once the great freeze began they could be trapped in the lodges for days. The rest of the party began to board and two large Canoos were loaded for the braves to return. I translated as the Jarl thanked the Micmac Chieftain bade farewell and at last boarded the Haggar. The village came out to see us off watching and waving as the ships were rowed into the estuary and the sails were hoisted.

It took us less than an hour to complete the journey across the bay and as we rounded the headland we could see that the Chief had chosen wisely. An inlet enclosed by two arms of land which met at a small entrance provided a sheltered harbour. Inside the enclosed harbour was an area of open ground sheltered to the north by a rocky out crop and this was a perfect place for the small winter settlement. The rock wall extended to a height of ten sword lengths and a fresh water stream plunged from this escarpment into the sea. On seeing this I proposed to the Jarl that a defensive barrier be built extending round from the rock wall enclosing within the circle eight huts. Four long huts would shelter the Jarl and his servants, craftsmen and clerics and the Men at Arms and four small huts for the knights and their Squires.

Trees were selected and logs cut and work began on the defensive barrier. This was completed in a week and the first building to be erected was a long hut suitable quarters for the Jarl and his servants. Large stones were collected from the river bed and built up to form sturdy foundations. Just as in the previous settlement the timber that had been felled was stripped of its bark and used for the main roof supports, the smaller branches had been cut into suitable lengths fixed in lines between the main roof timbers and the salvaged strips of bark woven between to form a strong base for the roof. Finally each roof was finished off with grass sods. I felt that if there was to be a bad winter the shelters would afford reasonable protection from the worst of weather.

By the end of August the building of quarters had been completed and when by the time we had moved into our respective lodges the first winter rains had started to fall. In the early part of September Running Deer decided to return with the braves to his uncle's lodge. He said that Missaguash clan would soon be moving to their winter quarters at ….. He would rest there until the great thaw when the Jarl was once again ready to explore the country and added that we would always be welcome at his uncle's lodge. He would try to return from time to time until the snows came and help us with any problems. The Jarl thanked him and gave Running Deer a Caribou that the hunting party had caught recently. We said our farewells and Running Deer and the braves climbed into the Can-oos and set out across the bay heading for the village.

The next day the Jarl ordered parties out again to hunt meat for the long winter ahead. Cari-boo meat and fish were prepared and salted then hung up in the storehouse. Fruits and berries from the forest were dried and stored. Furs and hides from the animals caught had been cured and prepared as ground covers and over blankets. By the time the first snows came we were as prepared as we could be for what nature would inflict on us.

With the onset of winter came days of violent blizzards when everyone was confined inside their lodges and each time the skies cleared, the snow had piled so high that we were forced to dig ourselves out. Nothing had prepared us for such harsh conditions. The incessant howling winds brought a biting cold that would split trees. It was the most inhospitable environment that I had ever experienced and I began to wonder if we would ever survive the winter.

Jeruba suffered miserably. For the first time since he regained his freedom he had been confined inside. Even in Orkney he had never experienced such cold. He spent his days huddled by the fire draped in a huge fur cloak unable to move. In the teeth of the blizzards he would rock back and forward moaning to himself in his own tongue. I tried to console him but was met with a stony silence. He appeared as if he was in another world. Fortunately we had a huge stock of firewood and fires were kept permanently lit.

With the stream frozen over, the fresh water supply was soon exhausted and we were forced to boil snow. Rations of dried fish and meat were passed out to each lodge and we prepared and ate our meals in our own lodges during the days when the blizzards came.

Christ's Mass and the New Year of 1399 came and went but apart from the religious festival held in the Jarl's lodge there was no other celebration. The Jarl was concerned that the preserved meat was almost used up. Fearing that we would have to send hunting parties out again he waited for a break in the weather.

It was another three weeks before there was a brief respite and with our supplies exhausted the Jarl ordered two hunting parties out. The break in the weather proved to be very brief as the very next day a blizzard struck. Nothing was heard from the hunting parties for three days, until one of the groups struggled into the settlement. They had little to show for their efforts but frost bite and two small Moose.

The following day the second party returned frost bitten and exhausted and without three of their men. The men had become separated while in pursuit of a herd of Cari-boo. The blizzard had struck with such force that the rest of the party had been compelled to remain in a small cave until it had subsided.

On the morning of the third day, the blizzard had receded enough to send out search parties. One of the parties found the men frozen to death barely a hundred paces from the safety of the temporary shelter. They had been caught out in the open by the unexpected blizzard it was a grim exchange, just one Cari-boo for the lives of three men.

An air of despondency permeated throughout the settlement, everyone was troubled by the news. We had become a close-knit community and for those who had shared the same lodge, the loss was hard to take. Some murmured that they would rather eat snow than the Cari-boo meat as they felt it was cursed.

The Jarl was saddened by the news. He knew that there would be dangers to face in this harsh new land but his men had died, not bravely in battle but by the unseen hand of nature. During another break in the weather and because the ground was too frozen to dig graves the bodies of the Men at Arms were unceremoniously covered where they lay with a rock cairn to keep the bodies being disturbed by wild animals.

As the short winter days of bitter cold eased slowly into spring the hunting parties were able to keep up a regular supply of deer meat, rabbit and turkey cock. Then a few short days of sunshine heralded the great thaw. The priors asked the Jarl for a service of thanks to God for our deliverance and the whole settlement was assembled for prayers and remembrance of those who had given their lives to maintain a supply of food.

By the middle of March salmon began appearing in the stream on their way from the sea to spawn. I had never seen so many and could scarcely believe my eyes. During that month can-oos were sighted in the bay and to their joy Running Deer and his men returned and were given a great welcome. They brought news of the men left at the Pectou settlement stating they had survived the winter and the men and ships were in good fettle. They brought baskets of eggs of the bustard which to me seemed as large as duck eggs. I marvelled that the eggs had survived the journey across the bay but was grateful for a slight change in their diet. The Jarl thanked them for the gift. He ordered that one of the lodges be cleared to accommodate Running Deer and his party.

As a result of the thaw the settlement soon became a sea of mud. Men at Arms struggled with great bulks of timber in an effort to make a roadway through the mud to connect the lodges. However things gradually improved the thaw had given them a fresh water supply once again and hunting parties were finding the lots of game in the forest and with the huge Salmon spawning in the rivers food was once again becoming plentiful. The harsh winter now becoming a distant memory the Jarl called his knights together and said he was ready to explore the land once again. He decided to send out a party to the east to explore and asked Sir John Gunn to undertake the mission.

Jeruba, Running Deer and I joined Sir James Gunn's party and we set out to explore a nearby headland. We trekked for about an hour and when we reached the top discovered to our amazement across a huge expanse of water was the misty outline of another large coastline running south as far as the eye could see.

Crossing the headland we came across a river and decided to follow it into the interior.

The virgin forestland saw little sunlight save for shafts of sunlight which managed to penetrate the leafy canopy or lit the occasional glade we would come across to rest in. So in this atmosphere of alternating gloom and sunlight we trekked on. We trekked inland for two days and found that the source of the river was a large series of lakes.

From time to time Jeruba would leave the party and go on hunting forays returning with large fowl that roamed the forests and the occasional deer thus keeping the food stocks up. One day he returned wide eyed with a tale that he had seen a giant bear in the forest much larger than the ones he had seen in Kirkwall chained and dancing for money. This one had stood at least three sword lengths tall. He said he had come across the creature attacking a bee's nest in order to extract the honey. The bees were everywhere and he had decided to keep well away but observed the antics of the creature with amusement until with paws and face covered with honey it had dropped down and ambled off into forest.

We halted for a while by the large lake but were plagued by small flies so we moved off keeping to the edge of the lake to avoid swampy ground and eventually found that it was the swampy ground that was feeding another stream that ran east the course of which we followed. From the start of our journey I had spent my time mapping our route where the other river leading into the lakes had flowed west. It was nearly three days since we left the settlement and we were glad to see that the stream had widened into a river.

We followed the course of the river for a day and camped where it now widened out into an estuary. The next day we came across a small Micmac settlement of about twenty wigwams. Running Deer and I went forward and were greeted the villagers. Running Deer introduced us both and was welcomed as the son of a Micmac chief would be. The headman of the village a bronzed broad shouldered man of medium stature stepped forward. He wore a deer skin apron and leggings, moccasins on his feet and a band of leather set around the jet black hair that framed his narrow face and deep set brown eyes. The hair band had several coloured kill feathers set in it indicating encounters with bears and other large animals and was beautifully woven with the same zigzag patterns I had seen in the other Micmac villages.

The headman who was called took us to his wigwam where his wife served us with pemmican and dried fish while Running Deer explained the nature of our visit. We smoked a pipe with him. As the rest of the party came into the village they were greeted like gods the villagers were amazed at seeing their first white men. The tired party were given food and water after which the Men at Arms set up camp just outside the village for the night.

The next day we followed the estuary which became broader as it neared the sea and finally arrived at the rocky shore. I considered that this must be the sea we had crossed almost a year ago. We rested in a makeshift camp by the sea for two days. While I charted some of our surrounding coastline Jamie Gunn sent out hunting parties to replenish supplies for the journey back.

Deciding that we had mapped enough of the coastline I suggested to Jamie Gunn that we should make our preparations to return to the settlement. As we retraced our journey westwards the red bearded knight regaled me with stories of battles fought against the unruly islanders of Prince Henry's Orcadian domains.

We arrived at the settlement to a cheery welcome from those who had remained and made for the Jarl's lodge as we approached he came out to greet us. We had been away for fifteen days.

"By God's grace you have returned safely and what of your adventures brave Knights come tell me?"

We bowed and he bade us enter the lodge to make our report we told of our sighting of lands across the open water to the south and of the rivers we had encountered on our way across to what we thought was the Western Sea. I showed the charts I had prepared. The Jarl seemed excited by the prospect that there was more land to be explored decided there and then that he would take the Haggar and sail south along the coast and explore this coastline hidden in the mists.

Running Deer was sent for and asked whether he was able to accompany us on this journey. Reluctantly he said he had promised his father that he would not leave the Micmac lands although he believed that other tribes of his nation could be found across the great water. However his two braves Husky Dog and Flying Squirrel were willing to remain and act as our scouts.

So we bade farewell to the Running Deer the native warrior who had given us so much help. I was particularly sad because we had done so many things to make the relationship between our two peoples a sound one. Running Deer clasped my forearm and said.

"You are my brother Ntutem and we will meet again if not in this life when the time comes for us to go to the land of the Great Spirit."

He took a small decorated bag from round his neck and placed it over mine.

"Take this talisman given to me by my father may it protect you on your journey as it has me."

I was reluctant to take such a precious thing but Running Deer pressed me and I accepted it with grace.

The Jarl presented him with a dagger similar to the one his father had received and he left the settlement with his braves to return to his father's Lodge while we set about preparing for the journey south.

Chapter Thirteen
The Land beyond the Mists.

Leaving the behind the two sand bars that formed the natural harbour protecting our settlement, the Haggar picked up a fair wind and we were soon heading south into the unknown. The weather was set fair for the journey with a stiff breeze catching the sail and moving us along at a steady rate.

I stood in silence with Jeruba in the bow of the Haggar gazing at the outline of the coast ahead both wrapped up in our own thoughts. After about an hour I could make out a rugged coastline of rocky inlets beset by dangerous shoals which from time to time with the rise and fall of the sea revealed the bared teeth of the rocks hidden below. We made good progress but the captain and the Jarl were being cautious about approaching the land for fear of foundering on hidden rocks and set lookouts on the bow to keep watch. So on we went following the coast searching for an inlet or cove that showed promise as a landing place.

The day passed quickly and we had not come across any suitable place to berth. With this in mind it was obvious that we were going to spend a night at sea so the captain prepared his seamen for the night watches while the rest of us lay down to sleep lulled by the buffeting sound of the waves against the hull. And thus we journeyed on.

With the dawn the mist departed showing us the real nature of the shore we were sailing past. The coastline was made up of rocky and forbidding inlets with no hope of landing. With day now turning into night the cautious Captain steered the vessel away from the shore and continued south.

By late afternoon the next day we were sailing past a large island. The Captain being warned by the lookouts of a line of skerries just off the island wisely steered the Haggar to the seaward side of the island. By the time we left the island astern and turned westward towards a coastline it was night once again.

I awoke at first light and saw that we were passing a shoreline of heavily forested land edged by wide strips of white sand. Suddenly we heard a cry from the lookout in the bow his sharp eyes had spotted a wide inlet which had promise as a sheltered berth for the Haggar. As we moved closer we could see the narrow entrance to the mouth of a wide river and the Jarl gave orders to the Captain to enter.

As we tacked westward and made our way cautiously through the narrow islets of sand into the river estuary it began to open out into a large bay. So wide was the river that forty ships end to end would not reach across. As the day gave way to night we sailed on and although the river seemed to narrow gradually it was still wide enough for several ships to maneuver with ease. The Jarl shouted orders for everyone to search the shoreline for somewhere to berth the Haggar but night had already overtaken us and so we laid offshore in anticipation of what we would find on the morrow.

I awoke in a mood of excitement and stood up to get my bearings. As the day dawned I found the Jarl in the prow gazing up river. We were anchored close to a small headland covered in trees.

'Join me Sir Guillaume,' he said beckoning me forward. I did so and he continued,' I am intrigued where this river will lead us and propose that we continue to explore its length.'

I could only agree for the Jarl's mind was already set.

The Jarl commanded his captain to follow the course of the river and the stone anchor was hauled aboard and we were soon underway making our way steadily up river. The captain took advantage of the breeze and the Haggar made good progress and with the aid of the shallow draft of the ship we had advanced upriver against the current some ten leagues. The river became more sheltered by the forest cover the wind dropped we were forced to set up the oars and row upstream against the river current.

We continued like this making slow progress upriver for the next three days following its meandering course through vast forestlands that stretched as far as the eye could see. Eventually we reached a wide section where we were able anchor.

Strange as it may seem we never saw any sign of the inhabitants of this limitless forestland. Jeruba's sixth sense however was alert and he said that we were being followed by a band of at least eight and possibly ten natives and although they had blended into the undergrowth his sharp eyes had detected them. I passed this news on to the Jarl and he thought for a moment and then said.

"Well I think it is time for us to make contact and find out what these people are like. Tomorrow we will go ashore. Summon Sir James for I would speak with him about the arrangements."

Chapter Fourteen
Our Mahican Friends.

The next day broke clear making our preparations easy. I watched as Jamie Gunn prepared his men for the trek ashore. There was an air of apprehension among the ten men that were chosen to accompany the exploration party as they assembled. What strange natives and creatures would they encounter in this vast forestland? Would the natives be fearsome or friendly like the Micmac they had encountered? Jamie Gunn however allayed their fears by addressing them saying they had fought their way through many skirmishes and this would be no greater task than anything they had dealt with before. He told them to always remain alert and they would have nothing to fear. With that he ordered the men into the two boats which had been made ready to be rowed ashore. As soon as they had settled in the boats we joined them and we set off across the bay towards the wooded shoreline.

After disembarking the party made its way into the forest with Jamie Gunn, myself, Jeruba and the two Micmac warriors leading. Progress was slow for there were no paths to follow. We were lucky enough however to find a small tributary off the river where we had moored and followed it inland. As long as we kept this in sight we knew we would be able to find our way back to the Haggar.

Once again I became fascinated with the flora and fauna of the forest although we found ourselves in a familiar forest setting I noticed once again that the trees, bushes and flowers were of different varieties to those I was used to seeing in Scotland. The oaks were much slimmer than the broad oaks we were used to and the most prolific tree in the forest had a huge three pointed leaf. It entered my mind that this virgin forestland had been untouched by man from its origin and perhaps we were the first humans to venture through.

But this was short lived for while I was musing I hadn't noticed that Jeruba had left the party accompanied by Husky Dog and had disappeared into the forest undergrowth. I was used to Jeruba's excursions and had no fears for his safety for he was truly a master in this environment. We continued on following the course of the tributary which we would judge to be in Scotland, a small river. After we had trekked for a while I noticed that the ground was beginning to get steeper and before long we had emerged from the forest into a small area of grassland. This was not a natural feature for the grass was a form of wheat and the area had been cleared specifically to grow the crop. There were also plants with large stems and big green leaves from each stem huge seeds pod hung protected by the leaves. We skirted the edge of the crop and were just about to enter the forest once again when there was a loud cry ahead of us and Jeruba and Husky Dog appeared together with several other natives. They looked and were dressed in similar clothes to the Micmac but there was one significant difference. The heads of the men had been shaved each side leaving a tuft of long hair across the top and a circlet of decorated leather held kill feathers.

Jeruba's face lit up with a smile when he saw me and he came running over.

"Husky Dog and I knew there were natives tracking our progress so we decided to go and find out who they were. They are the people of the Mahican tribe and these are their lands. The Mahican are kin of the Micmaq and speak virtually the same language so Husky Dog had little trouble in explaining who we were. We have been told to bring you back to their village and meet the Sachem."

I must say I was happy to see the tall Nubian. "Jeruba I knew that you couldn't resist going out to find who was following our progress through the forest. We must thank our Lord that the natives weren't hostile. Jamie what think you about this after all you are in charge of the party?"

"It is the Jarls wish that we should go and meet the natives of this forestland so I say we will go and see this Sachem whoever he is. It is better to have an ally than an enemy in this unknown land." He turned to his men. "Form up and follow me."

With Jeruba, Husky Dog and the other natives in the lead we once again entered the forest this time taking a well worn path that presumably led from the cultivated area to the village. Before long we were descending out of the forest towards a group of wigwams set up close to the tributary we had been following.

As we approached the village the natives came out to greet us. They stood open mouthed at the sight of their first encounter with us. They had never seen metal swords, helmets and shields let alone the strange dress that most of us were wearing. The children of the village ran forward unafraid and ran alongside us shouting and laughing.

As we entered the village a tall, heavily built warrior dressed in a doeskin shirt, cape, apron, leggings and moccasins which had been highly decorated in the recognizable zigzag pattern came out of a large wigwam set in the middle of the village. His head was shaven like the other braves and topped with several kill feathers. The right hand side of his face was marked with several representations of birds which had been etched into the skin with some kind of blue dye. He wore a short cape over his shoulders and this too was decorated with the familiar zigzag pattern. He appeared to be the Head Man of the village.

As we approached several braves stepped forward in a protective ring around him. I approached, bowed and in the Micmac tongue told him that we were travelers exploring this land. The Head Man raised his hand and said some words which I translated as a welcome and that he was happy to let us share his fire, food and water. I learned that the Head Man name was Wobi Mageso (White Eagle), he was Chief (Sachem) of the Mahican people of Wabanakiak. He said we had travelled far from the great waters through the lands of the

We made camp on the outskirts of the village. It was good to bask in the sunlight after days under the canopy of the forest. Some of us took advantage of the river to wash away days of sweat and toil marching through the vast forestland. The village was quite large and contained near to fifty wigwams housing about one hundred souls. The men sent out hunting parties to find fresh meat while the women cultivated areas of land with the strange type of corn. The large yellow pods enclosed in the green leaves were called maize and were harvested and used as a vegetable. They brought several husks for us in baskets similar to those that the Micmac used and I could see they were seed pods with large yellow seed which the women scraped off with pieces of bone into woven baskets. They showed us that they could be eaten raw or cooked in the ashes of the fire. When cooked they tasted deliciously sweet and together with the meat we hunted provided us with all the food we needed.

With the help of our two Micmac guides I told the Chief as best I could in the Micmac tongue about our people and that we had come over the great sea from lands to the east in large canoes.

We were exploring this country on behalf of our great Chief the Jarl of the Orkneys. The Chief was amazed to see our metal swords, daggers, helmets I explained that they were made from a special kind of earth called ore which was melted down in great fires until it was liquid and when it was cool it was fashioned into the objects he had seen. He was anxious to know where he could get this earth I could only explain that it was mined in special places from the ground.

Jamie, Jeruba and I together with the two Micmac guides spent many hours talking together with the Chief. He said that there were many other tribes in this great land some of which were hostile. His enemies were the 'snake people' who many times in the past had raided their tribal lands. They seemed to raid villages for the women although there had been no raids since he was Chief. In other parts of the Mahican Nation the snake people had been seen hunting in their lands. He explained we should be on our guard when we were exploring the country.

During our few days spent with the Mahicans we were treated with kindness and hospitality and a great friendship had grown between the three of us and the Chief. We departed in the hope that we would meet again on our return to the Haggar. On our departure the Chief supplied us with two large containers with maize pods and pemmican to sustain us on our journey. He appointed three warriors to escort us through the Mahican lands their leader was to be a tall warrior named Grey Wolf a stern faced man. I found it hard to communicate with him because he never showed his feelings but he was willing and eager to lead the party and at the same time hunt for game in the forest.

Once again we entered the forest. Grey Wolf said that we would follow the river to the edge of their territory the journey would take about three days. Entering the cover of the forest was hard to take at first for we lost the warmth of the sun and until we had accustomed ourselves to the situation it was for a while like a cold hand had touched us.

At last we broke through into an open area close to the river and Jamie decided it was a good place to rest. We went to the river and revived ourselves by splashing our faces with the cold water. When the men were refreshed and had drunk their fill Jamie commanded them to refill the leather flasks with fresh water from the river. The maize strips of pemmican helped to allay our hunger.

As we sat on the grassy swathe I could hear the men chatting excitedly among themselves about the journey and what they would discover, what great monsters they would encounter in this vast forest seeking comfort from the protection of the Blessed Mary to see them safely through.

After a short rest we moved into the undergrowth once again. We trekked on until nightfall forced us to find a suitable glade to make camp. A fire was lit and some of the maize pods were cooked in the fire and distributed among the men.

After a nights rest we trekked on spending a further two days following the course of the river until Grey Wolf said we were nearing the edge of his territory. At this point he started to lead us away from the river because he said he did not want to cross into hostile territory and after a short while we reached a huge rock. Here he indicated that we were about half a day's march from the boundaries of his nation and we should not go any further as we would encounter a fierce tribe they called the Mohawk which translated as 'Man Eaters' . As he would go no further Jamie said it would be a good place to rest and perhaps hunt for fresh meat. Grey Wolf and his party said farewell and together they journeyed back to their village.

Jeruba said he and the two Micmac warriors would like to try to get enough fresh meat to take back to the village. Several of the Men at Arms volunteered to join the hunting party as well. Jamie thought this was a good idea as it would free them for a while from arduous trekking through endless forestland so he decided to send six Men at Arms with the hunting party and keep four with us. The men drew lots and the six men were selected.

The next day the hunting party gathered together and moved into the forest. The four Men at Arms who remained at the camp were   sent them off into the forest gather wood for the fire and we settled back by the rock and talked about this vast country and the wealth of food, water and timber it had to offer. So engaged in our conversation we failed to notice that the men who had gone out to collect wood had not returned.

As Jamie stood up to stretch, I heard a noise from the undergrowth, Jamie let out a stifled cry and dropped to the ground. An arrow had pierced his neck and suddenly his life's blood was pumping away in great spurts. I jumped to my feet rushed to his aid and tried to stop the flow of blood but it was hopeless. His whole body began to go into spasm and then with a loud gurgling sound he gave a sigh and died. I was so distressed and overcome with shock at witnessing this terrible tragedy I wasn't aware that several natives had surrounded me. I felt a sharp blow to my head and everything went black.

Chapter Fifteen
The Keepers of the Eastern Gate.

When I came to I was lying with my head against the roots of a large tree. My hands were tied behind my back. I had no idea how long I had been out and there was no sign of any of my colleagues. My head was pounding from the blow I had received. The horror of what had happened overwhelmed me, my friend was dead I had been separated from Juba and the rest of the company and now I was a captive of a group of natives that I knew nothing about. I looked about me sitting cross legged by a tree were two braves their heads were shaved except for a long narrow crown of hair and they had strips of black marking their cheekbones and around their eyes which gave them a fearsome appearance. Inserted in their ears were decorated pieces made from bone.

At first glance I could see that they wore the familiar buckskin leggings and apron and a decorated buckskin cloak loosely wrapped around them. Their feet were covered by leather moccasins which had high sides pulled up against their legs and tied with leather thongs. Each of them had three kill feathers stuck in the hair. Hanging from their waist belt was a kind of club made from a short wooden shaft surmounted by a shaped stone which had been set into the shaft with strips of leather and alongside them were two crudely made bows and several arrows carried in a birch bark quiver. Leaning against the tree were two long wooden shafted spears with pieces of sharpened animal bone bound with strips of leather.

As I lay there I tried to pick up bits of their conversation but could not make anything out that was close to the Micmac language. I reached for my leather satchel which contained all my worldly possessions including my small set of masonry chisels but it was missing. The brave nearest to me had observed my movements and stood up and walked over to where I lay. He grabbed the satchel and began to berate me at the same time kicking me in the side. Before long the other brave had joined him and together they continued this unrelenting onslaught.

Fortunately another tall brave wearing similar dress but with a fringed jacket made of buckskin instead of the cloak approached shouting angrily and saved me from further attack. I was dismayed to see that on his head he wore Jamie's helmet and he was carrying Jamie's sword he took the satchel and pushed the two braves away from me. They withdrew scowling at their reprimand and returned to where they were sitting.

He said a few words to me which I didn't understand then tried another tongue that sounded like the Mahican language from which I picked up several phrases. I learned that he was Kahon Okwa a Kanienkehaka (Mohawk) of the Kanonsionni or five nations and that I was his captive and I would go with him to his village and work for the Mohawk people. I realized that these people were what Kolkohas had called the Mohawk although they called themselves Kanienkehaka.

Trying to use similar Mahican words I asked what had happened to the people that had accompanied me and he indicated that they were all dead. I was stunned by this but he gave me the impression that I had been saved because the sack that I wore around my neck indicated that I was the son of a Chief and a unique prize to take back to his village.

He pointed to the sword and the helmet showing signs that he wanted to know how the long knife was made. Using some words and lots of hand gestures I gave him the same explanation as I had given to the Mahican Chief that it had been made from special rocks from the earth which had been melted down into a liquid then cooled and made into strips which hammered together formed the blade. He was amazed by this and asked where he could get these special rocks. I told him that they had to be dug from the earth and were only found in certain places. Then he took the satchel from his shoulder and spilled out the contents on the ground pointing to them he demanded to know what they were for. I tried to explain the tools were for cutting rocks into shapes. Shaking his head he walked away leaving the satchel and contents on the ground and started shouting orders to the braves. I bent forward quickly and with my bound hands scraped the tools and other contents into the satchel and pulled it towards me.

Clinging to the satchel I was forced up by the two braves who had attacked me earlier and a halter of plaited rope was placed around my neck which appeared to be made of a type of grass. The leather thongs remained around my wrists we continued the journey into the Mohawk lands.

We marched for the next two days through great swathes of forestland only stopping briefly to rest and hunt. I was dragged along by one of the braves sometime falling to my knees and I soon became in a sorry state with my neck, knees and wrists bleeding and sore. I prayed that we would reach the Mohawk village so that this torment would cease.

Eventually the forest gave way to a large open area by a lake where I was surprised to see a small town made up of longhouses and surrounded by a palisade of logs set along the banks. As we entered the palisade the native women came out of the longhouses to see what the braves had brought back from the hunt. When they caught sight of me they sent their children back into the houses and then came forward and surrounded me shouting loudly they followed me to a longhouse in the centre of the village.

To my amazement a woman stepped out. She appeared to be of high standing. She was dressed in a long dress of buckskin covered in intricate designs. Although she was wearing similar moccasins to the other people of the tribe her legs were bound with a kind of decorated leather bandage tied around the calves. A cloak of animal skin edged with a zig-zag pattern hung loosely over her shoulders and on her head was a tufted crown of red bird feathers. She raised his hand and the shouting ceased.

The leader of my captors stepped forward and exchanged words with the woman occasionally pointing to me and to the sword and helmet he had taken from my dead friend. The woman appeared to be angry and began to reprimand my captor although I had no idea of why this was so, she then returned to the longhouse.

Later in the day I was brought to the longhouse where I faced a group of women seated cross legged either side of them were two men one of which was my captor, They also appeared of high status each wearing the feather headdress of a Chief behind them was what I considered to be a Shaman for he had a large pouch around his neck similar to one I had seen on the Shaman in the Micmaq village and his face was painted in intricate designs.

The woman who I had first seen emerging from the longhouse indicated that my halter should be removed and my hands untied that I should sit and I was offered food and water. I had not eaten anything but pemmican washed down with water during the journey to the village and now I was ravenous and feeling weak from lack of water and vittles. The food was a mixture of corn and beans and I thanked the woman in the best way I could.

When I had finished eating the woman began to speak. I believe that she was trying to question me but I could not understand. She turned to the Shaman and seemed to give him an instruction. He got up and left the longhouse but returned shortly afterwards with another younger woman.

I learned later that this woman had been taken from her Abenaki village on a raid many years before. The brave who had taken her for a wife had been killed on a hunting expedition over a year ago. She had still retained her old language and I was able to recognize words in the Abenaki tongue that were similar to the Micmac. She told me her name was Ehnita Yakon which translated as Moon Woman and explained that the other women were what I could only translate as clan mothers. The one that seemed to be doing all the talking was called Yoken Tsihstekari (Grey Owl) and was married to Kahon Okwa (Black Bear) the Mohawk Chief who had captured me.

The clan mother spoke and the younger woman translated. She explained that I had been captured by her husband who was a Chief of the Mohawk which was one of the Kanonsionni or five nations. The four other tribes that made up the five nations were the Seneca, Oneida, Onondaga and the Cayuga and these were governed by representatives elected to a Great Council. She said that each tribe had a separate language but at the Great Council only Mohawk was spoken.

The tribal homelands extended from where the Senecs guarded the Western Gate at a place where the great water flowed into a large river and over the water mountain called Nia-gara. Their lands took many days to cross and they the Mohawk guarded the Eastern Gate at the edge of the lands of the Algonkin where I had been captured.

Each Longhouse housed two families. In this longhouse she her daughters husband and children lived with another matron and her family. The matrons controlled the clans and the children took the names of the mother's clan. Each nation contained several clans that divided into two groups performing mutual services one group in political matters and the other in ceremonial rituals. In each village the clan mothers appointed the Chiefs.

I was asked about myself and gave my Micmaq name Ntutem I explained that I had sailed from the east where the sun rises across the great water to these lands in a giant can-noo with my father a great White Chief. He had many braves with weapons such as had been carried by the brave that had captured me. I said the Great White Chief would be angry at my capture and may send many warriors to find me.

I asked what would be my fate and the younger woman translated. The clan mothers were angry that a Chief's son had been captured for it would only bring trouble to the Mohawk. Then Grey Owl said she had discussed the matter with her Chiefs my status would be respected and to avoid any further bloodshed I would be returned to the place where I had been captured in three moons when a hunting party would next go towards the Eastern gate.

I thanked the Clan Mother for her wisdom in deciding my fate and said that I would tell my father of this on my return for I knew he would be pleased to receive me back. I was then taken to another Longhouse where I was given shelter with a family and a place to sleep.

Sleep did not come easily my mind too full of all that had happened I lay on the rough bed of animal skins at the edge of sleep trying to catch a dream that would take me away from the thoughts buzzing around in my head. But it was not to be I searched every event from the death of Jamie Gunn with whom I had become great friends to the fate of Jeruba and the hunting party that had left us in the forest. What would the Jarl do when he learned of the tragedy for surely some of the party would have escaped the massacre? I considered that he would think me dead and now abandon hopes of colonizing this particular part of the land and would return to the Micmac lands. If this was a true summary then what would become of me abandoned in this vast country with no close friends. All I could do was resign myself to my fate and pray to the Blessed Mother that my circumstances would change as my captors got used to my presence and so I drifted into a troubled sleep.

I became familiar with the ways of the Mohawk as the days passed picking up some of the language from my forays in the village. I noticed that the children played a game with what looked like sticks on which a net of leather thongs had been tied. They were passing and catching a round leather ball which they tried to get between two upright sticks. I learned from my translator that this was called Attsihkwa'e.(Present day Lacrosse)

Unlike the Micmac who mainly used bone as tools I was amazed to see how they fashioned tools from flint stones. They shaped an adze so that it had a flat side and a curved side and used the sharp end to smooth bark or shape logs. They used a primitive axe made from a hard wood handle which was wider at one end. A hole was driven into the wide end which was tapered so that when the flint head was inserted and the axe was used to strike a log it would drive the axe head into the handle keeping it tight. A primitive chisel was formed from a long piece of antler or bone sharpened at one end and used to peel thin strips of bark from felled trees to use for basket making.

I noticed that trees were felled by lighting a controlled fire at the base until it burnt through enough to push over. To light a fire they used a piece of flat hard wood with a groove in it and a stick attached to which was a leather thong which they looped around the groove and worked back and forward until it started to smoulder then they would place some dry moss against the end of the stick until it caught fire. This was similar to the Micmac way of creating fire by working a stick looped with a twine around another back and forward in a hole made in a flat piece of wood. Unlike the Micmac who used bone their arrowheads were small shaped flints sharpened at one end and fitted into the end of a wooden shaft then bound with a tough grass.

I discovered that some of the younger women would go out each day to the forest and harvest Aweryahsa (huckleberries). They also had small areas of land on which they cultivated vegetables including heads of corn, beans and like the Micmac a plant called tobacco the leaves of which they dried and used in their pipes. The older women would dress skins of the animals caught on hunting forays, make and repair clothes using thin slivers of bone threaded with thin strips of hide to pierce the skins, make decorated baskets to hold and carry things in, keep the fires in the longhouses well stocked with logs and cook the meals.

I was intrigued to know more about the brave was who had captured me. I was told that Black Bear was one of the two village Chiefs or Hoyaneh (Keepers of the Peace). As the days went by I found myself in his company more and more. He helped me with understanding the Mohawk language which I was picking up quite quickly finding many similarities with the Algonkin tongue. He told me that a Great Council of the Chiefs of the clans would meet soon at a place of the Buffalo and already amazed at the role of women in the tribal system I was curious to know how the Kanonsionni were governed.

Together with Moon Woman I approached the longhouse of the Grey Owl only to be stopped by a tall warrior who shouted something.   Moon Woman said that he was telling us to go away but

just as we were about to leave the Grey Owl
appeared at the door and told us to enter. She
told us to sit and asked why I wanted to see her. I
said that I had heard there was a gathering of the
Great Council of the Kanonsionni and if so
whether it would be possible to accompany the
party. She said there was and the clan mothers
would be sending representative Chiefs of the
Eastern Gate of the Mohawk nation. To
accompany them might be dangerous, for the
tribes that made up the Kanonsionni disliked
strangers and were jealous to preserve their way
of life.

Grey Owl thought for a while and said that there
might be a way that this would be possible. She
said that a Chief's son might be acceptable in the
eyes of the Council and as she had been
impressed by the weapons her braves had
brought back when they captured me, she felt
that I might accompany the representatives to
show them to the Great Council and to explain
how they were made. If I was willing to take the
risk that the Council would accept me I should be
ready to leave with the party two dawns from

now. I said that it would be a great honour for me and we withdrew.

Chapter Sixteen
The Meeting Place of the Buffalo.

With all the preparations complete I said my goodbye to Moon Woman and the other matrons who were assembled to see us depart and we set out on the journey to the Great Council. Making up our party was the Chief elected by the clan mothers to represent the tribe and myself with two other senior Chiefs elected from the five other villages that made up the Mohawk peoples of the eastern gate, We were accompanied by six braves carrying the weapons that had been captured.

I had been told it would take many days to reach the meeting place and we should be prepared to hunt while we were traveling. I decided to keep a record of the days by cutting notches on a stick. By now my fellow travelers seemed able to trust me so I was allowed my freedom during the journey and was even given a bow and several arrows to take part in the hunt for fresh meat. I enjoyed the freedom of the hunt and for my part caught two rabbits (kwa'yenha) and a large ground bird they called kawerowane. (Turkey). On my return the warriors grouped around me patting me on the back and shouting 'Ratorats' (hunter). They presented me with a kill feather from the bird I had shot which I wore proudly in the back of my hair not knowing whether this was a serious gesture on their part or that they were making fun of me.

With fresh meat to be used up the Black Bear suggested that we should rest up for two suns then continue. We camped by a large lake where we replenished our water containers and I was able to bathe and rid myself of lice and clean the wounds left by the occasional ticks that had sought refuge and sustenance on my skin.

That evening we sat round a large fire and ate well on the food that had been caught. By now I was able to converse a little in the Mohawk language and we remained around the fire into the early hours the warriors exchanging tales of their feats of hunting and discussing the forthcoming Council.

For many days we traveled through vast forest lands of broad leaf trees they called wahtha (MapleTree) the warriors explained that the women extracted a sweet syrup from the bark of the tree they called wahtha ohshehs which was used to flavour some of the food they ate.

We continued on following forest paths familiar to some of the braves and circumnavigating several lakes eventually reaching high ground

where our eyes had to get accustomed to the strong sunlight that we had greatly missed traveling under the trees. To the south, in the clear light we could make out a range of mountains. We skirted through foothills where at night the cold bit into our hands and feet and eventually we reached the tribal lands of the (Onenyotehàka)
Oneida. I carved another groove on the stick in my pouch and counted the grooves they revealed that we had been traveling for fifteen days.

Before long we reached a village and the Oneida chief with several of the village braves welcomed us. The women of the village brought us food of burnt (cracked) maize and pemmican, berries from the forest and we were given shared accommodation for the night in the various longhouses scattered around the village. I was taken in by two matrons and their spouses and their children who were anxious to know where this strange pale faced man had come from.

Once again I was forced to relate how I had traveled in a large can-noo across the great water from lands where the morning sun rose into the sky. I had traveled with a great Chief and his braves but had been taken from them by the Mohawk . Although, because of my status, I was told I would be returned eventually to my tribe I had asked to attend the Great Council of Chiefs. The clan mothers had agreed on the condition that I would show the Great Council how the weapons that I carried were made.

The families listened intently to what I said and the questions came thick and fast. It was if there was some status attached to the fact that they had taken this stranger from another land, every now and then the brave would leave the hut and report what had been said to his fellow braves who had gathered outside.

The questions flowed until the early hours of the morning until tiredness overwhelmed me and I could not keep my eyes open. My hosts quickly recognized this and the family graduated to the corners of the longhouse to their sleeping mats. I was left alone watching the embers of the dying fire and lapsed into a deep sleep.

I was awakened by the laughter of children and through sleepy eyes could see the mother and the young girls were busy preparing food over a rekindled fire. Judging by the laughter coming from outside the longhouse the boys were busy playing Attsihkwa'e, they were using the similar sticks to those I had seen at the Mohawk village shaped like a shepherd's crook with a net made up with leather thongs. This time there were a crowd of about twenty boys were split into two groups passing the leather ball by skillfully catching it in the net and throwing it to one of their side until they could make a strike on a nearby tree marked as the goal.

The matron whose fireside I had slept beside tried to explain that it was a popular game amongst the tribes and sometimes one village would compete against another to settle a dispute. The games could go on for two or three days until the dispute was settled. She offered me some cornbread and beans which I gratefully accepted for I was famished.

While I was eating my host the brave entered and informed me that the party would be leaving shortly and I should join them after I had finished the meal. I consumed the rest of the meal collected my belongings and thanked my hosts for their kindness.

I joined the rest of the party and after expressing our thanks made our way out of the Oneida village. We were joined by a party from the tribe who were also going to the Great Council. The braves chatted among each other as we progressed through more forestland.

After a while the ground began to rise and we found ourselves entering a pass between two bald mountains. We continued up the slope across a rock strewn plain until we reached the top of the pass. The air was a lot colder here and we were forced to don the heavy skins we slept under to keep warm. The mood changed and the conversation between the braves had long since ceased as we pushed on. Only when we had traversed the pass and were making our way towards the welcome sight of more forestland did the chatter amongst the braves recommence I think we were happy now we had left the pass behind.

We trekked for another three days and rested. This time I could hear a different sound over the chatter of birds and the occasional sound of the forest animals. It seemed to be a kind of dull roar I was curious and asked one of the Chiefs what it was. Black Bear said that we were nearly at the place where the Great Council was meeting. I was still intrigued to know what the sound was but was told I would find out soon enough.

I could hardly sleep that night the fate of my friends still haunted me with one recurring question. Would the Jarl have thought I was dead and abandoned me to this strange but earthly paradise where man had not set about destroying Mother Nature but lived in harmony with her?

I rose at first light and was surprised to find most of the braves in the camp had already risen and were decorating their faces and bodies in preparation for some kind of ritual. They were conversing in an exited way and from their conversation I realized we were close to the meeting place. The Chiefs were donning their magnificent headdresses made up of bird feathers and I knew that I was going to witness some great ceremony.

We traveled for another half day with the strange roar getting louder and louder. At last we crested a small hill and to my amazement below us were row after row of longhouses surrounded by a raised bank. Some were cone shaped others were dome shaped and others rectangular but all were made from pole frames and covered in the bark of a tree. In front of many of the longhouses sat the women of the various tribes busy preparing food. In the centre of this vast settlement was a great longhouse some sixty sword lengths long, fifteen sword lengths high and fifteen sword lengths wide surrounded by an arena which could accommodate upwards of 1000 braves.

Forming a wondrous background to the meeting place was a scene which filled me with awe it was a waterfall, a waterfall bigger than anything I had ever seen, a wide river fell unremittingly over a high cliff which spread into the distance in a huge arc for what seemed like a league sending huge columns of water down into an abyss of turbulent foam and white mist. I stood fixed to the spot unable to take my eyes off the scene mesmerized by the thundering cascade of water.

Black Bear stood beside me and said quietly. 'This is what you have been hearing, our meeting place of the Buffalo is one of the most spiritual places for the Kanonsionni as it lies close to the mountain of falling waters a place we call the Niagara, (I translated this as 'the water that thunders how true I thought to myself). Come we must make haste.'

At this point the Chiefs and braves of the Oneida lined up with the Mohawk and in a long column we went down the hill and into the vast field of longhouses greeted with whoops and yells from the other tribes.

We passed through areas where the men and women of the various clans traded with others showing animal skins, baskets, clothing, foot ware, drums and pipes, weapons and foodstuffs. As soon as they saw me they stopped and stared some pointing and yelling what seemed to be insults.

As we approached the large longhouse and arena we were met by a Chief of the Seneca our hosts who I learned later was one of the paramount Chiefs called Dancing Crow. He greeted the party warmly but then he noticed me and began to talk loudly, gesturing animatedly towards me. Black Bear stepped forward and showing Jamie Gunn's sword explained the reason why I had come.

The Chief calmed down and took the sword inspecting it closely. He then swung it at a nearby wooden post catching it with the sword edge and splitting it in two. His eyes lit up in amazement I could see he was impressed with this new material and was anxious to know more about how it was made. Black Bear said that he would have to wait until a meeting was convened of all the paramount Chiefs when all would be revealed.

Dancing Crow led us to one of the longhouses close to the arena and said that this would be the Mohawk quarters one of the Seneca women would attend to our needs and cook for us. He left us and continued on with the men from the Oneida taking them to their quarters. Inside we found sleeping skins and baskets with food that had been prepared for us, we each picked a spot to rest and settled down to eat what had been prepared for us. There were strips of pemmican, àyok (huckleberries) from the forest some cracked corn and a starchy root crop they called ohnennàta (potatoes). We ate heartily for it had been a long day and we had, had no time to eat.

After we had eaten Black Bear came over to where I lay and said that I should remain in the longhouse until the meeting of the Paramount Chief because the assembled representatives to the Great Council did not know why I had been brought here. I felt irritated by this as I was keen to explore the great village of longhouses.

I remained frustrated in the longhouse for the next two days. Black Bear would inform me of what was happening outside as we waited for the delegates from the other Nations to arrive. On the third day after we had arrived I was summoned to the Council of Chiefs. Black Bear came for me and took me to the great longhouse. Assembled inside arraigned in their regalia of feathered headdress and with decorated cloaks covering their normal attire were the Paramount

Chiefs. Black Bear introduced me and sat down among the Chiefs.

In faltering Mohawk I repeated my story of how the red rocks were melted down and formed a liquid metal which was cooled and made into long knives. Fortunately this was the common language used at the Great Council and the Chiefs sat in silence intently listening to what I was saying as the metal sword was passed around the assembly for closer inspection.

I finished my talk and was suddenly receiving a barrage of questions. Black Bear rose at once and raised his hand for silence. He said the best way to question me was to go round each of the assembled Chiefs one by one and they could present a question to our guest.
The Chiefs agreed and so the questioning began.

Where could the red rocks that produced the metal be found?
How was the red rock converted into metal?
How many red rocks would be needed to make enough metal for the long knife?
How was the long knife made?

Would the long knife cut rock?
Could other smaller knives and axes be made
with the metal?

The questions continued throughout the morning
I answered as best as I could thankful that I could
recall my conversations with Fergus the Jarl's
blacksmith back in Roslin where I had seen the
ironstone for smelting. I said that they should
look for soil that was red in colour for it
contained red and yellow rocks that made iron or
find hilly outcrops that contained rocks that were
a dark silvery grey colour. I put into plain words
that they would have to construct a small furnace
out of clay and charcoal to make the fire that
would be hot enough to melt the rocks also that
they would need to construct bellows from
animal hides to push air into the fire to raise the
heat.

After I had answered as many questions as I
could Black Bear led me from the assembly and
back to our longhouse. He told me to remain
there until a decision was made. In the meantime
he said there was much more to discuss in the
assembly about boundary disputes, domestic

problems and other matters affecting the five nations.

I spent another two frustrating days in the longhouse while each evening Black Bear would come back and report that nothing further had been said about the metal long knife. Then the next morning I was once again summoned to the assembly. I stood in the centre of the great longhouse all eyes fixed upon me waiting to know my fate.

The Seneca Chief Dancing Crow stood up and announced that a decision had been made. The Seneca Nation would learn the secrets of making the long knives. I would go out with a party and search for the rocks to make the metal. Black Bear would accompany me as he knew the Seneca language. On our return I would make the means to melt the rocks and show the braves how it was done. When the Chiefs were satisfied I would be released back to my Nation beyond the Eastern Gate.

Chapter Seventeen
The Search for the Red Rocks.

The Great Council had deliberated for six days and the decisions were passed to each of the tribal Chiefs to be communicated to the villages under their control. As the Great Council broke up there was one final gathering. A huge fire was lit in the arena and led by the attendant Shaman the people sang praises to the Great Spirit and danced into the night whooping and yelling until in the early hours they departed to their various longhouses.

The next day Black Bear assembled his braves picked two out to return to the Mohawk village and pass the message that the rest would return after the mission had been fulfilled. They said their farewells and left the village. Soon after Dancing Crow arrived with several Seneca braves and said we could join them in the search for the iron rocks.

I repeated what I had told the assembled Chiefs. Dancing Crow passed this to his braves and asked whether they had ever seen rocks like this. One of the Seneca braves said that he had seen rocks that wept a red deposit into natural springs the place was about two day's march away.

We gathered sufficient provisions to sustain us on our journey and joined the Seneca Chief and his braves heading out into the forest. We trekked until nightfall only stopping to refresh ourselves as we came upon a stream and rested to eat the pemmican cakes made by the Seneca women. The cakes were made with strips of lean dried meat pounded into paste, mixed with melted fat and dried berries and fruits, and pressed into small cakes.

I slept soundly tired after the previous day's trek and woke refreshed to the sound of my companions making ready to continue our journey. One thing I had observed ever since I first made contact with these people of the western lands, whenever they made camp they would leave the area in the same condition as when they had arrived allowing Mother Nature to continue unimpeded her cycle of the seasons.

About half way through the second day the Seneca brave who had been leading us gave a shout we had arrived at the place we had been seeking. It was a tall escarpment at the base of which a stream fed by the rocks above ran red onto the forest floor. On inspection of the rocks I realized this was made up of black rock which glinted with silvery flecks. This was a huge ironstone lode and elated that it was the purest form of the iron bearing rock passed the news to Black Bear who in turn told Dancing Crow.

I knew that we would have to collect a huge quantity if we were to produce an iron ingot. For the rest of the day the braves laboured at the rock with their stone hammers breaking off pieces capable of being carried in their leather pouches. The night was soon upon us each brave had filled their pouches with as much rock as they could carry and Dancing Crow suggested we should make camp there before returning to the village of longhouses. Although Black Bear agreed he pointed out that the water from stream close by would be no good for drinking and the braves should be warned of this. Dancing Crow made a tally of water pouches and found that with care we could last until we reached a clear source of water.

The next day we retraced our steps towards the Seneca village. Once again it was two days of walking until we reached our goal. We were greeted with whoops and yells from the inhabitants as we entered the village as if they were anticipating some powerful thing to be conjured up from the rocks we had brought.

Tired after the long trek Black Bear his braves and myself returned to our appointed lodge where we found the women of the village had prepared victuals for us. I was exhausted and too tired to eat I lay on my furs and drifted quickly into a deep sleep.

Chapter Eighteen
The People of Iron.

Over the next few days I constructed a crude forge made from clay. It was beehive shaped with a hollow inside with a large opening to allow a fire to be lit inside, two pipes led from the base to which were attached bellows made of animal skins.

I knew that we would need charcoal to heat the rock enough to yield its bounty. Again I was grateful for the trips made to see Fergus the blacksmith the smithy in my youth and remembering my visits to the charcoal burners who had shown me how prepare the mounds and light them to produce the necessary material.

I needed to explain to the Seneca braves how to make charcoal before the forge we had built could be used. I asked them to go and collect dry pine wood while I dug a hollow two sword lengths across in the earth. When they returned I told them to build a tepee shaped mound with the smaller branches I then told them to gather bundles of dead grasses and put them over the wooden structure place wet ash from their cooking fires over the structure leaving an opening at the top.

When this was completed a small fire was lit with twigs and dry grass on the top off the mound and was left to burn. After some time had passed I went to the mound and opened vent holes at the base to allow air to get to the slow burning wood. Later I closed the vents up and left the mound to burn. The mound burned for a day and a night. I prayed that it would produce enough charcoal to start the furnace.

My prayers were answered for next day when the mound was opened up we had produced six large baskets of charcoal. The braves who had assisted me were running around whooping as Dancing Crow approached and saw the results of our labours. I said that we could now use the furnace that I had built and produce a small amount of iron from the rocks.

I took a basket of the charcoal to the furnace and laid a small collection of sticks and moss inside.

One of the braves brought a fire stick and ignited the sticks. As it burned I placed a quantity of the charcoal inside and waited for it to start to smoulder. Before long the furnace was ready to receive some of the iron stones which were placed in a large clay bowl with a spout at one end which had been specifically made for the job in addition I had made a mould for the iron to be poured into. The bowl was laid on the charcoal while two of the braves were instructed to pump the bellows.

By now a large crowd had gathered around the furnace all engaged in animated conversation at what was happening. Relays of braves took over the bellows as it took some time to get the furnace to a temperature that would extract the iron from the rocks. I began to see the rocks break up into slag and a deposit of iron forming in the bowl. With a long stick I attempted to remove some of the slag from the bowl but it burst into flames. I called for the sword they had taken from Jamie to be brought to the furnace and this time I was able to clear some of the slag.

I could see now that the iron was ready to be poured into the mould. Using the sword I carefully tipped the bowl forward so the liquid iron and the residue of slag could run into the mould. I was surprised at the amount that ran out it filled half of the mould making a small ingot.

The crowd had watched silently while I was carrying out this course of action and as they saw the liquid iron run into the mould erupted in a series of whoops. I scraped the residue of slag from the top of the quickly solidifying iron and poured some water over it cooling it rapidly so that I was able to release it from the mould. I stared in awe at what had been produced and silently thanked God in all His mercy for making it happen.

Dancing Crow came over and slapped me hard on the back pleased with what had been achieved. He picked up the warm iron ingot and raised it above his head presenting it to his people. From now on he said the Seneca would be known among the Five Nations as the people of iron.

Over the next few days I instructed the braves in producing charcoal and using the furnace. I was surprised at how quickly they learned these arts for soon they were producing their own ingots. It was necessary to show them how the iron ingots could be formed into tools so I had to make a blacksmiths forge. A large square clay vessel with a pipe at one end was mounted on a large flat rocky outcrop. The vessel was filled with charcoal laid on sticks and moss and a bellows attached to the pipe. I needed some means of holding the iron ingot in the fire so I asked one of the braves to produce some tongs made of animal bone with flat rock inserts at the end. They proved ideal to lift the ingot the test would be when it was placed in the fire.

The fire was lit and when the charcoal had become hot one of the braves began to operate the bellows while I placed the ingot on the charcoal. It soon became red hot and I extracted it with the makeshift tongs and placing it on a nearby rock began to hit it with a stone hammer I had borrowed from one of the braves. The ingot started to flatten out and I replaced it in the forge.

This was repeated several times and eventually I had formed a shape like an axe head.

As the days went by several men were split into groups to carry out the tasks of making charcoal employing the furnace to covert the iron stone into metal and the crude forge to create objects out of the iron ingots. Those that were clumsy were dismissed and the few that remained became quite proficient at the tasks. Dancing Crow was pleased with the results and wandered around the village with a satisfied smile on his face. I felt now was time to ask him to release me so that I could return to my people.

He said I had carried out all the tasks that had been asked of me and I was free to go, I passed the news to Black Bear and we prepared to leave but not before Dancing Crow had laid on a celebration similar to the one I had witnessed at the end of the Great Council.

A huge fire was lit and the braves whooped and danced around it. The women prepared a feast and I sat with Black Bear and Dancing Crow watching the festivities. A shaman prepared a pipe and this was passed around the assembled elders of the tribe finally coming to me. I took a large puff and this time was able to blow the smoke out without coughing. The night passed quickly and in the early hours we made our way back to the lodges.

**Chapter Nineteen
Return to the Mahicans.**

We bade our farewells to the Seneca people and as we were about to leave Dancing Crow presented both Black Bear with a necklet of Bear's teeth. Black Bear said this was a great honour for the bear was a fierce opponent in a fight. I was presented with a necklet of various coloured and polished stones which was beautifully crafted by the Seneca women. We thanked the Chief and left the meeting place of the Buffalo and its magical setting of thundering waters.

Saddened by the fact that I had to leave Jamie Gunn's sword my last link I had with my late friend but cheered by the knowledge that our trip had been a great success, we set off on our long journey back to the Eastern Gate. By nightfall we were approaching the foothills that led us towards the Oneida territory. We made camp close to a fast flowing stream lit a fire and consumed the pemmican cakes that had been prepared for us.

I could not settle to sleep for my mind was active with the expectation that I would soon be back with the Mahicans and would learn of the fate of the Jarl and my colleagues. What little sleep I had was interrupted by the dawn chorus of birds echoing throughout the forest.

For several days we traveled along well trodden paths through hills and valleys and endless forest finally reaching the Oneida village where we had stayed on our journey to the Great Council. I was given a hearty welcome by the family with whom I previously resided and they welcomed me into their longhouse anxious to know all the news from the Great Council.

Throughout a meal of cracked corn, fresh meat and berries I was able to convey my impressions through an interpreter who could speak Mohawk but I told them that I knew nothing of the deliberations of the Great Council and they would have to speak to Black Bear if they wished to learn more. However I told them about the meeting place and the waters that thundered for they knew nothing of this wonderous place. I also mentioned that the Seneca were now proficient in making the material from which the sword was made. Once again we talked long into the night until I could hardly prevent my eyes from closing and was forced to leave the company and take my rest.

I awoke after a fitful sleep and was told that Black Bear was preparing to leave. I was given food for the journey and we said our goodbyes. It was a sad parting for I knew I would not set eyes on these people who had been so kind to me ever

again. I silently prayed to the Lord for their well being and comfort and we parted company.
After many long days of endless forestland, encounters with creatures therein and several hunting trips we finally reached the Mohawk village bringing with us the fresh meat that we had killed on our forays. The people were excited to see us and greeted us in the now familiar way of whoops and yells. Grey Owl came out to greet us embraced her husband and led him into their longhouse. The Mohawk braves ran to greet their spouses leaving me alone to return to my appointed lodge.

I had been inside for but a short while when Moon Woman entered bringing food and water. I thanked her and asked her to join me and as we ate I told her about the journey to the Great Council and everything that had happened. Her eyes widened when I revealed to her that I had seen the great waterfall called the Nia-gara that dominated the meeting place. The long journey had taken all my energy and I was ready to lie down and sleep. I think Moon Woman realized this and collected up the food containers and left me to take my rest.

I stayed in the Mahican village until it was necessary to form a hunting party to search for more fresh meat. Black Bear told me he would accompany me to the rock where I had been captured at the borders of the Eastern Gate and there we would part. It was with some sadness I realized it was time to leave because after my initial capture I had formed a bond with these people. They had showed me an alternative way of life where there were unspoken rules of respecting and living together in harmony with nature. At first I had believed that they were primitive beings but that they had proved to me that their way of life was in many ways better than the life I had led at Roslin and on Orkney.

As I bade farewell to Moon Woman I noticed a tear in her eye for she knew I would be going back to the people she had been taken from, her people the Abernaki. Her life, such as it was without a husband was now with the Mohawk and here she would remain until her death. I thanked her for her kindness and we parted.

Grey Owl stood majestically by her lodge as I approached her to say goodbye. She said that she would pray to the Great Spirit that my journey back to my people would be safe and free from danger. I thanked her for her wise council in allowing me my freedom and told her that I would keep the memories of my stay with the Mohawk and the rest of the family of Five Nations in my heart. As I made to leave Black Bear came out of the longhouse and joined us. He bade farewell to Grey Owl and we set off with the other braves following the paths into the cover of the endless forest.

Chapter Twenty
Creating A Memorial and an Unexpected Meeting.

Early in the morning of the seventh day we reached the great rock where Jamie had died and

I had been captured. Black Bear and his braves were anxious to return to their lands and quickly bade farewell before they were discovered and I was left alone by the rock. As I stood there I recalled all that had happened at this place.

Almost three months had passed since my capture and I knew in my heart that my colleagues would have departed believing that I too was dead. However my hopes were lifted when on searching the paths around the rock I found a small boulder on which a ship resembling the Haggar and an arrow giving a direction had been etched. It had been carefully placed on one of the pathways leading from the rock probably by the Jarl's men.

Once again I was drawn back to the rock and I felt that it seemed a fitting place for a memorial for a man of strength such as Jamie Gunn had been. I made up my mind that before I left this place I would used the surface of the rock to create some memorial to my friend.

I searched for my masonry tools in the leather pouch which had been returned to me with my

sword and belt, took out a small piece of charcoal
and began to draw. I sketched out the full figure
of a standing knight in full armour carrying his
sword and shield before him. On the shield I
drew the arms of the Gunn family then with my
mallet and a small pointed chisel and
painstakingly began to make a series of holes
following the shape of the figure I had drawn. I
spent the rest of the day so engrossed in my work
that I forgot my surroundings.

It was late afternoon when I finished and satisfied
with the result I rested taking a draft of the water
left by the braves. I was preparing to light a fire
and settle down to rest when I heard a noise
nearby it sounded like men moving through the
trees.

I stood up slowly and looked towards the area
where the noise was coming from. I searched the
tree line someone was approaching rapidly I
could see a shape suddenly a figure bounded out
of the trees a face I recognized immediately it was
Jeruba he was accompanied by several Mahican
braves.

I dropped my tools and ran to greet him.
'Jeruba is it you? I can't believe it I thought you had all died or abandoned me.'
We hugged each other and with tears in my eyes asked what had happened to the rest of the party.

Juruba sat down with his back to the rock and began to relate all that had occurred since my capture. He said that when the hunting party was attacked he and several others were heading back to where they had left Jamie and I. When he saw what was happening they had laid low in the brush. They witnessed the death of Jamie and my capture. When the Mohawk party left with me as a prisoner they had buried Jamie under a cairn and then began the search for survivors.

They had been joined by Husky Dog and Flying Squirrel who had also escaped the attack and together they found two of Jamie Gunn's men badly wounded the rest of the party dead. They set about burying the men and made their way back to the Mahican village with the survivors who had their wounds tended to. One of the men died but the other was well enough in a few days to return with a party of Mahican braves to the waiting ship to pass the grave news to the Jarl. The following day the Jarl came to the village with some of the men at arms who had been left on the ship.

Chief White Eagle introduced himself and impressed by the great lord welcomed him to his dwelling together with Jeruba. After some refreshment Jeruba was asked to relate what had happened. The Jarl listened intently while Jeruba had told his story. After he had finished there was a moment's pause after which the Jarl turned to the Chief and asked whether there was any hope of the captured knight surviving and if he sent a raiding party would he be able to find me. The Chief said that I had been captured by the Mohawk they were like snakes who had a reputation for feeding on human flesh. They were masters of their own territory and if a party were sent after them they would have little chance of survival for the Mohawk could appear and attack at any time.

The Jarl was saddened by this but said he would wait for a week on board the ship and if there was no word of my return he would take the ship back to the settlement. Jeruba had stepped forward saying that he knew that I was alive and would remain here until my return. The Jarl praised him for his loyalty but said if he did not return with him to the ship he could remain here for the rest of his life. Undaunted Jeruba said that he would not abandon his friend. The next day the Jarl returned to the ship accompanied by Husky Dog and Flying Squirrel who were anxious to return to their village. A week went by and there was no news and so the Jarl departed leaving him to his fate. So on every occasion the Mahican braves had gone hunting Jeruba had joined them and had visited the rock hoping that I would return. It was he who had left the marker with the ship on it and he always came to that place. Today he had heard the sound of a hammer on rock and had investigated the source of the noise to his joy he had found me.

I then related all that had happened to me since I was captured. Jeruba sat there hanging on my every word. He was amazed by my revelations that the Mohawk had not harmed me and particularly how organized there were. I told him of the dominance of women in the tribes and how they elected the Chiefs, that the Mohawk were part of Five Nations governed by a Great Council. How I in joining a party of Mohawks to this Great Council I had realized just how vast was this country and the natural wonders it contained. I told him of the meeting place of the Great Council mentioning the great waterfall and how I was forced to pass on the methods of making iron in order to obtain my release.

After I had finished my story I said that I must return to the task of completing the memorial to Jamie but first I would like to see the cairn where he had been buried. Jeruba led me over to a rocky out crop where close by was a mound of rocks. Here Jeruba said he had laid Jamie's body and covered it over with rocks so that it would be protected from wild animals. I stood there in silence and prayed that God would take him into his care and that he would rest with the angels.

Once again I mourned the loss of my friend as I returned to the rock. With my heart filled with sadness I stared at the finished carving. This would be *his* memorial and although the rock may suffer wind and rain, snow and heat I felt that the outline of the knight I had hammered into the surface of the rock would remain as a mark of respect to my friend.

We prepared a camp close by for the night and the next day made our way back to the Mahican village. Chief White Eagle was surprised to hear this for his father had been killed by the Mohawk and to him they were fierce savages. Once again I related my story leaving out for good reason the part about the making of iron. I said that although the Mohawk were savage fighters raiding parties were usually formed to capture women for brides so that the tribe had new blood. The Chief was not impressed by what he had been told and still judged the Mohawk as venomous snakes. However he welcomed me back and said that I could lodge with Jeruba. So we settled down to life as Mahican braves learning their crafts in hunting and the respect for all living things.

Chapter Twenty One
Mesatawe.

It had been three years since I left the shores of Orkney I had become resigned to the fact that I would never see my homeland again. Under the protection of God I had witnessed twenty three summers. We had, had no further contact with the Jarl and the expedition and felt they must have eventually returned to Orkney. One of my friends was now with God and I realised that I would have to spend the rest of my life in the new lands. That Jeruba my loyal friend had stayed had given me great comfort.

I had become used to ways of the tribes and having been accepted by the Mahican people of Wabanakiak I was happy enough with my lot. However I began to realise there was something missing I needed a companion who would share my life.

One young woman of the tribe stood out from the rest. Her name was Mesatawe which translated as Morning Star and she was the sister of Chief White Eagle. I first noticed her when I saw her stop her work and find time to play with the village children. My heart was gladdened as I watched her attending to one of the village children who had fallen badly with a caring and loving nature. I felt a stirring in my heart that I had not experienced since my foolhardy episode with the Lady Margaret at Roslin. Jeruba treated my ardour with disdain but if I found she was unattached I was determined to succeed in winning her favours.

I judged that she seen more than twenty summers and wondered why she was not attached to anyone. She was tall, slender and walked with such poise that one would think she was held upright by invisible wings. Her dark brown hair was tied back in a single plait and held in place by a decorated band of doeskin framing an oval face, with deep set eyes, a slender nose unlike the broad ones that were common among the tribe, full lips and a graceful neck and when she smiled her face lit up as if a beam of sunlight had danced across it. She wore a long fringed doeskin dress and bodice decorated with intricate designs made from pieces of small bones from animals and round her neck a necklace of polished coloured stones.

I was infatuated and began to take notice of her every excursion to the forest with the other women of the village. As time went by I tried to make excuses to Jeruba for always being where she was in the hope that she would somehow notice me but it was a vain wish for she carried on her tasks around the village as if I were invisible.

The women of the village were more astute and quickly realised what my little stalking game was about because every time I passed a group of women out berry picking there was a hushed exchange followed usually by laughter. Judging by this I was sure I had now become the focus of their amusement.

Eventually their gossiping must have got to the ears of the Chief and I was summoned to his Wigwam. He told me of the wild rumours that had been circulating the village that I had been following his sister Morning Star around like a lovesick fool. He said that she had been joined to one of the warriors Soaring Hawk but he was killed in a skirmish with the Mohawks over four summers ago. Since her period of mourning she had been under his protection but I should beware because Grey Wolf had also taken a liking to her although so far she had not responded. I was devastated because Grey Wolf who was a friend who had accompanied Jeruba and I on many hunting trips and was one of the bravest warriors in the village now he appeared to be my rival.

However love had taken me over like a curse and I was besotted with Morning Star but so far there was no response to my romantic posturing. Soon the rumours reached the ears of Grey Wolf and one day he approached me saying angrily that I should stay away from her or I would feel his wrath. I replied somewhat foolishly that my purpose was to win her heart and if necessary I would fight any man to make this happen. Grey Wolf became angry and told me that if I continued to follow her around he would certainly kill me.

I shrugged off his threats and walked away but he followed behind his shouts getting louder and louder, catching the attention of some of the village braves who surrounded us and began themselves to shout. Some of the braves seemed to direct their attention at me and they made threatening gestures others tried to stop the argument. Jeruba appeared at me side ready to oppose any threat to my person. The commotion eventually brought the Chief White Eagle out of his Wigwam who raising his arms, shouted a swift command for everyone to be silent then beckoned us both to come to him.

Speaking softly he asked what all the noise was about and when Grey Wolf told him he said that he knew us to be brave warriors and felt that now she was well past her period of mourning he had to choose wisely for his sister. He told us to wait outside and disappeared inside his wigwam. When he came out again he said that he had spoken with Morning Star and she said that although she knew Grey Wolf had expressed a liking for her was not happy to take him as a husband. She had also noticed the attentions of the pale skin Ntutem but it was up to the Chief to decide. Grey

Wolf raised his voice in an angry outburst saying I was an outsider and couldn't possibly be accepted as a suitor for Morning Star.

So in the few days since the news of my intention broke Grey Wolf's rejection by Morning Star had turned him from my friend to my enemy. The Chief expressed concern for what might happen. I felt I should speak out and said that Grey Wolf had never once mentioned his intentions and surely Morning Star was free to speak her mind.

He had never said that he loved her at all and when talking about Morning Star she was mentioned as just another village woman. I said I felt that if he wanted her for a wife he should have made some effort to win her and added that judging by his attitude I felt that she would be treated like a possession to be used when required. If I on the other hand were to take her for a wife I would love and cherish her and give the tribe fine sons.

Grey Wolf could not accept this and continued to protest angrily saying what would I know about his feelings anyway and as he had grown up with

Morning Star he had more right than I did to be joined with her. The Chief thought for a moment and said that he had taken into consideration what his sister had said. If we both wanted the woman the only way to settle the matter was to fight for her at a place and time to be arranged by the Shaman. Saying no more he turned and went into his wigwam. Heartened by what Nolkasis had said I waited with dread for the summons to fight.

It came at dawn the next day I was collected by two braves who led me to an open area just outside the village. Jeruba went along too but I explained to him that this was my fight. Concerned at my fate he trailed along behind me. The rest of the braves had formed a square and I was pushed inside. The Shaman approached and told me to take off all but my deerskin apron. He handed me a knife made of a thigh bone of a Moose sharpened to a point and bound with a handle of grass rope. I was given a small decorated shield of tough hide and told to wait for the Shaman's command.

In the meantime Grey Wolf had been brought into the square.
The Shaman approached him, furnished him with the same weapons then walked to the centre of the square. Raising both arms he muttered a ritual prayer then said to us both that the path to win the hand of Morning Star would be decided on the death of one of us. Either of us could pull out now and concede victory but as soon as he dropped his arms the fight would begin and continue until one of us was dead. Neither of us conceded.

As his arms dropped Grey Wolf raced forward I side stepped and struck him a glancing blow to the neck with the knife handle knocking him to the ground. Before I could gain advantage from the manoeuvre he had sprung up and was diving for my legs. To the roar of the braves forming the square I fell spread eagled on the ground and just managing to parry his knife thrust with my shield I rolled away. It gave me time to get to my feet and face him once again. As he came at me lunging with the knife I remembered the moves that Running Deer had taught me back in Pectou, falling on my back I caught him with my foot square in the stomach and threw him backwards. Not expecting this he landed heavily on the ground and I turned once again to face him. He sprung quickly to his feet and was ready in a crouch position waiting for me to attack. Wisely I did not counter and we stalked each other looking for an opportunity to strike. He gazed at me with eyes full of hatred and uttered a curse that he would make my death long and slow.

We remained like this for some time both getting our second wind then he lunged once more catching my right arm with the sharp blade and ripping my upper arm open to the bone. I staggered back waiting for him to come again and come again he did the full force of his body driving me to the ground. He was above me now with his knife arm raised ready to finish the contest and in that split moment I saw my advantage his neck was exposed and I thrust the bone blade into the side. He never finished his attack for his neck was an open wound spraying his life blood into the air like a fountain. He fell across me moaning his knife falling from his hand I pushed him over and tried to stem the flow of blood but it was too late. His whole body shook in spasm as his life force ebbed away and the mantle of death quickly overtook him.

All around the braves fell silent as Jeruba ran forward. I said a silent prayer for his soul my heart wounded by the outcome but I was in a savage land with different values to the chivalry of battle I had experienced in the Eastern World even so I knew I would greatly miss his company.

The Shaman directed some of the braves to lift Grey Wolf's body and take it away to be prepared to be taken to the sacred burial grounds. As they lifted him the Shaman raised his arms and let out a soft wailing song and was joined by the rest of the assembled braves sending the spirit of Grey Wolf on its journey to the hunting grounds of the Great Spirit.

The Shaman came forward and taking my arm he led me out of the human square and to the Chief. The Chief declared that I had won Morning Star in a fair fight and when the time was right she would leave his lodge and be handed over to the women of the village to prepare her for her joining ceremony. Jeruba took me to the river to wash away the blood that covered me.

As I immersed myself in the cool river waters my mind was filled with mixed emotions, to gain the love of a woman I had to kill a friend, it did not seem to me to be a fair exchange. When I had washed away the dust of the fight I was summoned to the Shaman's wigwam where he examined my wound. The cut had sliced the upper arm under the bicep and fortunately for me he muscle and ligaments had remained unharmed. The Shaman cleaned and stitched my wound and bound it with cobwebs and tree moss then raised it up in a sling.

It was two weeks before I met Morning Star again she arrived at my wigwam chaperoned by her mother who allowed us to walk together ahead of her. It was the first time we had been close and although initially she was shy with encouragement she soon found her voice. She asked about my wound and I told her it was healing nicely. She said that Grey Wolf had been a brave warrior I agreed and told her I was sad that I had been the cause of his passing for he had been a good friend. Showing little remorse she said because of Grey Wolf's stance she felt her brother had been wise in suggesting that this was the only way to decide the outcome. If it had not been settled there would always be ill feeling her people would take sides and the whole village would have suffered. She did not want to make more trouble for her people. I asked her if she was happy with the outcome she said it was for her to find out whether the paleface would make her happy.

While we stopped to converse I was able to study her fair countenance closely and my heart stirred at her beauty. Her smooth skin and tanned complexion were a joy to behold. It was the first time I had been close enough to observe her eyes a found they were the colour of emeralds. When I told her what emeralds were she laughed and said if her eyes were like emeralds mine were like the blue of a summer sky. I longed to hold her close and kiss her tender lips but was being observed all the time by her mother.

As we continued our stroll she talked about the forthcoming joining ceremony. Her mother had told her that the ceremony would take place seven sunrises after her next monthly visitation so she had calculated I would have to wait for twenty dawns to come before I would be summoned to the ceremony.

When all had been prepared she would be taken to a special   wigwam on the outskirts of the village where she would spend twenty four hours naked while water was poured over hot stones and she would go through a cleansing ceremony. As part of the ritual the women of the village would gather flowers and herbs from the forest and lay them round the Wigwam. When the cleansing ceremony was over her hair would be prepared and she would be dressed in an attire of a robe, moccasins and headdress specially made by her mother. A necklace of forest flowers would be placed around her neck and she would be brought to the wigwam of her brother the Chief by the Shaman where I would be waiting and there we would be joined together.

Each day as we waited patiently for the Joining Day to arrive I would walk with Little Deer. She would ask me about my life before I had come to these hunting grounds. I told her many things about my life at Roslin castle and on the Island of Orkney, about the Jarl leading a great expedition across the great sea with many men and how my friend Antonio had guided the great Can-oo to find these lands. She knew something about my capture by the Mohawks and how my friend Jeruba had remained here with me when all the others had departed.

Her eyes would light up in amazement she couldn't imagine what it was like to live in a stone house. When I spoke of my father and how he was killed when he was thrown from a horse she wanted to know what a horse looked like. So by the next time we met I had sketched the outline of as horse on a piece of birch bark. She couldn't believe that we rode on the backs of such animals. Like a young child she would absorb knowledge like a water meadow would absorb the rains. She was always keen to know so many things so our time together seemed to pass quickly. She told me of her joining to Soaring

Hawk and how unhappy she had been. He had been so cruel and when she stood up to him he had beaten her so badly that she was not saddened by his death but rejoiced that she was free at last from his vile temper. I told her that I would always love and cherish her and that she would have no cause fear me.

I noticed that Jeruba was becoming more and more agitated at my behaviour. I could understand why, he had given up his freedom to remain here with me and now I had challenged our friendship with my love for Morning Star. I tried to explain that it would not affect our long friendship and although I would be soon living in another lodge we would still hunt together when the women were about their chores. He was not convinced and went about the village with a hangdog look on his face.

Saddened by his attitude I asked Morning Star for her opinion. She said the problem would be solved if Jeruba took a woman as a companion as I had. I put this to Jeruba he could only reply saying who would have him as a companion after all he was from a different race. I told harshly that so was I but as a pale face I had been accepted by Morning Star. There were many young women in the village who would accept a warrior like him. He still wasn't convinced and I knew I had to do something about it.

As time went on my wound had healed sufficiently so that I could spent my time hunting with Jeruba and the rest of the braves bringing in fresh meat that would provide the feast after our ceremony. The women of the village were kept busy gathering fruits and berries and wild herbs from the forest nevertheless I noticed one unattached woman was always staring at Jeruba and approached Little Deer to ask who she was. Little Deer said her name was Yellow Bird she had been widowed when the hunting party where I had been captured was attacked. She was still in mourning but the designated period would end soon. I told Jeruba that Yellow Bird might make him a good wife and encouraged him to take an interest in the woman.

A new wigwam had been erected for us to live in on the edge of the village and the women had decorated the outside with ritual animals and birds representing harmony, fertility and long life. When one day I saw Little Deer being led by two of the older women towards the wigwam I knew the morrow would be the day of our joining. I couldn't sleep all night thinking that I would soon be holding Morning Star in my arms and she would be my love forever. The night passed quickly and I rose early and went to bathe in the river. Returning to the wigwam I made an effort to trim my beard and straighten my long hair. I put on a new doeskin suit that had been specially made for ceremony and as the sun rose that Shaman arrived and took me to the wigwam of the Chief and was told to wait outside.

In a short while the Chief appeared in full array wearing his great feather bonnet. He said that Morning Star was being prepared for the ceremony and would arrive very soon. As I stood in a state of nervousness Jeruba joined me smiling broadly for he knew he would not be left alone now that I was to take a wife for Yellow Bird had responded to his advances.

As the minutes ticked away I was consumed with the single thought that from today life would never be the same. Hearing voices raised around me in song I turned and saw a small group approaching led by the Shaman. In the centre was Morning Star flanked by her Mother and the wife of the Chief.

She was dressed in a bleached doeskin dress and bodice with a beaded front. Her hair was swept back into one large plait surmounted by a headband decorated with beads and shone like gold as the sun touched it and round her neck was a necklace of white flowers. As she approached she was greeted by her brother who placed her hand in mine.

The villagers went silent as the Shaman began to recite a blessing to the Great Spirit as he bound our hands together with a finely decorated leather strap in a loose knot. He began to chant in a low voice walking around us several times shaking his rattle around our heads and when the chant had ended stepped back.

The Chief came forward and lifting his arms began reciting a joining ritual:

"May the sun bring you new happiness by day
May the moon softly restore you by night
May the rain wash away your worries
And the soft winds blow new strength into your being
And all the days of your life
May you walk gently through the world and know its beauty
Now you will feel no rain
For each of you will be warmth for the other
Now there will be no more loneliness
Now you are two persons but there is only one life before you
Go now to your lodge
To enter the long days of your life together
And may your days be good and long upon the earth."

He undid the binding and handed it to the Shaman then placing his hands on our heads he said.
'Go in peace and remain together until you are called by the Great Spirit.'

The celebration of our joining began with feasting and dancing round two large fires that had been lit in the centre of the village. As we walked among the tribe they greeted us and recited a blessing on our joining. The celebrations continued on well into the night and as the fires began to die down I took Morning Star's hand and led her to the new wigwam to the cries and shouts of the men and women of the village who followed us banging small drums hooting and whistling.

I was glad to reach the safety of the wigwam and as we went inside and pulled the skin over the front the shouting stopped and the villagers drifted away to their homes. In the welcome silence of our wigwam I took Morning Star in my arms and we kissed. The first touch of her lips sent shockwaves through me and I felt a stirring in my loins which I could not suppress. She must have felt the hardness growing as we pressed our bodies together and suddenly drew back. She turned and quickly disrobed when she turned back she was completely naked.

Shyness overtook her as I gazed in awe at the beautiful roundness of her breasts and pert nipples and on down her body at the slender hips that divided at the focal point of her being and was fascinated by the thick growth of hair that covered it. I wanted to run my hands across her every curve but she pulled away and lay down on the cot covering herself with the bearskin.

I quickly undressed and pulling back the bearskin joined her. For the first time our naked bodies were entwined in an embrace from which I never wanted to part. I kissed her eyelids, embraced her mouth once again, moving away I studied her face and noticing a small mole just under her right eye kissed it before moving down to kiss her slender neck listening to her soft sighs at the touch. Working down her body I discovered another small mole above her right breast and kissed it gently. I felt her nipples harden against me and I closed my mouth over each one suckling them in turn, she moaned as I Kissed them gently forcing them to harden even more. My hand moved down between her thighs and she opened her legs welcoming my searching fingers into her.

By now my sword was erect and burning with desire I took it and placed it where my fingers had explored. As I entered her for the first time she let out a cry. I felt her thrust forward with her hips allowing me further access and for a moment passion gave way to a frantic thrusting until a searing joyous pain surged through my loins and my seed burst into her.

Thus we carried on throughout the night exploring each other's secret recesses and only when the dawn light entered through the top of the wigwam did we fall back exhausted and lapsed into a deep sleep. Our lovemaking went on unceasingly as the days went by while we discovered everything about each other.

I soon discovered that Morning Star was not the timid woman she had first appeared. She had suffered during her previous joining and having experienced the unhappiness that it brought, no more would she bend to a man's whims and desires. I found that she was passionate about many things and ready to speak her mind. She would view all problems with intelligence and common sense. For all my education and learning, in the world of the Mahicans I found she was more than my equal and I loved her for it. We vowed that we would never go to sleep on an argument and it would be resolved one way or another before sleep overtook us.

So wrapped up in our own world we didn't really notice the months passing. Jeruba had taken Yellow Bird for a bride and they had settled in a new wigwam close to ours. He seemed to have that broad grin on his face these days and the couple appeared to be very happy together. We still enjoyed each other's company and went out with the hunting parties on a regular basis together.

The summer was left behind as Little Deer and I grew closer and closer to each other. As the autumn days approached the time arrived for the tribe to move to its winter quarters in a sheltered valley several leagues away. An advance party had had been sent to prepare the site by setting up timber skeletons of several stout poles for our wigwams.

It was a two day march to the valley from our summer lodges. On our arrival everyone took a hand in setting up the wigwams. When this task had been complete the men went hunting for fresh meat while the women of the village began the routine of going into the forest to scour for broken branches to build up a store of dry wood to keep our fires alight throughout the winter days. Soon a large stockpile of wood began to take shape. It was providential for the winter turned out to be very harsh with continuous blizzards where the snows piled into deep drifts forcing us to stay inside our wigwams for days huddled around the fires.

When the weather allowed Jeruba and I and the more robust braves ventured out several times on hunting parties. Clad in heavy skin coats, trousers and boot to ward off the cold. These expeditions became less frequent as the winter closed in. As the snow became deep the party would fit Anghem-special snow shoes. When these were fitted to our winter boots we were able to walk across the snow drifts without sinking in.

The ingenious shoes had been prepared by the women by bending two sets of spruce branches in a loop and binding the two ends together. The edges of the loop had holes bored through at different intervals. Plaited strips of bark were fed through the holes and woven back and forward to form a net.

Whenever we went on a hunt in the snowy weather we towed small sleds behind us on which to place the animals we had caught. When we were lucky our sleds would carry back a deer or a small caribou but on most occasions game was scarce and we were forced to depend on our traps which gave us the infrequent cony, porcupine or squirrel. And thus we survived the worst of the weather until the big melt.

One day as spring approached Morning Star and I were walking by the stream that ran through the valley and provided us with fresh water which was now in full flood with melting of the snows. Soon the tribe would be starting the trek back to our summer quarters and we had taken a break from preparing for the move. Morning Star suddenly drew me close and whispered that her monthly visitations had stopped. We were to have a child and that there would soon be a time of confinement. I was overjoyed not only had I proved myself as a man but more importantly the next generation of de la Croix was about to come into being.

I told Morning Star that I hoped for a fine son who, with the mixture of our two bloods would be strong, intelligent and laughingly added, handsome like his father. She made a face and said she didn't want to bring a child into the world that would frighten the animals in the forest he would be beautiful like his mother and have all the women falling at his feet. I took her in my arms and kissed her. I held her there for a long time not wanting to let her go until finally she broke away saying there were many things to do to get ready for the coming of our child.

The tribe made the move to the summer quarters and the months approaching her confinement were spent preparing a place in the wigwam for our new arrival. Morning Star made a carrying harness to hold the child when doing work. I in turn had made a small enclosed cot of closely woven split spruce branches and covered it with soft furs. It was mounted on a wooden frame and could be rocked back and forward. As Morning Star's confinement neared the women of the village brought gifts of animals made of fur, tiny rattles, wooden dolls, and small items of clothing for the coming baby.

As the months passed through summer and into autumn the time of the birth was approaching I made ready by making up a separate cot ready for her confinement. One night I was woken suddenly by Nolkasis she was gripped by spasms of pain and told me that she felt her time was at hand and I should call her mother so I dressed quickly and ran to fetch her. Her mother arrived with another woman of the village and I was shooed out of the wigwam. As I sat outside in the cold night air I could hear screams coming from the inside and my heart leapt as I could not imagine what Little Deer was going through. I could do nothing but wait through the long hours of the night.

As the first light of dawn spread across the sky chasing the night away her mother came out of the wigwam and announced that I was the father of a healthy son. It had been a long and difficult labour for Morning Star and she would need plenty of rest. I prayed to the Lord that it had been a safe delivery and asked if I could see my wife and her mother lifted the flap of the wigwam and bade me enter.

As I entered Morning Star looked up and smiled at me then with a sigh closed her eyes and fell into a deep sleep. I kissed her forehead and turned to her mother who was holding our son. I took him into my arms for the first time and now knew what the preceding generations had felt when their sons were born. This small bundle was <u>OUR SON</u>. I wanted to run out and shout it all around the village, to the trees of the forest and the animals they protected but both mother and child needed to gain strength and rest. I handed the child back to Morning Star's mother and thanked her and her companion for their loving attention. I was worn out too from the long wait and laid my head down at the foot of the cot where Morning Star lay and was soon fast asleep.

**Chapter Twenty Two.
Tragedy.**

As the months turned into years we watched as our son grow into manhood. We had given him the name of the Brave I had killed to win his mother's hand but had added my father's name, so he was known as Gilles Grey Wolf. Growing up in the Mahican village with his companions he had showed himself to be a natural leader and had soon become eager to be taught about the

animals and respect for the forest environment
and as I had been told the story of the Le Croix
family by my father, so I passed our history on
for Gilles to tell future generations of our family.

Jeruba had taken him under his wing and he was
quick to learn the stealth and guile of the hunter.
He had the fearlessness of youth but wisely used
his judgement when tackling the more ferocious
of the animals. Soon he was joining the hunting
parties that frequently left the village in search of
game.

It was always a joy when we went hunting again
so accompanied by Jeruba, Gilles and several
braves we left the village bound for the great river
where I had last seen the Jarl. It was a place I
often went to in the hope that one day I might
see the Haggar moored there once again and the
tall figure of Prince Henry Sinclair standing in the
bows. It was a forlorn hope but nevertheless it
was necessary for me to do this to preserve the
memory of my past life.

We found the river in flood after the melt of the
winter snows. Jeruba as usual had gone off into

the forest with the other braves to search for game while I sat on the river bank with Gilles telling him, as I had many times before, about his de la Croix forebears and the noble band of Knights Templar. He was now sixteen summers and I felt it was time he knew more of how the knights were appointed.

I explained the ceremony I had undergone how on the night prior to the initiation I was made to stand vigil in the castle Chapel, and Holy place where we felt closest to the Great Spirit. After a long night of prayer I was taken blindfolded to a room specially prepared in the Castle there I was initiated as a Templar Knight by Prince Henry, the Grand Prior and two Knight Wardens.

I explained the virtues that had been the foundation of the Order, a strong faith, helping the poor and needy, charity, chivalry and honour in battle and how I had been slapped across the face so that I would always remember them. It was uncanny but when I recalled this moment I could still feel the force of that slap.

As we sat talking there was sudden cry finishing in a desperate scream emanating from the forest undergrowth. Alarmed by this we got up and raced towards the sound. After some time we came across one of the braves laying on the ground his leg was broken and the bone projected through the skin of his thigh. I told Gilles to stay with him and ran forward towards the sound of a great commotion. I approached a clearing from where the noise was coming and stood in horror at what I was witnessing.

A huge bull moose enraged by several spears and arrows that had pierced its body had trampled several of the braves and there was Jeruba who had grasped the infuriated animal by the neck and was trying to wrestle it to the ground. The Moose was roaring and flaying about every now and then raising up on its hind hoofs. Jeruba was holding on with grim determination trying to turn the beasts head to force the creature to the ground.

I drew my sword and rushed forward the beast was by now moving in a great circle trying to shake Jeruba off. Although I was close I its antlers prevented me from getting close enough to deliver a fatal blow. I could see that Jeruba was tiring and tried again and again to deliver a sword thrust at the animal.

Unable to retain his hold on the animal Jeruba let go and fell to the ground but was not quick enough to roll away and avoid the terrible trampling hoofs which struck him several times on the head. The trampling distracted the animal for a moment and I took the opportunity to move forward and thrust the sword into side of the Moose' neck retreating as the injury took hold of the beast and it succumbed and fell to the ground.

I ran to Jeruba and could see his injuries were bad. His skull had been crushed, he was unconscious and blood was trickling from his mouth and ears. As I knelt beside him I realised he could not survive such a terrible injury. I stared at that face that so many times had lightened my life his life and watched his life force slowly draining away and eventually with a long sigh he passed away. I was distraught and wept openly at the loss of a true and noble friend who for so long had been part of my life.

It took some time for me to gather my thoughts and I got up slowly turning my attention to the injured braves. Most of them had superficial cuts and bruises but one had a broken arm and leg. The remainder of the party began to gather some branches in order to make three improvised litters so that we could take the injured brave and body of Jeruba back to the village. The carcass of the Moose was tied on the other litter by the two of the braves and we made our way slowly back to the village.

As our sad procession reached the village I felt a mounting hollowness invading my body I had now lost my two best friends to the wild savagery of this New World. It was the suddenness of this disaster that I was unable to comprehend, one moment we were setting on a hunt cheerfully making fun of each other and in a short while my most loyal friend was dead. My only consolation was the fact that Jeruba had died doing what he loved – hunting game.

As we entered the village the news spread women appeared from their lodges wailing at the sight of the disaster that had befallen them. Yellow Bird who had heard the commotion, ran forward and observing her husband in the paleness of death she let out a scream that would shatter the soul and threw herself on the body of Jeruba trying to lift him as if willing him back into life. Realising it was no good she fell to the ground sobbing. Morning Star ran forward to comfort her but she was inconsolable she and several women of the tribe led her away moaning to her lodge.

Chief White Eagle appeared with the Shaman who promptly began a chant to the Great Spirit to protect Jeruba on his journey to the Spirit Lands. His body was then taken away by several women to be washed and prepared to be taken to the tribe's burial ground and placed on a special wooden structure made to keep the body from the wild animals.

Still numb from the loss of my friend I was comforted by Gilles and led to our lodge and was joined by Morning Star. I lay down on the fur covered resting place heavy with grief seeing in my mind's eye that great Nubian figure striding towards me with that huge grin on his face and knowing that now it was only a dream and he was gone from my life. I prayed that we would meet again in the afterlife for his loss was too great to bear.

For several days after the incident I was traumatized and wandered about the village like a lost soul. Morning Star and Gilles were my only comfort but I had lost my last contact with my previous life and I found in the loss of Jeruba a strange irony for he would have been the last to remember me as a Templar Knight. At last I was confronted with the fact that from now on I would forgo my life as a Templar Knight and become a brave in the Mahican world.

Chapter Twenty Three
Joy and Pain.

It had been a year since Jeruba had passed on and it still left an ache in my heart. Life went on as usual in the village as it had done for thousands of years. Gilles had now seen fourteen summers and had become an accomplished hunter; White Eagle had taken him under his wing and appeared to be grooming him to take over the leadership of the tribe when he had passed away.

Morning Star remained in my eyes as beautiful as she had been when I first met her. We spent much time together as we watched our son take on the responsibilities offered to him by Chief White Eagle. We felt we were gradually losing him as a son although he still maintained an affection for us on the rare occasions he came to see us.

I noticed in our conversations about our son that Morning Star seemed to be holding something back. I asked her if she had a secret to hide from me. In her forthright manner she asked me why. I said that I had observed that she was not as talkative as usual and wondered why. For the first time in our marriage she broke down in tears.

'Can't you see you fool', she said tearfully, 'I am pregnant and because of my age I am frightened'.

I took her in my arms and comforted her. I told her it was a beautiful thing and that she should not worry. I knew I was speaking from a man's point of view and that for Morning Star it could be a traumatic time.

As the months went by Morning Star seemed to have succumbed to her fate to be once again a mother and she carried out her tasks around the village as if nothing had happened. By the seventh month of the pregnancy her belly had grown large and she found that she would become exhausted very quickly. I beseeched her that she should rest more often but she would not heed my words.

One day she had gone to the forest with some of the village women to pick fruit while myself,

Gilles and some braves had gone off hunting. On our return we were met by one of the village women who told us that Morning Star had collapsed and had started to bleed the women had brought her back on an improvised stretcher and she was in her lodge being attended by the Shaman and her mother.

We ran to our lodge and found the door barred by the Shaman who told me that Morning Star had lost a lot of blood the baby had been born dead and she was fighting for her life. I pleaded see her and at last the Shaman gave way allowing only myself to enter. Morning Star lay on our resting place her face deathly pale but on hearing my voice she opened her eyes, I kissed her forehead and took her hand in mine but there was no warmth in those slender fingers. She tried to smile briefly and whispered that she was sorry. I told her she had nothing to be sorry about and that she must preserve her strength and get well.

I felt a touch on my shoulder and her mother said quietly that I should leave and let her rest. I kissed her once more and with a heavy heart took my leave. Outside the lodge I found Gilles and told him that for the time being his mother had to rest. We took up station outside the lodge and prepared for a long wait.

We remained there the whole day unable to take food while over and over I prayed that all would be well. Day turned into night and we huddled together to keep warm. I couldn't sleep concerned that there might be some news about Morning Star's condition.

It was close to dawn when her mother came out from the lodge she looked exhausted but she brought the news that Morning Star was sleeping easily and the shock of the premature birth was now subsiding. I went inside and knelt down close to her she was fast asleep but her cheeks which had previously been so pale were now showing the glow of health. I thanked God for her recovery but I knew there was a long way to go before she would be fully recovered Gilles came in and stood beside my much relieved at the sight of his mother sleeping peacefully. Shortly afterwards the Shaman entered and bade us leave so that he could begin the ritual of healing over Morning Star.

We left the lodge and walked out in to sunlight of a new day safe in the knowledge that the worst was over and Morning Star would soon be on her feet again. I vowed that I would never let this happen again and any thought of producing more children would be banished from my mind.

The days went by and Morning Star gradually built up her strength although confined to the lodge and taking the potions that the Shaman brought to her. Within a week she was back on her feet and walking around the village. I was amazed at her recovery but knew that her strength and resilience had brought her through this ordeal.

**Chapter Twenty Four
A Winter of Despair.**

I was now approaching forty five summers and my auburn hair was showing sprinklings of grey. Some of the tribe said it was an indication of wisdom that came with age but I took to be the natural fact of ageing. We were happy in the knowledge that our son Gilles had now joined with a beautiful woman called Dancing Water and they had a son called Guilluame Swift Eagle. We were thrilled to be grandparents and see the next generation of de La Croix take our place. Chief White Eagle was ageing too and giving more and more responsibilities for the well being of his people to Gilles who was accepted without opposition by the braves as the natural successor to the Chief.

Now Gilles had his own family to consider we were finding ourselves more and more involved in village life, while I was busy hunting fresh meat Morning Star would be tending the small garden that she had made on the edge of the forest where she grew maize and corn vegetables and herbs which she harvested and prepared for storage during the winter months. She would also dress the skins of the animals and produce fine moccasins, jackets and leather chaps to wear over the loin cloth. She also made dresses for herself and with the trimmings that were left over produced laces to sew the material together. Life in the village was tranquil there were no raids from the west and peace reigned over the Mahican tribe.

Soon it was time once again to make our annual pilgrimage to our winter quarters. We began to gather all that we would need for the journey and packed away the food that Morning Star had preserved for our stay there. Gradually the lodges were taken down, packed onto sledges and we began our journey. It would take us three days to reach the sheltered valley that would be our home during the winter storms. During the many years we moved to this place we had established small dwellings which withstood all that winter could bring. We quickly established ourselves in one of the shelters and as we had done each year Morning Star set about her routine to make the place habitable laying our fur skins in the area where we would sleep, making sure the circle of stones were set ready for a fire to be lit and pacing the stores we had brought in a suitable place. While she was engaged with this I went out and started to gather wood from the forest for we would need a great amount to keep the fires in when the winter storms began.

By the time the first snowfall had come we were well established and huge heaps of dead wood were set in areas close to the lodges. The lodges were snug and when the blizzards arrived we were ready. After years of experiencing these winters I knew that these blizzards could last for days and we would be confined to the lodges. On these occasions we would keep ourselves occupied producing things. I would set about making more arrows for hunting while Morning Star would produce warm clothes to combat the freezing weather outside.

One day while we were confined in the lodge Morning Star said she had a bad stomach and that she would lay down for a while but as the day wore on she seemed more and more agitated and the colour had drained from her cheeks. Worried I braved the weather and fetched the Shaman who started a ritual over Morning Star waving his feathered stick over the area of her stomach to drive the evil spirits away and blowing smoke there to purify the area. He left shortly afterwards saying she should rest. Morning Star was moaning a lot, seemed to grow weaker and weaker and soon lapsed into unconsciousness. Alarmed I tried to revive her but without success I lay by her side helpless calling her name but she remained still. By now it was late evening so I thought it best that she should rest as the Shaman had said. I took up station opposite trying to stay awake to keep watch over her but soon sleep overtook me.

I woke up suddenly a fear gripped me as I went to Morning Star's side I kissed her forehead and drew back she was cold. I realised that she was no longer breathing and tried to revive her but there was no sign of life I checked the beat of her heart but there was none. Then I just broke down and sobbed, the light of my life had gone out, my darling Morning Star was dead. I remained at her side all morning knowing that she was with her forefathers and I had lost her. I had to tell my son that his mother was dead so I got up and went outside the blizzard had gone and the sun was shining.

Gilles and Dancing Water were heartbroken and came back with me to the lodge. Gilles knelt beside the body of his mother and kissed her tears streaming down his face comforted by his wife. By now the whole village had heard the news and Morning Star's mother and two other arrived. At the sight of her daughter lying there she began wailing and chanting in a most distressing way. The other women joined in and we quietly left them to their sorrow and waited outside the lodge. The Chief joined us and put his arms around us saying that she would be welcome in the world of the Great Spirit for she had been a good person.

Over the next few days morning Star's body was prepared for the trestle that had been erected and placed between the others on the sacred ground.

Our procession wound its way up the hill Morning Star's body being carried on a litter by Gilles, White Eagle and myself and she was laid to rest with dignity, a bowl of food and her moccasins were placed with her to help her on her journey to the Spirit World. The Shaman performed the ritual to guide her on her way and sorrowfully we said our goodbyes and made our way back to the village.

I visited that place every day while we remained at the winter quarters telling her how much I loved her, how her son, daughter and Grandson were and what had been happening in the village. Soon it was time to return to our village and leave the winter quarters. With an overwhelming sadness I made my way up the hill for the last time and said my goodbyes from now on I was destined to spend my time alone with my memories of the beautiful morning Star.

Chapter Twenty Five
Fulfilling a Dream.

We eventually reached our village and set about making it habitable once again. I was now alone in my lodge. With all that had happened I was now filled with a longing to return to my homeland and expressed these feelings to Gilles. I explained my thoughts to him and with great understanding and wisdom for his age he said that he understood my reasons for leaving but his life would always be that of a Mahican warrior a life that he cherished just as I had cherished my life as a proud warrior Knight of my Order. He said that he understood but what he had heard of my world he was quite content with his life with his people. I loved my son very much but I knew he was a Mahican by birth and would always remain so.

Gilles said wherever I was I would always be remembered as the father who had made him the warrior that he was. He would always know where his father's family came from and would miss me a great deal if I decided to return there but his goal in life was to become Chief of his people. Now with his own family to consider he could not interfere with my decision.

Over the time I had been with the Mahicans there had always been rumours from the other villages that men from across the great waters had been ashore many times in search of fresh water. I was intrigued by these rumours and asked Gilles if he would go with me to the great waters to see whether the rumours were true. He showed a great reluctance at first but knowing my heart was set on seeing my homeland once again he said that he would.

When I spoke with Chief White Eagle about my intention he was at first shocked that I wanted to leave but then he was generous with his words. He said I had been a brave warrior and hunter and had brought good judgment to his tribe and if this is what I truly wanted he would not stand in my way. He added that if my quest was successful and I did not return I could rest assured that his nephew Grey Wolf would be treated as his own son the Great Spirit had taken away and would succeed him as Chief.

In the next few weeks Gilles and while planning our journey to the great sea I had thought long and hard whether what I was doing was the right thing. I knew I would never see the future generation of the De La Croix family grow and make their way in life and was saddened by this. Although I was heartened by the fact that they would grow up with a respect for natural world as I imagine Adam and Eve had in Paradise before their fall from grace.

I had seen what our civilization had done to advance the society I had grown up in, constant fear of war and pestilence and feudal lords controlling the lives of the population but I could see that there was nothing else I could do here to fulfill my life. Even after all these years with the Mahicans I missed the life as a Templar Knight and there were still unanswered questions that I had to resolve regarding the fate of the Jarl.

The day came for us to leave and I went around the village saying my final farewells to the friends I had experienced this life with finally ending at the lodge of Chief White Eagle. He came out and he hugged me saying that he had prayed to the Great Spirit that my journey would be free from danger and just as we had met in life when we were taken by the Great Spirit we would meet and hunt again together.

I said my prayers would be directed to this end. He re-entered the lodge and returned and presented me with a decorated leather medicine bag similar to the one I had worn when captured by the Mohawks many years before. He placed it round my neck and said this would protect me on my long journey and ensure a long life. I was embarrassed for I had nothing with me to give in return. Then I remembered a stone carving of a bird I made many years before often admired by the Chief when passing my lodge and asked Gilles to bring it to me. White Eagle's eyes lit up when he saw it and he gratefully accepted it into his keeping.

With a heavy heart I said my last goodbyes. The whole village had gathered to see us off and they began a chorus of wailing as myself Gilles and several warriors began our journey to the great sea.

Chapter Twenty Six.
A Strange Meeting.

We travelled overland to the river and found two can-oos which had been placed by the river to use for fishing. Now they would be used to carry our party down the great river to the sea.

We placed our things in the can-oos and boarded ready to undertake the long river journey. The current was strong and we needed little effort to paddle the can-oos downstream. By sunset we had traveled some distance along the river and we decided to make our encampment on the nearby shore. We gathered dry wood and moss, lit a fire and settled around it eating pemmican cakes talking about the journey ahead. I was the only one in the party who had seen the great water and the braves were talking excitedly about what they would do when they saw it for the first time. After we had eaten we settled down and one by one sleep overcame us.

It was almost dawn when I was awoken by the sound of footsteps crushing a twig close to our campsite. Several of the party had heard the same noise and had got up to investigate. As I got up from the forest floor voices began to talk excitedly. I glanced in that direction and saw to my surprise several braves from another tribe had surrounded the camp. Gilles was talking animatedly with the one who appeared to be the leader. The voices dropped to a normal level and Gilles strolled over.

'These are our brothers from the Penacook Abernaki. I told them we were Mahican people of Wabanakiak. They say they have seen white men coming ashore from the great waters they usually remain a few days ashore getting fresh water and hunting for food. They say there is another day's journey along the river past the great island and just before it meets the great waters. They would show us but they are hunting for their village and need fresh meat.'

I went over with Gilles and thanked the braves asking then whether they had broken their fast that morning. They said that they would wait until later for this was the time to hunt. We bade farewell, they disappeared into the forest and we packed up our few things and made ready to leave.

We continued our journey along the river. By now it had widened to about a league across. In the mid afternoon we came to the island that I recognized from all those years ago the one we had rowed past going up stream in the Haggar. We made good progress helped by the strong current and as the sun dipped over the trees decided to make camp.

I knew that it would be slim chance whether we would come across the white men we sought but Gilles and the braves said they would remain for one moon and if there was no sign we would return to the village and so remained camped close to the shore keeping a watchful eye on the estuary. From time to time Gilles and the braves would go hunting while I was left alone with my thoughts.

I felt split between two worlds. On one hand I was ready to face the perils of a sea voyage to resume a life I had known all those years before without knowing what I would find. On the other hand if we found these white men with boats I would lose all contact with my Mahican family forever.

The days passed quickly and as always I remained close to the shore with my eyes fixed on the horizon for signs of a boat but it seemed like all the white men had left these shores. I was beginning to despair at ever leaving this place. Gilles knew I was troubled and would spend as much time as he could with me. A strong bond had grown up between us while we waited, a bond which, if my quest succeeded would be never be broken, even though we would be many miles apart.

We were getting close to the time of leaving and there had been no sign of any men or boats. I began to think that I should allow Gilles and the others to go back to the village and stay here until I succeeded in finding a boat but Gilles wouldn't hear of it. He said that we could always return to this place at the same time next year.

The following day Gilles and I decided to follow the path to a nearby headland as we had done so many times before. As I reached the top I saw what I had been searching for all this time. Moored off shore was a small Cog and pulled up on the beach a small rowing boat. We ran down to beach shouting but no one was there. I knew they couldn't be far away and shouted once more.

Suddenly several men appeared from the cover of the forest carrying barrels. I went towards them and spoke in Latin asking them where they were from. They were taken aback for I was dressed like a native, tanned and my hair was plaited and crowned with a circlet and a kill feather. They began to speak a kind of Breton patois to each other. I remembered some of the words from when I would frequent the harbour Inns of Orkney all those years before. I tried some of the words I remembered and they began to listen. I managed to make them understand that I came from a place called Roslin near to the port Mussleborough in Scotland and had been left here many years ago. One of them noticed my sword and belt and came forward pointing to it and asking where I had got it. I said it was my own sword and had been with me all these years.

I told them I wanted to go back across the sea to my home before I left this world and asked them if I could join them. They talked among themselves and one man that seemed to be the Captain came forward. He said I was welcome to join them but they would be fishing for another month off these shores and I would have to work my passage as one of the crew. I agreed and we shook hands.

I told the Captain I would have to go to our camp around the headland to collect my things and would return with some fresh meat for the crew shortly. The Captain thanked me but said he would wait here but he must sail on the turn of the tide which was in two hours.
I promised I would return in a short time and we left the beach with heavy hearts.

On reaching the camp I asked for some of the fresh meat to take on board the boat and the braves gave me a calf deer that they had caught. I turned to Gilles, he wrapped his strong arms around me and clung to me as he had done when a small child. With tears in his eyes he said he would never forget me and he would make sure his children would always know the family history. We both understood that this is where we would part for ever until we met again in the afterlife. One by one I said goodbye to the braves who had escorted us and turned for a final time to my son. I kissed him gently on the forehead slung the calf deer over my back, picked up my satchel and the rest of my things and strode towards the headland not looking back for fear that my heart would break.

I reached the beach and joined the fishermen. They were pleased with the fresh meat and helped me get it into the boat. We shoved off and made for the Cog. The Captain explained who the stranger was to those he had left on board and they greeted me in their patois.   Once aboard I stowed my few possessions in a small area on the deck allotted to me and we set sail. I turned back to look at the headland and there on the top was Gilles and the braves waving and letting out a wailing sound that echoed across the water. They remained there until we were far out to sea and I could no longer make them out.

**Chapter Twenty Seven.
An Startling Discovery and the Return to the Sea.**

The Captain said he was making for an area of sea that was rich in a fish he called Colin and that we would fish the area until we had sufficient to return to his home port of St Nazaire. He explained I would work my passage by helping to haul the nets in and when we had sufficient fish in the hold to spend the time sailing back to St Nazaire filling the vats of salt water set along the gunnels on either side of the deck and filling them with the live catch to preserve them on the journey.

Thus I was to learn the hard life that fishermen chose in order to place fish on the tables of the rich. I had not been on the great sea for over eighteen summers and not long after boarding the vessel I became sea sick. It lasted for about three days when I rolled about the deck fit for nothing. The sailors would chide me and offer all kinds of remedies like tying a piece of meat to string swallowing it and pulling it up. It made no difference to my condition and all I got from this was a sore throat and chiding from the crew. They had caught another unsuspecting novice and made a fool of me.

When I had recovered sufficiently the Captain said I should help the others to haul in the nets. I was given a long, hooded coat to wear made from oiled sail canvas which I was told it would provide protection from the squalls we encountered. One of the sailors said that it was previously owned by a sailor that had been washed overboard on the voyage here but I wondered whether there was any truth in this but wore it just the same.

After two weeks at sea the Captain decided that we should take a boat and go ashore to replenish our stocks of water and see if we could catch some fresh meat. We came to a river estuary and followed its course and the Captain said we should land and try our luck there. I still had my bow and arrows among my belongings and collected them. The boat was lowered and four of the fishermen and myself set off for the shore to where a patch of sandy beach provided a good landing place. Cautiously we made our way up the bank, crossed the top of a rise and entered the forest. We found a small stream of fresh water which flowed into the main river and filled our barrels.

While two of the fishermen took the barrels back to the boat I decided to see whether I could find some game. I was joined by the other two fishermen and followed the bank of the main river before setting off into the forest. With the river still in view through the trees we followed its course. We managed to come upon a grazing deer and very quietly we approached it from downwind I took careful aim. The arrow struck the beast at the side of the neck it took a few faltering steps and fell to the ground with a grunting sound. I went to the flaying body and swiftly put it out of its misery with a sword thrust.

We found a pole and strung the beast on it ready to carry it back to the boat. We decided to go back to the banks of the river and follow it until we found the beach where the boat was moored. As we approached the river we could see a small glade ahead with something in the centre that nature had reclaimed with vegetation and on reaching the glade we were surprised to encounter a strange round tower which appeared to be constructed of stone standing on a hill above the shoreline. Cautiously we made our way towards the tower not knowing what it might contain. As we drew closer we could see that the tower had been abandoned many years before and now was at the mercy of the surrounding vegetation. I brushed away the invading growth and entered through a round doorway now inside I was able to see that the tower had many familiar features similar to those I had encountered on my journey around Orkney which we called Brocks. There were post holes in the wall where the remains of a floor had been and cut into the outer wall were two small window-like apertures. These two openings in the wall were set above the arches and I could see on closer inspection that the crude wooden upper floor which had been built inside had long since rotted and collapsed. I could see that the building had been skilfully constructed of stone and stood about twelve sword lengths high with a girth such that twenty men with arms outstretched could just reach round its base. The tower appeared to be supported by seven round pillars which rose into arches at its base.

Now I was puzzled, could Prince Henry have travelled to this river, formed a settlement here and built a watchtower? Then I recalled the tales my father told when my great grandfather had escaped to Scotland. He said the fleet had separated in a storm and some ships were never seen again. Could it be possible that some reached these shores and were shipwrecked here those many years ago eventually building a watchtower and succumbing to fate trapped in this perilous but beautiful land.

It was a strange feeling standing by a structure that may have been built by our people but we were some way from the boat and it was late afternoon. So reluctantly we left the abandoned building and followed the river until we could see the boat beached up ahead on the sandy shore. It had been a successful trip and as we left the shore and made for the ship my mind kept going back to the tower although I knew it was a puzzle I would never solve. Soon it was caste from my mind as we hoisted the mainsail and made once again tor the open sea to resume our search for fish. I had found at first pulling nets laden with fish onto a rolling deck was a precarious task. Wearing only moccasins I would slip and slide as the ship rolled and bucked and spent a lot of time on my back. In time I mastered the task by watching how the seasoned sailors braced themselves before hauling. My hands however became raw with the chaffing of the net and the continuous sea spray. The Captain provided some fish oil to rub on my hands and although it smelt rancid I persevered and my hands gradually healed.

In between the casting of nets and hauling I began to learn some of the Breton patois for sailing the ship. It wasn't easy for the sailors one particular sailor, a tall barrel- chested man called Gaston, would first say something to me and then

shout it in a loud angry voice and finally
exasperated he would gesture with his arms until I
understood finally turning to his fellow sailors
and throwing his arms up and looking to heaven.

We spent many days hauling nets and as the full
nets were brought over the side the live fish were
placed in vats of sea water and would be
preserved this way until we reached land once
more. The Cod was very large and many missed
the vats and soon the decks were awash with fish.
We scrambled to get them into the vats before
they made their escape back into the sea... Soon
however, the Captain was satisfied at last with the
bountiful catch and said that we would make   for
home. We were cheered by this and a mood of
hope for a safe passage spread throughout the
ship.

We had encountered heavy swells while we were
fishing but had avoided squalls and gales. This
was not to last for on the third day of our journey
to port the winds became strong and we had to
shorten sail. The waves whipped up as we headed
into the fury of the storm our little vessel tossed
about like a leaf in the cold winds of autumn.

It brought back memories of that great storm many years before that had struck the ships of Prince Henry's expedition. All we could do was lay low as the Captain struggled to keep the vessel on course.

The storm lasted for two days and finally blew itself out leaving us in a calm sea with little wind to assist us. The Captain called for a full rig of sails and tried to catch as much of any light wind as he could. We continued the task of placing the remainder of the life fish in the vats and those that had succumbed during the storm we threw over the side. All the vats were full now and we still had a quantity of fish to store these were stowed in barrels in the sail lockers in the forward hold where normally we would have stored the spare sail. This spare mainsail still remained spread over the after deck where it had been used to provide shelter between watches when the storm had hit. When the venison had finally been used up we had to satisfy our hunger on fish. Now fish once a week was bearable in my days at Roslin but now it was a daily meal which we soon got sick of continually yearning for a piece of fresh meat.

The wind had now freshened and the ship now made good speed under full sail and thus we continued for the next twenty days through rolling swells until land was sighted. The Captain recognized the land mass as Iceland and made for port to replenish our water supplies. We spent three days in port and the Captain managed to sell two barrels of fish.

The Captain said I had more than earned my passage and because of this he would pull into Mussleborough a port he knew could replenish victuals and fresh water and perhaps he could profitably sell some more of his catch. I was elated and thanked the Captain for his generosity. Replenished with water we left port and turned south east heading for the Pentland Firth the channel between Orkney and Scotland. After making good progress we sailed into the North Sea and I knew I would soon be home. The voyage had not been as fearful as I expected for after experiencing the first journey across I had been somewhat anxious.

As we sailed closer to Mussleborough my mind was racked with unanswered questions what would the Jarl think of my return, would I be accepted back into the court as the Knight I once was? I had been missing for over twenty summers and long forgotten by all I had known before. Would I be recognized for the years living with the Mahicans and the long journey across the sea had weathered my body, my hair was long and speckled with white, I had grown a beard and my features had changed? What would they make of this disheveled character still dressed as a native of the Mahican tribe.

We made port the next day and I said my farewells. A cheery Gaston slapped me hard on the back and presented me with a tusk of a sea creature on which he had carved a representation of a lady. I accepted it gratefully saying that it would always remind me of our journey across the great sea.

**Chapter Twenty Eight.
The Homecoming.**

As I walked through the port I was greeted with looks of surprise for   still clothed in my buckskin smock, trousers with my belt, sword and scabbard at my side, my leather satchel slung across my shoulder and wearing moccasins on my feet I was something of an oddity. Passing folk drew back from me, pointing at this strange disheveled bearded man in wonder and chatted excitedly in little groups.

I had now attracted the attention of a group of Men at Arms who started to move towards me in a threatening manner I was about to draw my sword to defend myself when down the street came a knight on horseback. He shouted a command and the men moved away from me. He stopped and asked me who I was I told him I was Sir Guillaume de La Croix, Templar Knight and a survivor of the expedition led by the Jarl Henry Sinclair of Roslin to the lands across the great sea.

The Knight was taken aback by this and I wondered for a moment if he would believe what I had said. Then he asked me a question which only Knights of the Order would know the answer. I gave him the right and proper reply and he dismounted and came over and shook my hand.

'I am James Mackie from the Preceptory at Haddington I am pleased to make your acquaintance brother come we will go to an Inn and you can tell me your story over a glass of ale.'

I said I would be glad to and taking up the reins of his horse he led me towards a nearby ale house. Over a glass of ale, my first for many years, I told my story watching the Knights eyes grow wider and wider. When I had finished I wanted to know the answer to the many questions that had for some time been perplexing me. I was deeply saddened to hear the news that the Prince Henry Sinclair had died on his return in 1400 and his son my boyhood friend Henry had passed away just a month ago. His son Jarl William was now laird of Roslin and Lord of the Isles of Orkney. I asked if I were possible to get me to Roslin where I could make my presence known to the new Jarl. James said he was willing to take me but I needed a horse. He said I was in luck for the purpose of his visit was to collect two breeding mares which had just been landed from France.

I had not mounted a horse since we left the shores of Orkney and was slightly apprehensive at riding bareback to Roslin. James allayed my fears for he also had to purchase riding tack from the saddlers and I could break it in on one of the mares. We duly collected the mares from the port and made our way to the saddlers where James purchased a fine saddle and bridle blanket and stirrups. A mare with a quieter temperament was selected to wear the saddle and it was fitted without difficulty. With trepidation I mounted the mare but found the saddle quite comfortable, the mare however not used to the heavy saddle became slightly fractious and slowly backed round in a circle. I stroked and patted her neck and she quietened down thus we commenced our journey to Roslin.

The route was as I had remembered all those years before. The track led us through the Pentland hills until we reached the banks of the Esk and there watered our horses before tackling the steep climb to Roslin Castle. I noticed that a new tower had been built and was told it was the work of the Jarl's father. We approached the Gatehouse where we were halted by a Man at Arms who asked us our business. Unsure at my presence his fears were quickly allayed by James. Satisfied with our identity we were admitted and crossing the bridge through the second gate we entered the familiar inner courtyard and dismounted. I noticed that as well as the new tower there had been many changes at the castle. The stable block blacksmiths forge and mason's and carpenters' workshops were still in the same place but the new tower had been built over the old scriptorium and library. The Great Hall remained just the same as I remembered.

After some discussion with a Knight who had appeared when we arrived James came over and introduced him and to my surprise he told me he was Malcolm the son of Sir Robert Melrose who had been one of the party that made the journey to West Scotland. He said that he would take me into his safekeeping and I bid James goodbye and a safe journey back to the Preceptory.

As he led me to his quarters Malcolm told me that his father had died seven years ago but he knew all about the journey because as a boy his father never ceased telling the story. He said that Jarl William was out hunting but would be back before dusk and he would tell the Jarl on his return. In the mean time I should refresh myself after the long journey.

The inside of my legs and my backside not used to riding for some time were sore and aching. When I had washed the grime of the journey away and ate some victuals we made ourselves comfortable in Malcolm's cramped quarters. He was anxious to know how I had escaped death. His father said that he assumed I had died when the Jarl was told that a savage tribe had attacked us. He said that I, James Gunn and many of his men had been lost. I began to explain what had happened. I knew now that I would have to repeat this story again many times over the next few days so I kept it as brief as possible. Malcolm was amazed that I had survived all this time and yet had made the journey back to Roslin.

Before long the Jarl arrived with his entourage after a successful day out hunting the woods around the Esk. A message was sent to the Jarl informing him of my arrival and eager to know more about me he invited me to attend a feast that night and sit at his table. I felt a little out of place dressed in the now very soiled and worn buckskin clothes I had journeyed in and asked Malcolm where I could borrow some clothes to wear. He gladly lent me leggings, a red smock with a hood and offered me leather boots which I found too small so I was forced to wear the sad looking worn out moccasins. I put on the clothes and fitted my sword and belt around my waist. As I was dressing Malcolm had noticed the medicine bag I wore around my neck. I told him it had been given to me by my brother in law Chief White Eagle of the Mahican tribe to keep me safe on my long journey. Malcolm was surprised at this and said that surely I had put myself in God's safekeeping, he did not hold with what appeared to be witchcraft. I told him that

the tribes he had met believed in nature and a
Great Spirit who guided them in the same way as
we trusted in   God. The bag contained natural
healing plants and was worn just the same as we
would wear an emblem of St Christopher the
patron Saint of travelers to protect us on our
journey. It had kept me safe throughout my long
journey home and it was a link with my family
back in the new world.

That evening as I was led into the Great Hall by
Malcolm I felt a deal of trepidation at meeting the
new Jarl. A tall lithe young man with a familiar
countenance that displayed many similarities to
his grandfather Prince Henry stood up and
greeted me. He shook my hand and bid me sit
next to him. My uncertainties were soon allayed
for the Jarl soon put me at my ease telling me that
as a boy he had heard the name of Guillaume de
La Croix many times when his father had spoke
of his childhood at Roslin. He pointed to a
polished granite plaque on the table and I
recognized it straight away as the Sinclair crest I
had made for his father all those years before. He
said that his father had spoken of his sadness
when I had left the Castle to attend his

grandfather at Kirkwall and was deeply affected when he had heard that I had been lost on the expedition.

As we ate he spoke of his grandfather how he hardly knew him and was only a small boy when he returned from the new world for he had died before he could get to know him. The Jarl was anxious to know what he was really like he had discovered across the western sea and the fact that the set. I described him as I knew him and said that he a leader of men who would not suffer failure that it was through his perseverance that the settlements in West Scotland had been established and now sadly through his demise had been abandoned.

The Jarl told me how on Prince Henry's death his father had assumed the title of Jarl and had been appointed Admiral of Scotland. He did not follow up his father's quest for lands in the new world and was satisfied with carrying out his appointed duties as Admiral. It was he that had rebuilt some of the Castle and he had been very proud of the achievement. He had died suddenly during the previous last month and the court was still in mourning. I told him that it was with great sadness I had received this news from Sir Malcolm.

Eager to know the answers to the many questions that wracked my mind I asked what had happened to Antonio Zeno his Captain of the fleet. Jarl William said that as far as he could remember on the death of his grandfather, the navigator had asked his father to be released from service and return to Venice where he could end his days and his father had granted his request.

Soon it was my turn to tell my story and the Jarl listened intently without saying a word. Only when I had finished did he speak asking me about my son. I told him that he was destined to be Chief of his tribe and that he was truly committed to his people I would miss him for he was a comfort to me after Morning Star had died but I knew that his life was with the Mahican people, he had never experienced our kind of life only knowing a life that communed with nature. I said I knew he would never countenance coming across the great sea to the place I called home so

I had left him to the life he understood and was happy living.

We talked on through the night about this great new world across the western sea. I painted a picture of great forests stretching as far as the eye could see, of native tribes living in harmony with nature using primitive tools and living a most simple life. I spoke of the Mohawk who were deemed savage by the Mahicans and to some degree they were. On the other hand I said that they were of a group of tribes calling themselves the five nations and they governed themselves in a most egalitarian way. I surprised the Jarl by saying that the women of the five nations appointed the Chiefs of their individual villages to which he replied it would never do in our world for the ladies of the court were not capable of such a task. I thought to myself what would Morning Star have said about this.

It was soon time for us to take our rest but before the Jarl left he said that I should stay at Roslin and assume once again the role of a Knight. He asked me to return and see him when we had both rested and he would find a suitable position for me. I thanked him for his generosity and made my way wearily to the temporary quarters Malcolm had provided for me.

Chapter Twenty Nine.
A New Beginning.

The news of my arrival had spread around the castle and I was being treated by the court with some acclaim. I hated this notoriety for I did not seek fame I just wanted to live the rest of my days serving the Jarl in some capacity. I was soon to learn my fate when I was summoned before the Jarl. He said he felt I had earned my spurs as a Knight and now he felt I should settle down in a task that would satisfy my talent as a craftsman. He would appoint me take charge of the fabric of his Castles and island defences as his Master Mason. I was honoured for I was to continue the same task his grandfather had given me in Orkney but with responsibility for Roslin as well. I thanked the Jarl saying that I would serve him to the best of my ability for the rest of my days.

So for the last thirty years by the grace of God I have carried out my duties traveling to familiar places in the islands, to the Pentland Estates and enjoying the countryside around Roslin but the memories of my adventures in the new world still haunt me. I lie awake on my pallet during many long nights thinking about the family I left over there and how they might be faring.

Now the task before me is to complete the fabric of the building the Jarl William has put his heart and soul into. It is to be a wonderful place dedicated to God, nature and the Knights of my great Order and just a small part of this wonder will be a portal which will be a vision into the new world that we found and explored. It would be my personal dedication to that great man of courage and tenacity Jarl Prince Henry Sinclair who chose me to be part of that great adventure.

So my story is finished and I Guillaume de La Croix will place these sheets of parchment in a secret cache that no man will discover until this great Chapel of Roslin is razed to the ground and under the protection of God through his faithful servants the family St Clair I predict that that will not happen for many centuries to come.'…

Chapter Thirty.
The Memorial is Finished.

In his cramped quarters in the Castle of Roslin Guillaume removed the lens from his tired eyes and carefully rolled up the bundle of parchment tying it with a thin strip of leather. He snuffed out the candle it was already dawn and shafts of light penetrated the slit window and lit the surface of the table. His record of that great adventure was finished and he was satisfied that his memory had not failed him.

Returning to the site he watched as the first of the blocks making up the base of his memorial window moved to the place where they would be inserted into the building. It was then he made the decision that he would place the parchment scrolls within a cavity below the window before all the base blocks were set into place.

Later in the day when the other masons had left the site he returned with the parchment scrolls rolled up in a piece of soft leather and secured with lacing. Inspecting the point at which the outside wall had reached the base of the south west window he located the gap between the walls that had been in filled in the usual way with small stones and gravel. Scraping away the infill until he had made a cavity large enough to take the scrolls, he placed them carefully inside. He spoke a dedication and a small prayer for the souls of all who had joined in that great adventure so many years ago and covered the scrolls up with the infill until all trace of the whereabouts had were completely concealed.

Over the next two months he watched the walls of the Chapel slowly rise and soon it was time for the base blocks and the frame of the window to be set in mortar. Only now he could be satisfied that his secret was safe.

He now set about finishing the design for one of the two pillars which would stand either side of the altar. The Jarl had prescribed a basic design for both pillars and Guillaume worked hard on a drawing that would satisfy his wishes. Following the instructions laid down by the Jarl he had produced a drawing of a square pillar with roundels at each corner and each face inset with tracery representing Norse symbols and interwoven floral designs. The capital had been shown with intricate floral tracery and the base was represented by heavy round footings.

As soon as the drawing for the first pillar was approved by the Jarl Guillaume set about the task of selecting suitable stone blocks ready for carving the tracery. For two long weeks he made the journey back and forth to and from the quarry inspecting each stone as it was cut. It was tiring work for he had to be sure that the blocks were properly sized and that there were no blemishes that might cause them to shatter. Having selected the main blocks he placed a mark on them indicating the position that they would take in the pillar. First he selected two large rectangular blocks one that would make up the plinth of the pillar and the first section of tracery and the other that would form the capital. He then selected six narrower blocks for the main body of the pillar. Now satisfied with his choice he bade the carters to take the stone back to the Chapel site.

For the next three months he set about carving the plinth and lower support from the block he had marked. Once finished he made a copy stone for the middle section of the pillar continuing the same intricate pattern and passed it to his group of masons and apprentices to carve the remaining five blocks.

The capital stone took much longer for the winter snows set in and made progress on the stone virtually impossible, but as spring arrived he began to carve with a new fervour. It took another four months to complete the capital and the stones were assembled in a compound where they remained ready for the time when they would be inserted in to the building.

The Jarl had visited the site regularly and was pleased with the completed work. He now began to talk about the second pillar and produced rough sketches of how he would like it carved. It appeared to be a standing column with garlands of vines wrapped around the main body. At its base he said that he would like mythical creatures from Scandinavia in the form of eight dragons. These represented the dragons of Neifelheim linking the Chapel with his ties with Orkney. Describing his thoughts for the capital he said he would like to see figures from the Old Testament.

For Guillaume the task was to be a challenge and he took the drawings to his quarters to study. He noted that this time the pillar must be carved from one piece of stone and there could be no mistakes in the workmanship for one mistake would ruin the whole work. Because of this he vowed he would carry out the whole of the task himself.

This time he was to spend every waking hour over three months carving the capital on the rectangular block of stone. The carving created many problems, the block had to stand erect to be worked on therefore scaffolding had to be built around it. The capital was nearing completion and before he started on the main column he went back to the task of supervising the rest of the tracery. Having now completed most of the stones for the roof cover his group of craftsmen were concentrating on the lintels and doorways. He was greatly pleased with their work and praised them for their care and attention to detail. After his visit he felt a great tiredness overtaking him as he walked back to his shelter and went straightway to lie down on his pallet of hay. The tiredness drifted over him and he fell into a deep sleep.

As noon approached a message was passed to Aiden that he should inform his Master that the Jarl had returned to the Castle and was coming to the site later in the day. Aiden sped to the shelter to inform his Master of the Jarl's return and forthcoming visit.
The old man appeared to be asleep on his cot and Aiden spoke softly summoning him to wake up but he did not stir. Aiden shook him gently and as he did so the old man's arm which had lain across his chest fell to the ground. The faithful Mason saw that his Master was not breathing and a sudden panic set in, he rushed out from the shelter and bade one of the apprentices fetch a Prior Apothecary who on his arrival pronounced the old man dead.

Prince William was saddened by the news and immediately summoned his knights to arrange for Sir Guillaume's body to be prepared for burial by the Prior Apothecary, after which it was taken to the Chapel to await burial. Prince William and a group of Knights spent some time with the body in prayers for the safe passage of his soul.

Chapter Thirty One.
Tribute to an Honourable Knight.

The following day in pouring rain a procession of Priors of the Templar Order preceded the coffin of Sir Guillaume de La Croix which was carried by the youngest initiates to the Order their ashen faces echoing the white tabards emblazoned with a red cross now covered with black shawls.

Immediately behind the coffin was Prince William of Roslin, Jarl of Orkney walked alone followed behind by another procession of Knights and his group of Masons, fellow craft and apprentices.

They slowly wound their way the few miles to the Templar Chapel at the Preceptory at Haddington.

After the burial service was said by the Senior Prior of Haddington, the Jarl gave a moving tribute to a Knight whose family had served seven generations of his family and Sir Guillaume was laid to rest in the family grave in the cemetery and a stone with an engrailed cross above which had been set the Merica star which had been beautifully carved by Master Aiden and placed over the grave on the orders of the Jarl.

As a tribute to his Master Aiden the Senior Fellowcraft Mason took up the challenge to carve the rest of the ornate tracery on the second pillar and set about finishing the task as his master would have done. It took six long months to finish the pillar but the result was spectacular and now cold winds swept over the Pentland Hills and began to strip the trees as the autumn days gave way to winter the pillar was moved with great care to the holding area and being carved from one single block it was carefully wrapped in several fleeces to protect it from the damage that frost could inflict.

Although the Jarl had only seen the pillar in various stages of the work he had not seen the finished piece as he had been away on duties among the islands of Orkney. He had now arrived back in Roslin and Aiden was ordered to prepare for the Jarl to visit the site to see the completed work so he set about making preparations the visit. The fleeces were removed and the pillar was lifted to an upright position to show the Jarl how it would look when installed in the Chapel.

There had been some concern by the Master Masons around the site that a Fellowcraft should take over this task but after seeing the skillful way the Mason had started on the tracery, the Jarl had directed that he should be given the opportunity to finish it. On seeing the finished work the Jarl was well pleased and knew he had made the right decision.

Over the next thirty years work continued on the collegiate Chapel of St Mathew at Roslin although it was never finished to the specifications laid out by the Jarl by the time he died in 1484. His son

Oliver St Clair saw to it that the roof of the choir was completed but the work ended there.

Epilogue.

Making his way through the dark forest a hunter with bow and arrow at the ready pursues a young buck with a full head of antlers. He takes careful aim and sends the arrow straight and true striking the buck at the back of the neck. It drops to the ground helpless and is quickly dispatched by the hunter using a metal dagger with an ornate handle. He stoops over the animal chanting a message to the Great Spirit to take the soul of the animal to his care.

Guillaume Swift Eagle strides into the village pulling a crude stretcher on which lies the buck. He is greeted at the lodge of the Chief by his mother Dancing Water and joined by some of the other women of the village who take the beast away to prepare, carve up and distribute throughout the village. As she praises her grandson for his prowess as a hunter his father the Chief appears at the entrance to the lodge and greets him warmly.

Soon they will be moving to the winter quarters and the fresh meat will go towards the supplies they will take with them. His father invites him to take a pipe but he declines for his eyes are fixed in another direction. A young woman sits outside a nearby lodge busy scraping a buck skin, preparing it to be made into moccasins. She looks up sensing that she is being watched and just as quick lowers her head blushing slightly at the attention.

The Chief and his wife return to their lodge smiling at what they have witnessed. Soon there would be another generation of De La Croix not one expected by all those generations who had passed before with that name. This would be a new generation growing up in a different world one that was happy to commune with nature rather than destroy it.

Bibliography

Source References.

Books.

Prince Henry Sinclair by Frederick J Pohl
Davis Pointer 1974

The Sword and the Grail by Andrew Sinclair
Random House 1993

The Rosslyn Chapel by the Jarl of Rosslyn
Rosslyn Chapel Trust 1997

Europe in the Fourteenth Century by Denys Hay
Longman 1966

The Temple and the Lodge by Micheal Baigent
and Richard Leigh
Corgi 1990

Internet Sources.

www.geocities.com/CapitolHill/Parliament/2587/crusades.html
Lebanon and the Crusades
www.undiscoveredscotland.co.uk/roslin/roslyncastle
Rosslyn Castle
www.tayci.tripod.com/boy2knight.html
Initiation of a Knight
www.geocities.com/Athens/Parthenon/5923/history/shjps.html
Ships of the Fourteenth Century
www.joeye.com/nyri2002/ri/pages/17-old-mill-2.html
The Tower at Norfolk, Rhode Island. USA
www.westray-orkney.co.uk/updates/culturalheritage.htm
Orcadian Language and Culture.
www.tsj.org/sancto.htm

Prince Henry Sinclair
www.geo.ed.ak.uk/-exped/stclair/SirHenry.htm
Prince Henry and the Expedition to America 1398.
www.class.et.byu.edu/mfg201Lecturenotes/lecture23.htm
The End of the Middle Ages the 14th Century.
www.//egla.bok.hi.is/cgi-bin/zoom.cgi?language**17&std=1
The Zeno Map.
www.vaarmouries.com/cloth/ccloth03.html
Historical Clothing 14th Century.
www.//museum.gov.ns.ca/arch/infos/Micmac1.html
The Micmac Native Americans.
www.//collections.ic.gc.ca/heirloom_series/volume2/section1/2-6.html
Micmac Aboriginal Life.
www.//mrc.uccb.ns.ca/miscellany.html
Sources of Micmac Language.
www.ilhawaii.net/~stony/lore21.html
Micmac Creation Story-Glooscap Legend.
www.//evfn.ca/Algonquin%20Language.html
Sources of Algonquin Language
www.native-languages.org/abenaki_animals.htm
Abenaki-Penobscot Animal Words.

Downloads -Freelang Dictionary – The Mohawk Language
www.//commons.wikimedia.org/wiki/File:Iroquois_5_Nation_Map_c1650.html
Map of the Five Nations. C. 1650
www.//members.tripod.com/~clangunn/westfordknight.html
The Westford Knight.

Author's Notes.

The Name Rosslyn and Rosslyn Chapel.

Whereas Rosslyn is the modern spelling of the Sinclair's lands and title I have used the old spelling Roslin to put the name in its medieval context.

Rosslyn Chapel was commenced in 1446 at the behest of William St Clair 3rd Prince of Orkney and was dedicated in 1450 as the collegiate Chapel of St Mathew. Prince William died in 1485 before the Chapel had been completed and was buried there. The Chapel which lies to the south of Edinburgh is open to the public and well worth a visit.

The window referred in the book as 'The Merica Portal' lies in the south west corner of the Chapel and is decorated with a plant that looks very much like maize a plant which could only be seen in the Americas.

The trials and condemnation of the Order of the Poor Knights of Jerusalem has been documented in many publications. I have woven this tragic period into the story to show how it affected the family of de La Croix. Some Knights Templar are known to have escaped the inquisition and settled in parts of Scotland after the fall of the Order in 1307. It is assumed that they also continued to practice their rituals. Templar gravestones have been found in several areas indicating that they spread far and wide throughout the Scottish countryside. It is common knowledge that Templar Knights fought at the Battle of Bannockburn and were instrumental in winning the day.

There was a Temple Preceptory near Hannington south of Edinburgh where many of the escaping Templars settled there after the Order was condemned.

The incident of the Knights taking Robert Bruce's heart to Jerusalem is well documented by both Christian and Moslem sources. Henry St Clair did go on a crusade to Alexandria and it is thought that during that time made a pilgrimage to Jerusalem.

Life for the poor of the Fourteenth Century was predictably short. It was a period that had seen famine, pestilence and war spread throughout the known world. Is it any wonder that the clergy believed that the Revelation of St John predicted in the New Testament was beginning to happen and the Four Horsemen of the Apocalypse were riding across the land. The Black Death had visited on two occasions during the century laying waste to the population of Europe. This was the background to the world that Guillaume and his forebears had been born into. However the residents of Rosslyn Castle had remained remarkably unscathed by these events in the latter part of the century. Because of the reduction in the population it was a time where the poorer peasants could dictate terms to supply their labour and throw off the burden of serfdom to become freemen and women.

The routine in the castle throughout the seasons is well documented in both Pohl and Andrew Sinclair's books mentioned in the bibliography.

How the controversy regarding the voyage of
Prince Henry Sinclair started.

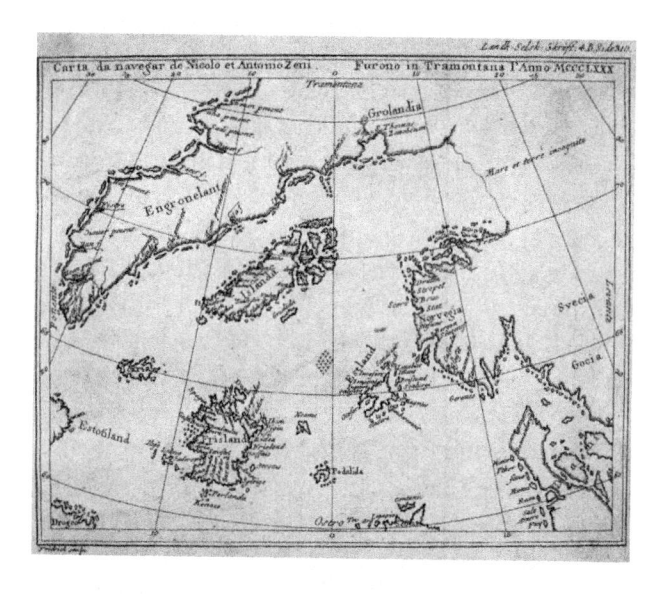

The Zeno Map.

The Zeno narrative describes how Nicolo Zeno was rescued by a Scottish prince believed to be Henry Sinclair and how he served the Prince as a navigator and visited and mapped the coastline of Greenland. It also tells that his brother Antonio Zeno served the same Scottish Prince and that Nicolo Zen had died in his service. Antonio in his correspondence writes that he made a journey across the western sea with the Prince discovered lands which he dutifully mapped and marked Estotiland. In the best traditions of the ruling class of this period I would imagine that Prince Henry would have made claim to the newly discovered lands.

I have thought about this and I believe that if a Venetian had heard the name West Scotland he might translate it as Estotiland and so later in the book I have used this translation.

The naming of America has always been associated with Amerigo Vespucci and mistakenly assumed that the name taken from Maps produced for the sailor was the name given to the land to the west. Another theory has been advanced that America was named by the Vikings from a Spanish sailor bearing the ancient

Visigothic name of 'Amairick'. I have taken a more subtle approach which would connect more with the world of the Knights Templar I quote from Christopher Knight & Robert Lomas' books, The Hiram Key: Pharaohs, Freemasons and the Discovery of the Secret Scrolls of Jesus.

"Josephus, the historian of the Jews in the first century, observed… '…that the Mandeans believed that the inhabitants of this far land were so pure that mortal eyes would not see them and that this place is marked by a star, the name of which is 'Merica'." Thus I have chosen the origin of the land across the western sea to be 'Merica' and that has been incorporated in the title.

Prince Henry sails in the type of ships used during the fourteenth century, the Drakkar (a modified Longship as used by the Vikings) was mainly used in northern waters as a cargo ship but quite capable of long sea journeys. It had a very shallow draft and could easily sail up rivers and estuaries. It was capable of being manhandled when navigation on water proved difficult. The Cog was a small merchant ship with high decks ideal for coastal work but very difficult to handle on the high seas. I have based the Roslin on a Venetian Galley and made it the largest ship in Prince Henry's fleet well capable of sailing the high seas.

Navigation was tricky in those days but the Venetians had mastered the skill using simple instruments and the stars. They were also very skilled at map making as can be seen by the Zeno map.

Pohl thinks the island where they encountered the hostile natives may have been the Faeroe Islands.

The origins of Jeruba - Many Africans of this and later periods right up to the Nineteenth Century (and in some cases even today) were taken from the villages and made captive. Arabs traders would raid the villages to supply the market for slaves and in Jeruba's case the raids were carried out in what we now call Sudan. Many of the stronger young men were sold as oarsmen to the Levantine Pirates and if they survived after many years at the oars and reached an age where they had lost their strength they would be cruelly cast overboard and drowned. Levantine Pirates operated from the Mediterranean Coast of North Africa and attacked all merchant shipping mainly out of the northern Mediterranean seaports and there were often clashes with the Venetian fleets.

Atlantic storms occur all year round and the coastal waters off Newfoundland are renowned for fog banks which can suddenly appear and engulf a ship so it is very likely that the adventurers would have encountered sea conditions like those I have described.
Sailing the uncharted coastal waters of what we now call Newfoundland and trying to make landfall on the rocky northwest coast would have been a hazardous undertaking. It was a common task for navigators such as Antonio Zeno to make charts as they sailed along observing the coastline. The north coast of what we now call Nova Scotia has many inlets and the fleet would have finally found a shore where they could land and restock with water and possibly fresh meat.

It would have been a strange experience landing on these shores for the first time seeing an unspoiled land with such an abundance of trees and strange animals must have seemed like an earthly paradise to the new arrivals but they were unaware of the dangers that awaited them. The forest land was vast and a complete change from the windswept barren landscape of Orkney and they would have certainly made an exploration of the area. The sight and sounds of strange animals and birds would have been unnerving to the highly superstitious among the Men at Arms whose belief in dragons and other beastly apparitions was rife.

The Inuit, Micmac, Abernaki, Mahicans and those tribes spread along the East coast of the continent were probably the first Native Americans to encounter white men from the East. Apart from the voyages of the Viking Eric the Red who is thought to have made landfall there it common knowledge that from the twelfth century fishermen from Orkney, Brittany and Norway fished the Newfoundland Banks. It is likely therefore that they would have landed there to obtain fresh water and victuals and would have encountered the Natives of the region. I don't think it is unreasonable to suggest that some may have been shipwrecked on this shore and never returned to their native land.

The tribes encountered in the fourteenth century would have seemed to the voyagers a simple race compared with the people they were used to in their idea of a developed society but the real qualities of these people of the New World was only understood later by those few who had a chance to live with them for a time. Although they were poor in appearance they were rich in their knowledge of hunting, trapping animal for their skins and bone to make useful clothing, shelter and artifacts and using natural medicine obtained from the forest plants and trees and to sustain their existence in the forestlands. They had respect for the land and the animals and never abused this trust. They may have been dazzled by the ships, armour and weapons of these visitors to their land but it would never change their close links with the natural world.

I wove the piece about the loss of the deck cannon into the story because a similar cannon with a bound barrel thought to have been made in Venice was found by divers in an inlet off the shores of Nova Scotia.

Although no remains of a settlement have been found it is likely that a permanent settlement was built at Pictou to accommodate the Prince and his men for their long stay. There is a legend among the Micmac people that a great lord called Gouloscap or Kuloscap (Shining Helmet) visited their people and brought peace and justice to them. On the western shore of Nova Scotia today there is a trail named for this savior of the Micmac people. There is some suggestion that this great lord might have been Prince Henry Sinclair. This is a Micmac poem written about him:-

'Kuloskap was the first,
First and greatest,
To come into our land -
Into Nova Scotia, Canada,
Into Maine, into Wabanaki,
The land of sunrise, or Light.
Thus it was Kuloskap the Great
Made man: He took his arrows
And shot a tree, the ash,
Known as the basket-tree.

From the hole made by the arrow
Came forth new forms, and these
Were the first of human kind.
And so the Lord gave them a name
Meaning "those born from trees".
Kuloskap the Lord of Light
Made all the animals.
First he created
All of giant size;
Such was the beginning."
(Page 50, "Kuloskap the Master")

The Micmac even today are skilled in the art of basket weaving and produce wonderfully zig-zag patterned examples of this art.

I have spelt the words canoe (ca-noo) and tobacco (to-bacco) they might have been pronounced by the native tribes.

Punishment for transgression in the fourteenth century was very severe and it there is no question that the offence of rape would have resulted in the transgressors being hung, drawn and quartered and their bodies caste out for the animals to take. It would also show to the native tribes that Prince Henry was fair and just and would not favour his men.

It is strange that Antonio Zeno was sent back to Orkney with part of the fleet rather than stay with the Prince charting the newly discovered lands. I would imagine this would have been to pass the news of the Prince's discovery of new lands to encourage settlers to come. Nevertheless he was sent home and his part in the adventure was over.

As well as the Venetian Gun I mentioned Jarlier I have woven into the story other places of interest including the Westford Knight which was found etched on a rock in Westford Massachusetts and is thought to show the Arms of the Gunn Family who happen to have been keepers of the St Clair Estates in the Pentland area of Scotland'
The Norfolk Tower Rhode Island is circular in construction and very similar to defence towers in Scotland called brochs. Circular Towers were a feature of many Templar buildings.

Printed in Great Britain
by Amazon